MW00328830

PRAISE

You can definitely tell that the author did her research on personality disorders ... both personalities are well-thought-out and written distinctively. Very gripping and keeps you on the edge of your seat.

— READERS' FAVORITE, 5-STAR REVIEW

Exquisite tension between the two experiences is well-crafted in a story which delicately walks the line between a psychological exploration and a thriller. Compellingly realistic.

— D. DONOVAN, SENIOR EDITOR, MIDWEST
BOOK REVIEW

My Top Read of 2020. Gray boldly takes on abuse, mental health, the small town hive mind, and racism ... with grace and dignity.

— LYNN, 2 GIRLS & A BOOK

Holy book hangover! Here I am 10 days days later and I am still thinking about this book.

— CRYSTAL, 2 GIRLS & A BOOK

THE GIRL
AT THE
HANGING
TREE

MARY GRAY

MONSTER IVY
PUBLISHING

Cover design by Cammie Larsen

Cover image from shutterstock.com

To Toni, for giving me the pieces.

*C*onsciousness hits me like a swift creek rolling over smooth and jagged boulders.

Hand on doorknob, back against door. It appears Tansy's decided it's time for me to take over.

Salt and pepper shakers go to war in my arms, so I shake them out. Grasp the nearest pillar.

Looks like my alter has left me on the side porch this time.

Settling my nerves, I remind myself, once again, of the few key details I know.

My name is Gemma Louise Coldiron. I live in Deep Creek, Texas, on the dead of a once-thriving Main Street.

Home is *here*—a boarded-up Victorian with a cupola and an iron fence that keeps everybody out. Tansy remembers everything that happened in our past, while I can barely remember much of anything.

My job is to go out to fetch food every two weeks. Of course, I'd like to come out more than that, but I do understand why Tansy never leaves. She has an extreme fear of the outside world and spends all her time drawing, painting, and embroidering pictures of dead bodies.

Glancing over my shoulder, I find that the second-nearest pillar says our house number is still 199. The holly bushes continue to be a mile high, and our cracked footpath expertly leads guests *away* from the house to the largest of our "No Trespassing" signs. Tourists like to stop by to take pictures of our house, but we do any and all things to keep them away. Tansy says they give her a migraine.

Well, I'd better get going if I'm going to get my hair done and shop before I return home by 6:30. Hopefully the store still has Tansy's favorite—split pea soup and lemon chamomile tea.

It only takes me a few seconds to trot down our path and find the key beneath a palm-sized rock under the gate. The pokey iron fence digs into my hand, but it doesn't take long to lift the corner of the rock and unearth the key.

I jiggle it into the padlock, which pops open. Sure, I could bring the key with me, but Tansy worries I might lose it. So I slip the key back under the rock, click the gate closed, and mostly close the lock.

Darting to the road, I drink in the sun, never more hungry for exercise. Tansy may have bad knees, but I'm able to shake them out well enough. Loosen my ligaments and joints.

Once I reach the railroad tracks, the grackles and I fly.

A newer, white-pillared mansion hunches on the left. The funeral home lurks like a bad omen to the right. The pink granite courthouse is just ahead, and, with its numerous towers and arches, it's probably another relic from the late nineteenth century.

I jaunt past a sculpture of a pair of giant metal dice while the clock tower on the courthouse bellows out three rings. 3

PM already? Looks like I should have just enough time to finish my run, do my hair, and get the groceries.

My sneakers fit like armored socks; pink running shorts brush the gooseflesh on my skin mid-thigh. I probably look like any average woman on a run, but I tend to memorize every detail in case it goes away.

I love the wreath-adorned windows.

My, how the red, white, and blue Texas flags flap so jubilantly.

The wood-smoke wafting over the square could only come from *Sweetie Pie Ribeye's,* and the pin-striped candy canes in front of *Hey, Sugar* remind me that their truffles are more dangerous than knives.

Three Victorian houses bow like old friends from the north end of the square, alternately painted red, blue, and green. Of course, *The Hair Lounge* back by *Hey, Sugar* is where I'm headed once I'm finished running.

Tansy's idea of grooming is adorning our head with a crown of roses without brushing once—or even washing. I sincerely hope she hasn't been sleeping with the cats again and gifted us with fleas.

Millwood, with its red brick and stone façade, seems to be waving for me to come over, but I tend to avoid the mental health facility.

By the time I've finished my three or so miles, I stumble into *The Hair Lounge*, covered in sweat and stinky enough to sidetrack a wolverine. Luckily, hair product has a way of covering that up, and Francesca, my hair stylist, is too nice to ever bat an eye.

"They're putting in a taco joint!" Francesca shimmies back and forth while singing in her rich, alto voice. Squeezing me with her muscular arms, she hugs me like I'm a long-lost relative—or a serial killer she really wants to see die. Calming shea butter lotion wafts off her umber skin, sending me off to a Caribbean beach.

Releasing me from her iron-clad grip, Francesca sashays over to her hair-cutting chair. Stomps on the foot pedal. "It's about *time* we got a restaurant with food that's not barbecue or fried."

Not about to argue, I take a seat.

"Back in Atlanta, this cute little taqueria was my go-to place. After a long day, I'd get me fixed up with one of their bean and jalapeño burritos, mmm, mmm."

"You sure you don't want to go back to *Josie's*?" I wink while she cloaks me with her slick, nylon cape.

The cape goes on a bit tight. Not that I blame Francesca. *Josie's* was recently shut down after employees put Miralax on their pizza, mmm-mmm.

"Don't you go harassing me, Missy!" Humor alights my good friend's eyes until the moment I tug the elastic from my pony, and both of us set our sights on the undead creature in the mirror.

Long, dark hair streams down a woman's face; jet-black circles rim her eyes. Her skin's so pale, you could call her Dracula's cousin, and the whole town would be on board for a reenactment, county-wide. I *suppose* this sickly twenty-five-ish creature is me, though it's a tad hard to believe. I'd rather grab a kayak and float down the Trinity River than be a potted plant, sitting indoors all day.

What *is* clear is that, once again, Tansy's failed to brush— or wash—our hair since our last visit. Not to mention the thick, almost black caterpillar growing over our eyes.

Francesca staggers backward. Her enormous eyes canvass all three-hundred-and-sixty degrees of my hair monstrosity. "Gemma Louise, now what'd you go and do? Stick your head in a turbine?"

"I'm a deep sleeper." I tug a lingering rose petal from my hair. "And I like running."

"But"—Francesca tentatively dabs at my hair with her palms, like she's been asked to wrangle a dead porcupine—"it looks like you've been *trying* to tangle it for weeks."

The back of my head gets itchy, and I reach up to scratch it when Francesca gives me the evil eye. I drop my hand. Best not exacerbate the point.

Huffing, she plants her feet shoulder-width apart and cups her chin with her hand, clearly trying to think how to help me. Nodding once, twice, she seems to decide everything at once when she says, "Don't you worry, baby." She glances around like we've been surrounded by WWII soldiers, and it's time to head to the bunker ASAP.

Hair products pile in her arms, including a detangler, tweezers, and about thirty different wax products before she lifts her chin to the back row of sinks. "Ready?"

I follow without question. No more Dracula's cousin, whoop, whoop! Or even that seedy girl from *The Ring*.

*S*ince Francesca's Wonder Woman, she has my hair and eyebrows done by 5:29. I'm going to be cutting Tansy's 6:30 deadline pretty close, so I give Francesca a generous tip and a million thank yous before tearing away for groceries.

Grady Dean's is on the other end of the square. They accept two dollar bills, which is convenient, since that's the stack of bills Tansy's provided me. The split pea soup sits on a shelf at the back, and the middle of the store houses all the herbal teas. Problem is, one of the workers is currently restocking the soup, and he's *not* Francesca. Small talk with strangers isn't exactly my forte.

Avoiding any and all eye contact, I can't help noticing that the guy's burgundy uniform, greasy collar-length hair, and long, slender arms give him an uncanny resemblance to Olive Oyl on *Popeye*. True, I'm able to remember old-timey and current pop culture references, but what I would give to remember *one* additional detail about my recent life.

Halting a full five feet away from the stranger, I set to work securing the fourteen cans of soup for Tansy. I settle the first in the cart. Make as little sound as possible, but I have to grab another and another—he's going to want to talk to me.

It would be helpful if I knew how well I'm supposed to know him. In truth, I could have bought groceries from him for eons and have forgotten. Unfortunately, Grocery Boy's flat gaze clings onto my shirt like iron shavings, and everything from his slouch to his skeevy expression makes me want to wash up in a pool of bleach.

I drop what I believe to be the fourteenth can into my cart and speed away like I'm a driver in a NASCAR race.

Deodorant. I need some deodorant.

I grab some, a few hairbrushes, and Tansy's herbal tea. I think I may have successfully avoided all contact, when, the second I roll up to the counter, Grocery Boy comes strolling like the king of England past the cupcake display.

His skinny chest does this rattly heave as he watches me place Tansy's cans, one by one, on the conveyor belt. His fingernails are crusted over with brown and yellow stains. Why are we the only ones in here? Why isn't anybody else shopping?

I could tell him that the store looks really great, except that the strewn wrappers on the floor looks like he's just survived a visit from a toddler—or an angry litter of puppies.

"You sure don't deviate from your usual diet," Grocery Boy says.

Oh, his voice is lower than I expected. And his chipped upper tooth doesn't look like it'll be hanging around much longer than the Fourth of July.

Though I'm sure I shouldn't be so judgy. For all I know, he's a really nice guy. Since he knows my eating habits, I must have bought food from him loads of times.

His movements are almost gentle as he scans the next soup can, the machine letting out a mechanical beep. "You goin' to the tree lighting ceremony?"

I hadn't even realized it was December already. Then again, the trees didn't have any leaves. That's the thing about winter in Texas—it can hand-deliver a blizzard, then, a day after, be in the 70s.

Grocery Boy still hasn't set down his latest can, so I give him my best reply. "I'm so sorry, but I can't seem to remember ... remind me of your name?"

Pausing, he continues holding the can while the check-out machine scans the same can at least four more times.

"Olly ..." He furrows his brow and leans forward, reeking of something much worse than engine grease. Whether we've had this conversation before, or we've known each other for years, I really cannot say. Though "Olly," really does sound like Olive Oyl, so maybe that's why I associated him with the cartoon character in the first place.

Regardless, I scramble for my wallet. It's almost time for Tansy's money. "I'm not sure if you know, but I lost my memory."

Olly bares another chipped tooth as he stretches his mouth unusually wide. "Aw, *sure* you did!" While he chuckles, inky hair falls into his eyes. "'I lost my memory ...'" He claps like that's the funniest thing he's ever heard. "Ya know, I'd say that, too, if I were like you and wanted to avoid the slammer. You're a resourceful one, Mrs. H!"

*J*run much faster than the grackles on my way home to Tansy. Doesn't matter that I'm carrying groceries or that I don't have time to linger at my favorite bridge. Doesn't matter that my hair's already a tangled mess and will probably be in even worse shape when I see Francesca next time.

Avoid the slammer? What did Olly mean?

I must have done something awful before I lost my memory.

Mrs. H?

Am I married? I glance down at my ring finger, but there's not so much as a tan line where I may have worn a ring.

I know my first and middle names are Gemma and Louise, and Tansy always insists our last name is Coldiron, but maybe the H stands for Hardin—just like the name of our estate. That would make sense, but I always felt like there was a reason why Tansy staunchly avoids using that name. Maybe H stands for something completely different. Harris. Or Harvey.

From a pocket in my running shorts, I pull out a piece of

paper with the three foundational rules Tansy wrote for us to
live by. Lengthening my stride, I clutch it tightly in my fist,
trying to think.

Rule Number 1, she wrote, *Stay in Deep Creek*. Naturally, this
rule is for me. I once ended up lost and disoriented in
another town. The police had to bring me home, completely
disillusioned, to an extremely worried Tansy. I don't
remember how long ago that was, but Tansy insists it was
traumatizing.

Rule Number 2, I know the next one says, *Don't let anyone in
the house*. This one's for Tansy. People don't exactly understand her macabre style of art. She says she depicts people
without their arms and legs because she likes to make sense
of unhappy endings, but sometimes I think she creates all
that stuff just to get a rise out of me.

Rule Number 3 has big, fat, red underlines. I slow my run.
Set my cans on the shoulder of the road to unravel the paper
so I can see. In Tansy's wonky letters, she's written, *Do not
discuss our history*.

Another rule for me. When I didn't understand why I had
to disappear every two weeks, Tansy underlined this final rule
and explained, *You have an almost unmanageable thirst for adventure. I know it makes me seem like the villain, but not answering your
every question is for your own good, G. You can count on me to keep
you whole and safe*.

I suppose there's wisdom in that. Both of us will do
anything to prevent the avalanche—even more alters taking
root in our already crowded mind.

~

*W*hen I return home, the bronze wall clock in
the hall says it's 6:28. I take off my shoes.
Splash some much-needed water on my face.

Navy-colored yarn splays halfway across the parlor rug from the settee, and the stove's front left burner's been left on. Quickly, I switch off the orange-blue flame.

While I couldn't say what causes Tansy's take-overs, one thing I can say for certain is, I'm never allowed to wander freely around the house on her time. Feels strange that she hasn't already pushed me out—hijacked the dinghy.

A car engine suddenly booms and rattles outside. I take an extra step toward the coffee table. Not that the sound of a car engine should startle me—we receive countless uninvited visitors, day or night—but my tolerance hasn't exactly been built up. By now, I suppose I'm used to entering the void.

While the stranger's car rumbles away, I set to straightening up the parlor's damask throw pillows, washing the dishes, and cleaning out the cobwebs in the library.

Tansy says people used to call all the time, asking for a tour of the place—but, lucky for her, we no longer have a landline. I suppose a tour could be fun for the average tourist, what with the sixteen-foot tall ceilings and meticulously maintained hardwood floors. Anybody could appreciate the intricately carved door moldings, thick rope pillars, and Texas Lone Star motif. What I don't get is why Tansy insists on covering up the half-moon stained glass windows. Her fear of the outside world means we get to live in a cave.

A few feet in front of me lays a beige book on the floor, splayed open wide. If I were to guess, I'd say that Tansy threw that—hit the window to spook an unwanted tourist. She *can* get rather crotchety. Maybe the tourist was getting too close? Climbed over the fence? There's nothing Tansy treasures more in this world than privacy.

Setting out across the room, I bend down to retrieve the book and re-shelve it on the imposing bookcase.

Tansy screeches inside my head, *Having fun playin' detective, G?*

I bump into the desk, which jabs me in the side. "I ... couldn't find you. I followed curfew and got back in plenty of time."

Catching sight of myself in a wall mirror, I find the abundant curls Francesca gave me have already wilted to sad, limp waves. I could use some eyeliner and mascara, though, I've got to admit, for the first time in forever, my eyebrows look great.

"Well, I don't know about you, but I'm starvin'!" Tansy seizes control of our lips and mentally taps me on the shoulder like she's ready to send me to Canada till summertime. But I'm not ready to go just yet. Not after what Olly said to me.

Digging our nails into the book, I square my shoulders. "Someone said we belong in the slammer, Tansy."

To prove I'm serious, I turn for the mirror to study our pallid face. Must see if her reaction gives anything away.

But all I get back is indifferent, soot-colored eyes.

"Well, what did he mean?"

Lifting our chin toward the clock in the hall, Tansy coolly says, "Rule. Number. Three." She rolls the "r" like she's part of the aristocracy.

Still, diplomacy just might be my middle name. "I know we're not supposed to talk about our history, but he was talking about *prison*, Tansy."

In the mirror, my other half's gaze flickers inside mine. Our lips are slightly chapped, and, yes, we still have cartoonishly large eyes, but neither of these facts should distract her from the fact that I have a point.

Tansy huffs, "You must be speakin' of Olly Joliffe."

I give a swift nod.

"'Skinnymalinky went to the pictures n' fell through the seat!'" She recites one of her favorite nursery rhymes. Rolling our eyes, she adds, "Kid wouldn't know amnesia if it smacked him up the backside."

I'd like to settle into the easy chair, hash out every single particular of what she means, but I have to be careful. Tansy doesn't like me threatening her authority. But I'm not willing to back down, either, so I get right to it. "Why does Olly claim that I'm lying about losing my memories?"

Tansy takes her sweet time running her tongue along the front of our upper teeth. "'Cause the boy's a bona fide imbecile, that's why."

"Why would he say we deserve to be locked up?"

Primly folding her hands over our stomach, Tansy looks down our pale nose at me. "How should I know?" Seeing how that's not enough of an answer, she huffs, "The Joliffes have *always* been morons." She waves our hand. "Too many of the same people in the family tree."

"But *you* know what we did in our past." If I had control of our hands, I'd point a finger at her face. "You're not willing to tell me."

"Do you *want* the avalanche?" Tansy's voice always comes out more Southern when she shrieks. She paces to a jewelry box on a shelf and stuffs on a mess of gaudy bracelets and rings. "I thought you were smarter than that, G."

"Look, you know I don't want the avalanche, but I thought—"

In one swift move, Tansy snaps the jewelry box shut while pulling out an ornate necklace with gems and beads. She leads us past the floor-to-ceiling bookcase. "Why don't you go and get some rest, hmm?"

I try to lift my hand to argue. But she tucks me into my corner while slipping on the necklace that's heavier than a boa constrictor, dead or alive.

When I come to, I'm in Tansy's curve-backed reading chair, again in the library. A tiny knit cat sweater lies in my lap, and my hair's so greasy, it sticks to the side of my face.

As I look down, I find that I'm also clothed in one of Tansy's Victorian dresses—one she must have gotten from a closet in the estate. This one's mustard colored with pleats. Last thing I feel like doing is searching every single room for my running clothes—Tansy left them in the trash last time—but the sooner I get out of this dress, the better. The corset and fabric—not to mention the massive necklace—are worse than an iron maiden torture device.

While the house boasts sixteen rooms and spans something like nine thousand square feet, neither Tansy nor I ever really clean. All the arches and pillars are too much work—not to mention the sickly shade of green that's splattered on the walls, curtains, and wood paneling.

The beer steins on the ledge halfway up the wall scream that the den's a man's domain. It's the taxidermy moose mounted on the back wall, though, that gives me pause. *Was*

Mr. Hardin my husband? What exactly did Olly mean? What if Mr. Hardin was a ninety-year-old invalid, who later learned he'd been conned into marrying a moody gold digger with questionable hygiene?

Egg-and-dart patterns scrawl across the chairs, matching the timeless Victorian theme, and an enormous rug lies beneath three couches that form a "U" shape.

At the back corner of the room, though, lie my running shorts in an untidy heap.

I stoop to pick them up. Peer up to the second-floor balcony. Maybe in a fit of artistic flair, Tansy stripped down to the nude and tossed my shorts over the side.

One of my socks spills like frozen water over the edge of a beer stein. I snatch up the sock, only to knock into the ledge. Oops—another mug slips off, but I catch the weighty cup just in time.

Setting it back on the shelf, I thank the good Lord that my reflexes are so speedy. I slip off Tansy's bracelets and necklace and place them on an antique table. Peel out of the dress and drape it across the antlers. Take that, Tansy.

I could wear the dirty shorts and sock I just found, but last thing I need is to greet Francesca with twice the stink. Down to nothing but a slip, I head for the main-story bedroom to see if I can find some extra running clothes. Maybe.

For once, I'm actually glad for the boarded up windows. A throng of voices ring like excited carolers from outside. They're talking about the cupola, and, chances are, in about five seconds, they'll be dreaming about the chances of getting a look inside.

From the derelict condition of the grounds, most assume Hardin Mansion's been vacant for a while. If it were up to me, I'd trim the bushes—make things a little more presentable— but Tansy likes to keep up appearances that no one lives here.

I'd try to make her see reason, but coming out for a few hours every fourteen days doesn't give one much time.

The bureau near the bedroom door seems promising. I pull open the top creaky drawer, only to find a pile of petticoats and wool stockings.

Drawer after drawer is the same.

A mess of crumpled-up dresses strewn across the floor serve as a testament to how Tansy feels about doing laundry. There's a cream dress, a pink dress, and a brown one that reminds me of something the Brontë sisters would have worn back in the day. What I would give to slip away from here—grab a guitar and experience more of *my* vibe. Maybe visit the Grand Ole Opry ...

Seeing how running clothes are in short supply, I sidestep the dresses and aim for the stairs. My favorite running joggers and visor *might* be hanging over a curtain rod, if I'm lucky. Though Tansy once told me that the basement's where she keeps things she doesn't like.

All right, I'll go downstairs—just as soon as I find a flashlight.

I take a sizeable step into the hall, only to sideswipe a mounted longhorn skull, its stately horns jutting left and right.

My shirt and socks sway from the horns—almost like Tansy knew I'd be leaving her dress a similar way.

I stifle a giggle. Snatch up the clothes, and pay my respects. "Thanks, Tansy."

I reward myself for running longer than usual by stopping by *Hey, Sugar* for a treat. Their Chocolate Thunder truffle is gooey, salty, glorious, and it sticks to my teeth. Part of me wants to sample each and every baked good, but I'm not so sure my stomach could handle it. Tansy's limited diet makes celery seem spicy.

The store owner keeps watching me like a hawk, though I'm not sure why. The shop's baby blue walls drown out the dull blue of her eyes, and her short, cropped hair is nearly the same pale color of her skin. While she munches on a fistful of rock candy, I can't tell if she's watching me because she wants to sell me more chocolates, or if there's something more somber on her mind.

When, after a full twenty seconds the woman still hasn't looked away, I think to try some small talk—since we all know that's my forte—but her eyes are brimming with water and her arms are going stick-straight.

Her face is beet red.

The same bright, primary color in Tansy's latest painting.

She's clutching her neck, and she really must be choking. I should do the Heimlich maneuver. Do I know the Heimlich maneuver, or have I lost that memory?

Now *my* arms are pinned like pieces of wood superglued to my sides.

Another customer with a handlebar mustache and hair buzzed on the sides darts around the counter and seizes the lady from behind. Hands locked together, he repeatedly squeezes her stomach between the naval and ribcage.

I grab the ledge of the counter. Dig my nails into the granite while the woman's face flushes the color of purple frosting.

The man continues to squeeze her stomach. Again and again, and I can't believe I'm not doing anything.

On the following squeeze, a piece of rock candy dislodges from the woman's mouth, and it sails through the air, nearly smacking me in the face.

The man gasps. "Are you okay?"

"Yes," I say, noting how his mustache gives him a decidedly "Mr. Pringles" vibe. Oh, but he wasn't asking me. He was asking the woman, which is right.

Her face washes from scarlet to her earlier pale sheen. "Yes." She wheezes, shoulders and elbows drawn up while she clutches the counter. "At least, I'm alive."

Pure, cold hatred shoots from the man's eyes. "*You* weren't going to help her!" He juts a crooked finger in my face. "What were you going to do? Let my wife die?"

The woman and her husband exchange conspiratorial looks while my head spins sideways.

I only came for chocolates. I didn't mean to cause a problem. All I wanted was to help the business, not hurt anybody.

"She really does deserve to be locked up," the pale woman says, just like what Olly said.

"What were you going to do next?" The man lifts his arms. "Destroy our business? Get outta here before I call the police!"

I scramble for the door, but not before knocking into a stuffed unicorn in a cowboy hat and Texas flag bowtie.

"*E*ver consider putting your hair in a braid?" Francesca surveys my hair with a toothy grimace, showing off the cute gap in her front teeth.

To be fair, I put my hair up before I left the house, but Tansy must have misplaced all the brushes I bought. And I forgot to check my reflection in the mirror for the millionth time.

"I know, I'm sorry." I paw at my hair for the elastic. It's in there, but just barely. I don't really want to see how I look, but beggars can't be choosers, so I take the plunge and look in the mirror anyway.

Hmm. Guess I'm looking a little more "Edward Scissorhands" today. I've got this gigantic poof with several messy tendrils slipping down the side of my face. All I need is the black lipstick and I'll be set for the next big goth party.

At least my eyebrows still look nice.

Francesca rests a weighty hand on my shoulder. "You'd be beautiful even if we shaved off this unruly mane."

My heart does this happy, skippy beat. "Now there's an idea ..."

Francesca waves her hand like she just ordered a shooting. "No, no, hon—WAIT!"

Her voice carried louder than usual, and she giggles, reaching up to smooth back her coiled hair that's tied into a natural puff updo. Her manager—Wanda? Rita?—scowls so big, I'm afraid she's going to ply us with dunce caps for misbehaving, so I shoot her my most friendly smile to show that Francesca's doing a fabulous job.

When Francesca tries tugging her brush through my hair, though, it's like moving an elephant through concrete.

"Shave it," I beg. "Please."

"Don't you talk no sacrilege!" Francesca gives another painful tug. "Your hair is gorgeous. It just needs a little TLC." Wrenching the brush free, she steps backward a few steps and cups her chin with one hand, pondering. "You *do* own a brush, right?"

"I'll buy another." I sink further in my seat.

Maybe I can stick it in the bathroom cupboard before Tansy takes over next time.

While Francesca wordlessly fastens the back buttons of my cloak, I can't help thinking that she's the one person I can be myself around without being judged all the time. In the past, I've made it a point to keep things between us light, but, I have to ask, "Do you happen to know Olly Joliffe?"

Francesca's earrings jangle as she fastens the top button. "Who?"

"Olly. Joliffe."

She bites her bottom lip. "Can't say I do."

I run my finger down the slick front of the nylon cape. "He said that I deserve to be in the slammer. So did the *Hey, Sugar* owners. Do you have any idea why?"

At once, Francesca's beautiful, brown eyes drift to meet mine. "Why you telling me this? You messing with me?"

"No!" I shift in my seat. "I swear. But I have to tell you, everybody in this town keeps giving me the evil eye."

Francesca glances to the back of the store where Wanda-Rita straightens the purple shampoo bottles on the back-wall display. Three of her colleagues are whispering in a group at the back, and that doesn't look very inclusive, if you ask me.

"Honey, she isn't giving you the evil eye," Francesca says. "She's doing that *all* for me."

Sensing there's something underlying what she's saying, I wait a breath for Francesca to elaborate.

She leans in, her jasmine and shea butter lotion wafting over me. "Look, I'm new in town, so I don't know everything, but"—she peers over her shoulder at Wanda-Rita, then her colleagues—"not everyone in this town is as they seem ..."

What, do they have a thing against outsiders? I've been here for—well, six—seven—ten?—months, at least. So, yes, Francesca and I would both be newcomers to an already tight-knit community.

"Small towns." I sigh.

Francesca holds my gaze a bit longer, as if I'm supposed to read between the lines. But she's not the one they're saying should be locked up. Unless they think she does, too, just for associating with me.

Before she can say anything else, Wanda-Rita comes charging up like she's manning the busiest hair salon in New York City. "You have customers waiting!" Her nostrils flare, and her blonde A-line bounces, reminding me of a Fraulein of the Nazi party.

Francesca mutters under her breath, "Then why don't you ask *Jessica* to come back from her twentieth smoke break?"

Wanda-Rita stiffens. So does Francesca, and she'll soon be out of a job if she doesn't learn to play nice. I open my mouth to say something about how Francesca's made me look a lot less like a I belong in a street gang, but I doubt that'll impress

Wanda-Rita. Plus, Francesca doesn't seem like the sort of person who likes other people fighting her battles.

Gritting her teeth, Wanda-Rita clomps off while Francesca stomps on the chair pedal, giving me the roller-coaster ride of my life.

"Let's get you a wash," she says.

Last thing I like is seeing Francesca angry, so I make sure she's looking at me before leaning in, flaring my nostrils, and importantly cupping the bottom of my faux A-line.

Francesca howls with laughter. Neither of us dare to look at Wanda-Rita, but my good friend does lean in conspiratorially. "Let's get you fixed up with some caramel highlights, hmm?"

I give her about thirty nods before stealing one final look in the mirror. No more gigantic poof, no more messy tendrils. "Buh-bye, Eddie."

$\sim$

Once I'm certain I'm out of sight, I take off for another run. No need to stress Francesca about my hair tangling. Wish I could go somewhere different than the four square miles of Deep Creek.

Really, I'm grateful to get out, but I wouldn't exactly complain if I had to go to a beach in Cabo. A park in Spain. Shoot, a mountain pass in Oklahoma would do the trick, but I shouldn't look a gift horse in the mouth. I'm out of the house. Blessings.

By the time I make it to *Grady Dean's*, Olly's shift must be over, because an old lady with the world's worst arthritis rings me up, practically moving backwards in time. When I jog toward home, groceries in hand, at last, my good spirits are reblooming. The sun's out. Nutcrackers line a pretty, paved driveway, and a pair of loose pups become my new running buddies. One's a gorgeous German Shepherd. The other's a beautiful caramel-colored mutt with a lab head shape.

I can't help but smile. "Hey, guys."

The duo sniff at my bags, obviously hungry. I wish I had a treat, but Tansy only ever lets me buy kitty litter and her food. Unable to help myself, I slow to a stop. Set down my bags on the shoulder of the road and scratch behind their ears, greedy for their company.

"Who's a good girl?" I ask the German Shepherd, whose tongue is lolling to the side. "Oh, are you a good girl, too?" I ask the lab mix, making sure to give them both a thorough scratching.

Their tails are practically battery-operated, wagging double-time. I pat their beautiful stomachs. Scratch their furry sides, when a stout woman in a purple jogging suit comes bouncing down the red brick mansion's driveway.

"Jewel!" she cries. "Macy!"

Oh, looks like I've found their owner. I wave.

"Here they are." The woman's cherry lipstick matches the friendliness on her face. Exhaling in relief, she reaches for her fur babies with a double-sided leash. "Little devils slipped through the door the second I opened it."

I can't help digging my fingers into their glorious fur. "Bet they're fast."

The woman secures Jewel, the German Shepherd's collar says, first, then Macy. "Oh, you have no idea." Standing up straight, she somehow levels me with her squat five-foot-nil height. "I get seizures, see. And dogs? Well, I've always been terrified. But I got Jewel here to help me." She pats the German Shepherd's head. "Had to stop my fearful side from holding the reins."

I scratch behind Macy's soft, caramel ears. "I'm sure you had a reason to be worried."

The sun's starting to set. Looks like it's about that time. Grabbing my bags, I take a few steps toward home and Tansy.

"They're beautiful animals!" I stumble on a pothole but right my footing. "Actually, I wish I could have a pair of dogs. But my ... *friend* insists cats are all we can handle."

I stumble again. Swing the bags in lame apology. "Anyway —" I accidentally slam the cans into my legs. Try not to wail in agony. "You know how it is. Gotta listen to keep the peace!"

7

By the time I wander home and into the den, the last thing I want to see is Tansy's latest batch of "No Trespassing" signs. This is her way of telling me there are too many tourists, and this, she hopes, will chase them away. But we already have half a dozen signs posted around the property.

Half-empty paint buckets perch precariously on the floor, no drop cloths in sight. Yellow paint splatters across one of the couches, and I have to wonder where Tansy scrounged up the metal signs. Maybe they were in the shed? But she doesn't like to venture out. Maybe she half woke me up to get them, then tucked me back in before I became cognizant of what was happening.

Something ... smells like it died.

I track the scent to the back porch, where the odor only intensifies. Reminds me of a skunk under water. The pit in my stomach grows wider. I sincerely hope Jerusha or Hawkins haven't died.

I open the screen door, hinges shrieking, and there, on the

deck, lies a squirrel, splayed across the welcome mat, intestines spilling out. The smell of putrefying flesh has me placing my arm over my nose. I spy an old, chopping knife about two feet from the squirrel, stuck into the wooden porch like a trophy.

Tansy.

Actually, there's a sense of pride in the precision of the cut, like she wanted to photograph the scene. But I know why she did this. *Anything to scare away the tourists*, she would say.

Drifting outside, I let the screen door fall, bouncing shut behind me, and spot another black and white lump on the porch. Flies buzz on black and white feathers, hungry.

I grind my teeth together. It's a once beautiful, living magpie. "Okay, I understand your discontent with the tourists, but, *Tansy*, this is just awful!"

One of our neighbors—a bald guy in tan overalls—rolls his dumpster out to the road. I duck behind the pillar just as he looks our way.

"We are going to officially be known as the creepy squirrel and bird lady!"

Neighbor Guy jerks his head up to look even closer at me, but Tansy has us spinning on our heels and lurching us back through the screen door.

I'm a marionette, and she's pulling my strings.

Wishing more than ever that she hadn't done this, I let her march us past the paint buckets and into the kitchen where the counters are strewn with used chamomile tea bags and stains.

"You think you're clever," I say. "You think this will keep the tourists away—but, in case you haven't noticed, I *am* you. When you give me extra chores to do, it eats into *both* our time!"

Tansy stews beneath my surface, fuming. Our hands are

balling into fists and a low snarl is curling at the back of our throat. "What if I told you I *didn't* do it?"

I lift my hands. "Then we'd both know you'd be lying!"

"I could say you're doin' the same thing. Besides, the both of us know about your lil' trick of bringin' home fewer cans than usual just so you can get the drop on me!"

"I ... didn't do that."

"*Thirteen.*" Tansy's voice gurgles with anger. "Don't you dare try to deny it. I know how you've been covetin' my time."

"I got fourteen!" Unless, somehow, I miscounted while trying to avoid Olly. If so, Tansy should have calmly brought it to my attention, not kill the first defenseless animals she sees.

I spin to stalk into another room. "We *both* want more time."

Tansy spins me back. "Stay!"

Curling our fingers into fists, I prepare for her to push me out when a rush of excited voices whoop from outside. Car doors slam, and Tansy stills like a sunken log inside me. Someone's already saying how pretty the cupola is while Tansy takes deep and calming breaths.

"They won't stay long," I try to comfort her while she pulls in our arms and breathes raggedly.

"Hope you're right."

My stomach twists. I never like to hear her frightened voice. Someone out there complains about needing to pee—guess they're too far away to see what Tansy did to the squirrel and magpie—but after a long time, car doors are slamming again, and a diesel engine roars to life.

"I'll go clean it up," I reassure my other half with a sigh.

Tansy has us jutting out our lower lip. "*I'm* fine with you waitin' at least a week."

"But there's blood on the porch," I hiss, pacing to the den. "It'll stain."

Tansy wildly waves our hand in the air. "With all your social proclivities, Nostradamus, you can be *such* a killjoy." She reaches toward an antique side table and snatches up a pair of satin opera gloves and starts pulling them on, of all things.

I tug them off. "And *you* need to get back to reality. Remember, we have to live in this town, Tansy."

She grasps for the gloves. "I like anonymity."

Exasperated, I toss the gloves to the table and give her a look that rivals the time I caught her licking each and every one of our bowls clean. I had to give her a thirty minute discussion on germs and hygiene.

Tansy slumps, but she's still eyeing those opera gloves, so I snatch them up and stuff them inside the table's drawer. "How do you think I'll bury the bodies without being seen?"

She sniffs. "Oh, don't be so lily livered. I'm sure you'll find a way."

8

I do feel a little terrible for not digging two graves, but I'm in a rush, and, for all I know, Tansy will soon be insisting that the squirrel "belongs" with the magpie.

At least I'm out of the house. Gaining a little independence, one secret step at a time. Truth be told, I've been stockpiling change for a while—all the dollars and cents from buying groceries. Tansy may be the one who knows where the bulk of the money is, but, slowly yet surely, I'll be able to accumulate enough to go on a trip. Nashville's been calling to me for ages. Maybe I'll eventually be able to prove to Tansy that we're healthy enough to leave Deep Creek. I'll know more about what happened in our past, and she'll agree that her regimented schedule is a bit extreme.

Shoveling the remaining dirt over the corpses, I try to think how to get Tansy to split more fair hours with me. I get every-other-weekend? But she already accused me of cheating her to steal time ...

A twig snaps, practically a bomb going off in the copse of trees.

I spin around, only to find naked tree limbs crowding

round like prison inmates. I'm on the southwest corner of the estate—toward town, but away from the road. Not sure why anyone would be on this side of the property.

No one moves.

No one so much as breathes.

Must have been a squirrel ... just a squirrel ... one that hasn't been split open with a knife.

Turning back to my shovel, I aim to finish the job when another twig-snap practically blasts a crater in the mess of dirt and leaves.

I reel around. Accidentally bite my tongue as a man with a mop of dark hair lurks like a thorn amidst the grapevine. He dons a brown jacket, snug-fitting blue jeans, and I'd say he's handsome, except for the complete and utter lack of warmth in his eyes. It's like looking into a glacier—cold, brittle; slow moving.

Only a few inches taller than me, the stranger eventually slurs, "What're you buryin' out here, Gemma Louise?"

I take my time smoothing out the rest of the dirt with the edge of my shovel. "Oh, just a little roadkill," I lie.

"Ya know"—he licks his lips—"the vultures will make fast work of any"—licks again—"dead bodies." The man's gaze is so cool that an unexpected chill travels up my spine. He rearranges a lump of chew to his left cheek before spitting it out and nodding about three times. "Can't hide in that house forever." He hooks his thumb in his front belt loop and squares his shoulders like he deserves a medal. "Some might say these weekly excursions of yours are a tad bit risky ..."

The wind rustles the leaves—the ethereal sound of an oboe's double reed. A larger animal might be foraging for food in the forest, for all I know. A bobcat. Or a coyote.

Again, the man licks his lips, revealing sores on the corners of his mouth. "An' I *know* you killed WT."

I don't know what to say next. If it weren't for the fact

that I just finished burying two corpses, I'd have a much quicker reply.

As is, I grip the rough shovel handle between my hands. "I'm sorry?"

"It may've been when the bushes n' such were, eh, 'bushy,' but I know what ya did. Four months ain't that long. Not that it matters, as long as you stay tucked inside, mindin' your own business." Reaching into his coat pocket, he pulls out a badge with a silver star that has five points.

He's the town sheriff. The bloody town sheriff, and, while I'm not exactly sure about everything he's saying, I do know he's accusing me.

~

Stomping past the paint buckets, I accidentally end up knocking one over in the hallway. Yeah, I should clean it up. But Tansy can do it—especially if she has time to dress for a ball every freaking day.

The drawer handles in the kitchen rattle with my every step. I'm half-tempted to take a swing at all her pretty teacups, but I take a few deep breaths to calm myself before I say what I need to say. "I talked to the sheriff. Why didn't you say that the *cops* were watching me?"

Tansy's consciousness lazily floats up like the triangular window of an eight ball. I can practically feel her filing her nails in luxury. "Oh?" *Scratch, scratch, scratch; scrrrape.* "And what, may I ask, did the illustrious Jesse Beauchamp have to say?"

I smack the marble counter. "He said that I *killed* a 'WT'!" Really, I can't believe I still don't know the identity of Mr. "H." But WT has to be him. Right? "Tansy, tell me. Is WT 'Mr. H'?"

A strangled laugh tears like a train wreck through our teeth. "You need to calm down, G."

But I can't tell if she's mocking me. "How am I supposed to calm down? *You* didn't just get accused of murder!"

Sighing, Tansy rocks back on the heels of our consciousness. "He accuses you, Rosebud, he accuses me."

All too soon, a hot flash burns across my cheeks. "*You're* not the one who just talked to the guy." I veer around the counter to let out some of my pent up energy. "He seemed to really believe that I'm guilty." I smack the marble again. "I have no idea if it's true! Am I guilty? You've *got* to level with me."

"It isn't true," Tansy says far too sheepishly. "You simply let WT walk outta our life ..."

Bracing myself against the wall, I wait for Tansy to explain, but she doesn't so much as look at an old family photograph, a meaningful teaspoon, a shot glass. Nothing.

"Were we married to him?"

"This is what I was afraid of," Tansy says way too rationally. "Rule Number Three." She rolls the "r" again, seriously testing me. "Do not discuss our history. We risk you bein' overloaded, and neither of us wants that, G!"

"But it's like"—I think of the woman in the purple jogging suit with the seizures and dogs—"my brain is going to seize. I can *feel* the answers bubbling up, about to explode." I pound the wall, and brittle wallpaper and plaster crumble in my wake. "Maybe we should let the answers come. Tell me exactly what's going on. If it happens here, it'll be safer, right?"

Tansy leans against a canopied bed she's constructed in a frilly corner of our mind. "We married him about a year ago. The most handsome man in all the world. Wherever he may be."

"So, we *were* married! ... Or are ..." I wish I had access to a picture of him in my head. The clothes he wore. If he had a kind face. "Wait, you mean you don't know where he is?"

Tansy shrugs like picking out handkerchiefs would be a better use of our time. "He might be dead. Or he might very much be alive ..."

"So, then, why is the sheriff pointing a finger at me?"

Tansy snatches up a parasol that she left on the kitchen counter and tosses it in the air, making it flip, before catching it just in time. "All of that information will come, Rosebud, in good time."

"Stop calling me Rosebud!" I rip the parasol out of her hand and toss it to the corner.

Tansy glowers. "You and I both know that these details are somethin' I simply cannot explain. You need to artfully use your cerebral icepick to chip away at the memori—"

"How long ago did it happen?" Sheriff Beauchamp talked about the bushes "being bushy," so it had to have happened last summer—or spring—but I *have* to see if Tansy's being honest with me.

"I suppose," Tansy says with deep regret, "it happened in the month that bears Julius Caesar's grandnephew's name."

". . . July?"

"August, Rosebud, the grandnephew's name is Augustus. Honestly, it's well-past time that you brushed up on your history."

It looks like she's being honest, so I'll accept that. Okay. "So why do you think WT isn't dead? Have you heard from him recently?"

Tansy smooths our hand over the fraying wallpaper with its pale pink flowers and olive green leaves. "There's never been a body."

A body.

An uninvited shiver scurries up my spine.

All right, I can work with this. There's never been a body.

Maybe I should stop while I'm ahead. Stay calm and collected, one puzzle piece at a time.

Except, now that I've got a whiff of the truth, no way will one puzzle piece be enough for me.

In an effort to appear calm and collected, I run my fingers through our tangled hair. Seems I have a husband that may or may not be alive—and the town thinks I killed the guy.

But I haven't been locked up, which means they don't have proof.

I *knew* I should've been paranoid about burying that squirrel and magpie.

Everything's spinning out of control. I can't believe I still don't know much more than I knew when first waking up last time. There's a decorative bench right across the hallway, so I wander over to its iron clutches to try and think.

"Tansy ..." She has to see logic—that I'm not merely digging for another puzzle piece. "Why did you have to go and kill those animals?"

"I didn't, I swear to you!" She sniffs, something she often does when she lies. "And the tourists were goin' to storm the castle. It happened to Marie Antoinette"—she waves an arm —"it could happen to me!"

"But we don't live in France." I fold our arms. "And this is not an aristocracy."

"*Oui, mon cherie, oui!* But they could all be Guy Fawkes', plottin' to make us go ka-blooey!"

I raise a hand to argue, when I accidentally hit a shelf— and knock off an angel figurine. It smashes on the ground.

We both flinch at the noise.

And all we can do is stop and stare. Pull up our legs. From the way it broke, it now looks like a mask is covering the angel's face.

Tansy whoops. "Looks like the Guy Fawkes' are already inside!"

I try to stay calm, but, I can't help it. In a bit of hysteria, I'm also laughing. "We *really* need to work on your fear of strangers."

"I know ..." Tansy knocks our head against the wall as the plaster crumbles. "But the whole lot of 'em give me the willies."

I could tell her there's nothing to worry about, but I can't know that. The only things I know are what Tansy tells me.

Still, any argument we have seriously impairs my ability to know what's going on, so I reach out and pat her on the leg.

Tansy closes her eyes, and begins humming a jazzy tune before suddenly breaking off mid-refrain. "Say, Gemma, do you think you could call me 'ladybird' when you feel a deep and abidin' affection for me?"

Not exactly sure why she wants to be called that, but I'm not in the mood to argue. "Sure, Tansy."

"Do you think we could watch the birds for a while? Just till things calm down. There's a skylight in the den through which I like to watch the vultures fly."

I give her a half nod, when, all at once, she has us lurching us to our feet. She extends our arms, "flies" us past the rope pillars, and giggles as we knock over another bucketful of paint.

9

"*L*et's say I know someone," I tell Francesca while getting my hair done on a Thursday ... or Friday. "And let's say that person is very controlling."

I feel bad about turning on Tansy, but, apart from sitting with her and learning the markings of every raven, crow, and turkey vulture in Wise County, I've progressed very little in my quest to know what's happened these past few weeks.

Francesca glances up from her handiwork, her inquisitive eyes sparkling even brighter next to her rose gold earrings. "Family member?"

"In a way ..." I shift in my cushioned seat. "And let's say I need them to talk to me about something, but they absolutely will not explain."

Francesca pulls back another piece of hair to add to my Dutch braid. I don't need a cut, and she's determined that this can help minimize any future tangling. "I'm assuming this person needs to stay in your life."

An image of Tansy stubbornly tugging on those opera gloves flashes through my mind. "She's not going anywhere."

"Mm-hmm." Francesca secures another piece of hair. "And when all's said and done, what's this person care most about?"

"That's easy. Her space ... though, really, I'm the one person in the world who makes it possible for her to stay home and *have* said space."

Francesca juts out her lower lip in this adorable, commis-erating sort of way. "Sounds like this 'friend' of yours needs to be whacked upside the head by the ol' gratitude tree." Clucking her tongue, she plants a bangled hand on her hip. "And it wouldn't hurt for you to say so straight to her face. She needs *you*. Remind her of that. If she really wants a rela-tionship, then there needs to be a hefty amount of give and take." She grabs the squirt bottle and spritzes my hair enough to reenact the conditions of the Amazon rainforest.

With the side of my hand, I wipe the water from my eyes. "But what if she doesn't listen to me?"

Francesca puts her other hand on her hip. "You *absolutely* cannot cut this person out of your life?"

I can't help but laugh. "That would be nice."

"Sounds like she doesn't know how good she has it," Francesca mutters, grabbing the squirt bottle and generously spritzing. "Hon, I can't see how *anyone* wouldn't want to meet you at least halfway. Then"—she growls, eyeing the stylist next to us, who's grabbing a pack of cigarettes for another smoke break—"you gotta bring home a little MMA."

Not sure what that is. "What's MMA?"

Francesca roars with laughter before planting a hand on her hip. "Mixed martial arts. You really don't get out much, do you?"

I look around guiltily for Wanda-Rita, but the salon tyrant doesn't seem to be close by, thankfully. And I can't really smack around Tansy since we share the same body. "I'm not really sure that would be a good id—"

"Symbolically speaking." Francesca brings her long-nailed

pointer finger to my lips and shushes me. "This girl's obviously using you, and from what you've said, sounds like things aren't going to change without you building your own fighting ring. Time to make your *own* rules." She gives a piece of hair near my ear a firm tug. "Give the con artist the double leg takedown she's least expecting."

Well, then. I've got to admit, I wasn't expecting Francesca to speak so passionately. Still, whatever I've been doing with Tansy hasn't been working. Plus, I'm tired of things being on *her* terms all the time. I open my mouth to say as much when Francesca slips a bottle of Nair out of her pocket and sets it on her neighboring hair stylist's counter with no one in sight. The handwritten label says, "Wonder if your shampoo bottles have any inside???"

"Francesca!" I can't help laughing as she giggles and pulls back a piece of my bangs. "So how do you know about fighting?"

She waves her hand. "Husband. He's a fighter. Or was ..." She grows quiet and focuses on tying off my hair to secure the braid. "I'll have him teach you some moves, sugar ... once I can get him to talk to me."

Sensing Francesca's problems run deeper than she's saying, I grab the Nair bottle and nod for her to put it back before Wanda-Rita goes on a rampage. "What's going on?"

Francesca accepts the bottle and stuffs it back in her pocket with a resigned sigh. "You just focus on your friend. Double. Leg. Takedown. Mmm-mmm."

10

"I'm ba-a-ack!" My nose burns from the cold as I step inside the house. I brush past the coat rack. Tug on one of the pegs that looks positively empty.

Sure, I've brought Tansy's soup, and there's a chance she won't undo my braid, but, better yet, I have a plan, a mighty suggestion to make. Tansy may feel like I can't handle the truth—that pushing too hard will bring on the avalanche—but, if we calmly work together, that won't happen. Francesca has convinced me.

An earthy aroma wafts from a bouquet of mums Tansy must have hung from the doorway. Pinecones crunch beneath my sneakers. I guess Tansy must have grabbed all the vegetation from the windows. Girl's been busy.

Except all of this must have happened before I left this morning. Didn't know until I got back. Sometimes I forget the two of us share the same body.

The twinkling of a wind chime chirrups from an open window, and looks like Tansy's been brave enough to summon the fresh air, even if it's freezing.

Luckily, there's no blood or paint spilled on the carpet—at

least, not this time. Even the rugs have been shaken out. Maybe Tansy's feeling grateful that I looked at the birds with her for all that time.

Not really sure what to say by way of a chipper greeting, I do my best. "Looks great, er ... ladybird."

But she doesn't so much as flinch a reply. A wind chime clinkety-clinks through the window—it's handcrafted with a slew of forks and knives.

Lifting the grocery bags to the counter, I set to straightening the teacups, coffee maker, and toaster with a fist-sized rust stain. Most of the soup bowls look like they've been soaking in grease, and the near-empty dish soap bottle on the counter tells me I'll soon need to badger Tansy for more grocery money.

The sink needs to be washed out, and it doesn't look like the counters have been wiped down since last January. Though a crumpled tea cloth does hang from the oven handle. "Two more points for fine and dainty living, Tansy."

Still nothing.

That's when I notice the board and rope-made swing that's recently been installed, dangling by the nearest window from the plaster ceiling. The ropes have been twisted into knots and coil around each other in double helix strands like DNA. The wooden seat's a bit warped, but Tansy stirs from our subconscious and plops us down anyway.

I'm afraid the screws in the ceiling are going to pull loose from the plaster as Tansy enthusiastically pumps our legs. She settles an ivy wreath on our head, flings a feather boa over our shoulders, and pumps three more times. Five or six kicks in, I've had enough.

"I ran into Jesse Beauchamp again today." It isn't true, but it's the only thing I can think of to distract Tansy from swinging. "He actually admitted why he thinks I killed WT!"

Tansy gasps, clambering up from the bridge of our throat. "What happened?"

I jump from the swing and set to stacking a pink flowered teacup in the cupboard—in the name of keeping our hands busy.

"Gemma Louise Coldiron, you better be fixin' to tell me."

Meticulously, I stack another cup. "Oh, you know. He threatened to bring me in. I threatened to sue him for wrongful imprisonment." Not sure if that's a thing, but I give it a whirl before adding a third teacup to the stack that's getting dangerously high. "And then, when we were ..." Crap, what was I saying? "When we were ..."

"WHEN WE WERE WHAT, G?" Tansy nearly makes the stack fall sideways. I catch the wobbling tower, but only just in time. Shift it over a smidge to prevent all the dishes from falling. "You *don't* remember, do you?" She pulls our hands down and balls them into fists. "You were just baitin' me by calling me my most treasured name."

I wish she wasn't right, but she has to see that she's not the only person who matters in our life. Besides, what did Francesca say? "Sometimes a girl's got to do a secret jab to stay in the ring."

"'Secret *jab*'?" Tansy moves our mouth like she's trying to say something in Chinese. "Tell me, in all our time together, have I really treated you so terribly?" She gestures at the shaken-out rug and the dried mums. Also the red and white checkered book she's apparently lain out with long, slender letters on the cover. *Deep Creek Eats.* I don't believe it. Tansy's actually inviting me to go out to eat.

But when would I do that, really? And it's not like it would be fun when the entire town thinks I'm a murderer, and I still don't even know my favorite color or the date of my birthday.

Marching to the trapezoidal mirror in the hallway, I kick

off my shoes and hold onto them with one hand. I need to have something of mine to hold onto to stop Tansy from pushing me out before I'm ready.

Staring into our deep brown eyes, I make sure she's paying attention when I say, "Everyone looks at me like I'm a murderer in this town, Tansy."

She flinches—I'm onto something—so I squeeze the tops of my shoes, refusing to be backed into a corner.

"And I know how you're going to help me regain my memories."

Tansy shakes our head a teensy fraction to the right.

I grip my shoes so hard, the soles actually imprint on the side of my leg. "All you have to do is write down a list of the most important people and places in our life. I'll do the legwork."

Tansy purses our lips. "Why-y-y?"

"Because I really think this is what it takes to be healthy."

"'Health'? You think this is about health?" Tansy smacks the table, rattling a decorative hummingbird broach to our right.

Ignoring the broach, I press our one free palm into the cool mirror glass. "Please."

Tansy seizes the broach and pins it on the feather boa I forgot we were wearing. "You can sit your sweet hindquarters down, 'cause I ain't goin' *anywhere* outside my domain!"

"You don't have to." I rip off the feather boa and strangle it while I try to get her to see reason. What to say? "I'll go."

Again, she slaps the table. "Agrippina! Catherine de' Medici! Bloody Mary!"

"I'm not being an evil dictator, Tansy. You've told me practically nothing. I understand. You don't want us to risk an onslaught of other alters, making even less of you and me. But I *can* stay levelheaded. You forget that I've long-honored our rules."

"But the soup!"

"I didn't bring home less soup. And I *never* break our rules. But if you don't give me a place to start or even a small list of names, I will be forced to figure things out my own way."

Tansy's nose twitches, her gaze practically bulldozing mine. She eyes the feather boa, the broach, and a letter opener on the table I half worry she's going to stick in our eye.

Wringing our hands, she side-swipes the velvety feathers of the boa. "FINE!"

Shocked, I accidentally drop one of my shoes to the floor. Well, now it's even easier to slip on before I leave.

"You can start with the cemetery," Tansy huffs, sagging against the table in defeat. "That is where you'll find your most *cherished* name."

I slowly slip on my shoes, careful not to knock into the table. Don't want her to change her mind. Tiptoeing to the front door, I do everything in my power not to let my tennis shoes squeak. Slip the feather boa to the coat rack. Twist the brass doorknob like turning it too fast will trip an alarm and bring the police.

Once I've got the door cracked open, I step outside.

11

*I*n lieu of crossing railroad tracks, I cut across the neighbor's yard and head east—away from town, away from the square, and away from the courthouse's pretty towers scraping clouds in the sky.

Cutting across fields, I trample over dead leaves, logs, and crisp, dry hay. A steep, downward slope plunges into a creek on the shoulder's far side—a forty foot drop. Far enough to break my neck if I don't watch where I'm going.

As I pause before a second bridge with a healthy amount of litter on the riverbanks, I survey the graffiti on the metal rails, following a bend in the road that twists like a snake.

All at once, something about the wind changes, and a hazy peacefulness tolls through trees. A curved, metal gate stands before an array of tombs, and to the right of the gate is a rock-made sign.

Deep Creek Cemetery.

Short, squatty gravestones sprout like witches' fingers from the grass and purple-tipped henbit. My pulse quickens. Wonder what I'm going to find.

A wind-worn cedar stands like a commanding general

amongst the graves. Its counterparts seem to be bowing and saying, "My liege." Post oaks create a dot-to-dot on the grounds. Ravens cross-stitch parallelograms in the sky.

As I draw nearer, I scan the names on the graves: Paschall, Sparks, Boyd. Another has a few more letters—Finkelstein.

"You have finally come back to me."

An older woman comes out of nowhere, and I spin to get a good look at her. Long, paprika hair contrasts with pale, pink lips that tilt upward from an oval face. I'd say she looks to be in her late sixties, and, really, I would love to look that gorgeous at her age. As she shuffles across the grass, though, she limps—as if whispering about a long ago injury.

Pulling her cardigan closed, she tilts her chin up, as if addressing a crowd from a stage. Sensing my lack of recognition, she stoops to set a bouquet of champagne-colored mums at the front of a grave. This one has a sleek, new front with blocky, crisp lettering.

Edgar, warns the tombstone's face.

Edgar Coldiron.

An unwelcome shiver scurries up my spine.

How exactly do I know that name? I know it almost like it was once mine. Is this who Tansy meant by my most "cherished name"? But why does my subconscious twinge with worry?

The dates on the grave say Edgar was born in the '60s. His death appears to have happened two years ago, February.

Still, something tells me I shouldn't feel too eager to admit he and I share the same last name.

"Who's Edgar?" An unkindness of ravens swoop down from the low-hanging sky.

Pain twists across the older woman's face. "What did you do with your wedding band?" She folds her hands together with an ageless grace.

So I did have one ... but I still haven't had time to think about rings or vows or even a *life*.

The woman's jade eyes become sharp and all-knowing as she searches my face. What if Tansy took my wedding ring and hid it? What if she's hiding mountains of evidence, and *plans* to continue hiding evidence until the day she dies?

Leaves crackle in the wind as the woman braces herself against the top of Edgar's grave, and she's my best lead, so I'd better not scare her off.

"Here, let me help you find somewhere to sit."

Her bangs flutter in the wind as she shakes her head defiantly.

"I'm sorry." I get to the crux of the matter as the wind continues to whistle between its teeth. "But I don't remember anything."

"I know, my darling."

I flinch. Am I supposed to know her? "You ... believe me?"

"Of course I do." The woman extends an arm like she means to pull me in for a hug, but I don't move. Still trying to match a name to a face.

True, between her skinny build and leg injury, I highly doubt she could hurt me, so I try to patch together a response. "I know I was married to WT ..."

The woman looks past me to the harsh, steel wool sky. "It was a beautiful wedding. Way back in the grasslands, through the piney forest last February."

A lump forms on my throat. February—just like when Edgar died. Only he was the year before, I think. I take a tentative step closer to the woman. She knows who I am. But who is she to me?

"You didn't know him well," she says, "your WT. But he reminded you of the father you never had, while bringing out your more adventurous side." Watching me closely, she extends her aged hand and wraps her veiny fingers around mine. Rubbing her thumb over the tops of my knuckles, she somehow stills the tremors that have begun traveling up my arms. "He was the love of your life. I only wish you had more time."

She's saying that I loved him—that WT loved me—and our life together was cut short. By accident, or ... ?

"Gemma." Her voice is a caress when she says my name. "What do you think you need to do to get healthy?"

"That's the exact same thing I brought up with Tans—" I clamp my mouth shut. How well does this woman know me? She could be nothing more to me but an insurance agent. My high school lunch lady.

Releasing my hand, the woman attempts to brace herself on the gravestone, but she misses, staggering.

Somehow, I catch her, and her smile is warm buttermilk. Reminds me of kneading bread in a red and white checkered kitchen—

I reel back. A memory ... a memory's teetering on the edge of my chest, almost like someone's just given me an enormous hug from the inside.

Trails of flour powder a gingham apron while the woman hums a gentle song that reminds me of wildflowers in spring. Her face is younger, pinker, and her footsteps—clip, clip, clip—come at a much faster pace.

"Grammy?" The name flies out of my mouth. I know this woman; she used to feed me graham crackers when I was young, teaching me to say her name. "*Gram.*" *She shakes the cracker.* "*Me.*" *She points both hands at her chest.* "*Gram.*" *She points again to the cracker.* "*Me.*"

"Oh my gosh, it's you!" I gasp. "I *know* you, Grammy ..."

She cries out in shock, gripping my shoulders. Her fingers curl around my arms, and she tugs me into her thin frame. Lifting her arms, the woman I formerly thought was a stranger cocoons me in a hug of cinnamon, cashmere, and bones so thin, I'm afraid she's going to break.

I sag into her shoulder, too starved for human touch to pull away. "I remember you." I say this into the crook of her neck, where her pulse throbs wildly. I'm probably strangling her where we stand, so I release her. "Do you remember me?"

Grammy gently folds her thin hands over mine. "I could *never* forget you, Gemma Louise."

"Who's Edgar?" A knot forms in my gut, and I take a step back to look her in the eye.

Snow white hair. A masculine, stony, square-shaped face. He holds a twitch in his hand, ready to subdue the horses. But he's sliced through their coats already. He whips them—whips them—whips them. I ask him to stop, but he turns, like he's going to use that twitch on me.

"Edgar." My stomach bottoms out, and I'm finding it hard to breathe.

Grammy releases my hand and pats my cheek. "You remember." Shoulders hunched, she hobbles a few steps toward his grave. Running her pointer finger along the top of the gravestone in an invisible pattern, she traces the shape of an infinity ring. "Sometimes the forever we choose is a mistake."

An elegant black dress and high heels make Grammy the most sophisticated woman on the stage. Her necklace bears the shape of an infinity ring. Green, glittery eyes shine like moonstones in the lights as she performs the world's most eloquent monologue on the stage.

"You were an actress," I say, though I can't remember the exact name of the play. I do sense the long hours she spent rehearsing. The worry that crossed her face when she came home to see how Edgar was treating me.

Smiling weakly, Grammy says, "Lead me to my car?"

I take her hand, trying to make out if my parents are still

alive. But the only thing I can sense is a thick wall of secrets
—impenetrable and stubborn. Tansy.

About thirty paces later, we come to a blue Impala with
silver trim, a vehicle that would have been all the rage back in
the '70s. The row of unkempt bushes beside it must be why I
didn't see it when I first arrived.

I try to think where Grammy lives or how far she has to
drive, but, again, all I can find is that black wall of marble.
"Where is your house, Grammy?"

She waves her hand in dismissal. "What *I* want to know is,
how are you getting along? You don't look like you've been
eating."

I open my mouth to say some vague hint about Tansy,
when my mouth's shooting off, "*You* look like the next big
wind could blow you to Albany."

"You're so skinny, you'd look like a zipper if you turned
sideways." There's a moon-sized twinkle in Grammy's eye,
and my heart skips a beat. This is what we do. We tease.

I whisper, "How did I know to do that without even fully
remembering you?"

Grammy turns all ninety pounds of her slight body to face
me. "Because deep in there"—she places her hand over her
heart—"you know me." Clearing the emotion from her
throat, she says, "Have you been able to locate your money?"

Why's she asking that? Oh, she's just my grandmother,
looking out for me. While I don't want to get into Tansy's
methods for rationing, I do reassure her, "I have what I
need."

But when Grammy watches me, it's like she's dissecting
every part of my soul. "I *know*, Gemma." A gust of wind
tousles her hair as she glances left, then right. "I *know* about
Tansy ..."

A bowling ball's sitting on my chest. I wasn't prepared to
discuss Tansy. Truthfully, I'd hoped to keep my more avant-

garde other half to myself. While Olly, the *Hey, Sugar* owners, and Jesse Beauchamp think I'm a killer, never once did they bring up Tansy.

"What exactly do you know?" I cup her thin elbow with my hand to keep her steady.

"I know that you balance someone *here*"—Grammy connects her thumbs and fingers in the shape of a triangle, a house, I think—"and you balance someone *here*." She raises her hands to either side of her eyes and waves them outward, like she's a flight attendant, pantomiming my relentless desire to see and do new things.

I don't know how she does it, but tears are automatically springing to my eyes. Grammy really does know my secret, but does she know that Tansy and I are two completely different entities? That she has a complete mind of her own —and she's in charge most of the time. If Grammy does know, what now? Has she been waiting for me to come out here, just so she can drag me off to Millwood for the rest of my life?

Glancing to the stone cemetery sign, I cut to the long and short of it. "Jesse Beauchamp accused me of murdering WT."

Fireworks practically shoot from Grammy's eyes. She hobble-stomps toward her Impala like it's a monster truck, and she's about to bash into anybody who dares stand in her way. "I'm *tired* of this town's bullies."

"So ..." A tiny spark of hope shoots from my heart. "He's not a good guy?" Tansy said as much, but to have another source confirm her suspicions would be great.

Grammy wrenches open her rusty door. "You leave that waste of space to me."

12

"Have you ever noticed there are no photographs in this house?" I slip off my shoes before barreling past the pinecones and twigs in the hallway. "Not in the entire place! I think you're holding out on me, Tansy."

I stumble past the table and mirror, thinking again about what Grammy said about this town being run by bullies. How many of them are there? What's their connection to WT?

I'm making so much ruckus, an embroidered picture of a Texas bluebonnet rattles from its wire hanger, but who was the one who embroidered it? There are a few busts of old-timey people in the parlor, but nothing from this century.

Lifting my foot to march up the stairs, I pray there's a clue on the second story when Tansy sags within me like deadweight.

I try to push past her—raise my foot another three inches —but she knocks my foot down, pinning both my feet.

"Come on, Tansy. I saw her—Grammy. She was visiting Edgar's grave."

Tansy's grip on one of my ankles falters.

"I also know that I *have* to find him." I rotate my left foot in a circle. "WT."

No way am I going to tell her how Grammy seemed to know about Tansy's and my condition—or how she talked about WT's and my wedding. Instead, I try lifting our foot even higher, when Tansy smacks down our leg so hard, I'm stumbling. The polished mahogany banister jabs into my side. Tansy must think I can't handle whatever's up there. But going upstairs isn't even against our rules.

I grab the rail, once again trying to climb.

"You *need* to be quiet." Tansy's anxious tone steals over my voice. I didn't notice it before, but she's trembling.

I look up at the balcony, and nausea and vertigo swing in a pendulum from her consciousness toward mine. What is this? I suppose this means Tansy's afraid of heights. But I thought she regularly went upstairs to find clothes to change ...

Jerusha, the bigger of Tansy's mottled tortoiseshell cats, darts down the steps, tail puffed, and nearly plows straight into me. She's clothed in a beige, knit sweater, ears poking out, oddly looking like a sphynx.

"*Gemma* ..." Tansy frantically says. "*Don't go up there. Please!*"

But I haven't been searching for clues only to ignore a hefty one when it's right in front of me. There's something up there. Has to be.

Feeling only semi-terrible for doing it, I give a swift mental kick to Tansy's head, and she falls away. I should apologize, but I have to find whatever she's hiding from me.

Squeezing the rail, I ascend the first half-flight. Climb the second half of stairs after turning ninety degrees.

It's getting darker. I should have brought a candle. Or flashlight. I wonder why Tansy was freaking out. All I really want is photographs or something similar to jog my memory.

Beneath my sneaker, an old floorboard squeaks. I'm

halfway up the second flight, when everything becomes stale and cobwebby.

Rattle, rattle. Shew; creak.

Someone's up here—unless Tansy's been stocking up random crows and such to do a bird show for the tourists when they stop by.

Cracks in the plaster reveal horizontal wooden slats of the wall's frame. Texan stars dot the wallpaper, but the door-frames up here don't have the fancier, hand-carved moldings. A chunky wrought-iron horseshoe juts from one wall. One of the brackets has come loose so that the candle sconce hangs sideways.

When I enter the first room, a rug with peacock feathers greets me with a miasma of monster eyes. A tufted bedspread lays between a heavy, ornate frame. The wooden back of the headboard looks absolutely perfect for sitting up and talking.

I ... don't know if it's our room—WT's and mine. The linens and headboard do seem familiar. Maybe we sat there and talked. Maybe he brought me breakfast in bed. Toast with deviled eggs.

Mostly, I wish I could remember his face. Maybe he was a great love—somebody I never wanted out of my life. Maybe we liked to shop together. Travel, explore, hike.

To my right lies a hefty, black metal fireplace—narrower than the ones downstairs but still more substantial than it needs to be. A stack of worn books lay in a neat pile on the mantel. I flip through them. One's about prehistoric humans. The other two are about the African Bush Elephant and the Bone Hall at the National Museum of Natural History. *My* interests. I think ...

The desk boasts an old lamp with a heavy, bronze base. *Long fingers reach out to turn it off*, but I can't tell if those fingers belonged to him or me.

"Surprised to see me?" comes a thick, Southern voice.

I accidentally bump into the lamp in hopes of finding WT, but the tanned figure in the doorway is leaner than I expected. Bowlegged. Pink-nosed and fat-lipped ... something about him tells me not to trust his supposed honest face. Spurs attach to cowboy boots, and his snug Wranglers are covered in stains.

I know him. WT's ranch hand. "Dwayne."

In the briefest of flashes, Tansy throws herself forward in our mind. She wants to slap him, *pommel* him, hug him, stuff dirt in his face, but just as fast, she's gone—nothing more than a specter that once tried escaping her grave.

Unsure of what to make of Tansy's mixed up feelings, I can't help spotting the brief flash of hope that's dwindling in Dwayne's eyes. So he *was* hoping for a reception—a passionate reception somewhat like Tansy wanted to give him. But something stopped her. Me?

"What are you doing here?" I don't know what to do, so I fill the uncomfortable silence with my voice.

Dwayne's spurs jangle as he takes a sizeable step toward me. Far as I can tell, he let himself inside, and I'm not sure if I should be concerned. I suppose he could have a key.

Raising his eyebrows, he says, "You always said you loved my unpredictability. Why don'tchya tell me?"

In another heated flash, Tansy hits me with a vision—of the hours he tended to the cattle, his branding iron wielding the Hardin double H. *He looks up at her and smiles. She gives him a toothy grin, and it's her—her, with her slouched demeanor and more exaggerated movements, saucier ways. "Oh, Dwayne," she purrs into his ear in the barn, making him shiver amidst the hay bales and feed. All the while, he blindly believes she is me.*

I brace myself by leaning into the hard edge of the desk. It's clear, he's had some sort of dalliance or affair with Tansy. The wood's digging into my back, and Tansy's grappling with some truth, something she never wanted to admit.

"*All right, you wanna know what it is?*" she yelps inside my mind. "*He's much stronger than I realized.*" She shows me a flash of him restraining a bull with an unnatural strength. Hits me with another image of—*a wooden post with horizontal slats, almost like a totem pole.* Then, the marble wall. Nothing.

"*Why is he here?*" I try to pry the truth out of Tansy, but she's a ghost, disappearing in a cyclone of grief.

Frowning, Dwayne runs his thumb and index finger along his jawline. "Are you goin' to tell me what happened to WT?"

I inch my hand toward the lamp in case I need a club of some type. A spark of hurt flares over Dwayne's eyes. "Gemma Louise, please talk to me." He hasn't exactly been long on words, but this I know. He didn't call me Tansy.

Still, I'm not sure what he wants, so I nod to the settee at the foot of the bed. "Why don't you sit down, Dwayne?"

His shoulders slump. His hands hang a little too heavily at his sides. "Ya never shoulda seen what you seen."

A flare of hope rises within my ribs, and I clutch the bronze neck of the lamp while standing up straight. "Tell me what happened? Or, at least, can you please tell me what you mean?"

Wiping his brow with the back of his grease-stained hand, he says, "The boss shoulda protected you. Sheltered you. He should know you're too delicate a flower to witness such things."

A newfound blaze of irritation washes behind my eyes. I may not be the most well-informed person in the world, but "delicate flower" isn't exactly what I'd want on my grave.

While Dwayne stares somberly into his lap, another brief flash comes unbidden into my mind.

He teaches me to ride horses. No, not me. Tansy. She's wearing a giant pirate hat, a fancy, double-breasted coat, and fishnet stockings. He settles her narrow hips in the saddle before showing her the perimeter of all nineteen hundred acres of the Hardin property. They pass giant thistles and pink, white-washed poppies. A squirrel spooks the horse. Dwayne steadies Tansy's wild grip on the horse's reins.

The peacock rug slips a little on the hardwood when I take a step back. "I can't even remember what he looks like." This I say about WT.

Another wave of hurt erodes Dwayne's pink face. "That's what Zeb said you'd say ..."

"Who?"

He narrows his eyes in confusion. "Your shrink."

*a*ccording to Dwayne, my therapist lives at 1229 Babbling Brook Lane. I need directions. I don't need directions. The address rings a bell. It's on the other side of the town square, I believe.

Somehow it really has gotten to be Christmas time. Scraggly cedars dot the square like gnomes with overgrown beards, and about six hundred people are stuffed in the one block in front of the courthouse. *Of course* there's a throng of people right when I need to go, as if Tansy's called them to block me.

The pink and blue storefront of *Hey, Sugar* has a line that wraps around the corner of its neighboring brick building. Even though *The Hair Lounge* is closed, with Francesca manning a cart out front and passing out hot chocolate. She's found the Christmas spirit by wearing reindeer antlers. Keeps searching the crowd, possibly for her family. I wave to my friend, but a man with a dragon tattoo and foot-long triangular beard blocks my way.

This isn't the time for friendly visits, anyhow. Hopefully,

Doctor Calhoun—that's what Dwayne says is Zeb's professional name—isn't here on the square. I pray he's home, reading a book, wearing fuzzy slippers, and brewing some tea.

A horse-drawn carriage suddenly blocks my path, and, before I know it, a policeman on a horse is marking me with his steely gaze. He licks his lips, and his helmet strap weaves across the patchy scruff on his chin. Jesse Beauchamp, with his sepia hair shaved on the sides. His bullet-proof vest makes him the most protected man on the street.

After wading past a few vendors selling cinnamon popcorn, licorice, and fudge—smells amazing—I round the corner of a red brick store to head up Babbling Brook Lane.

"Excuse me, Ms. Hardin?"

I turn at the sound of the almost-friendly baritone voice.

A young man with a crewcut and a face like a squirrel flashes me a badge that says "FBI." An arctic chill wraps its fist around my spine. "I was wondering if I could ask you a few questions related to a missing person's case."

Oh my heck, the *feds* know about WT?

I stumble past a woman with bright-red hair and a purse that says, "Rumor has it God is Texan." Can't talk to him. He won't even let me have a lawyer before locking me away.

A few paces off, a baby in a stroller cries, creating the distraction I need. I dart around the stroller before the agent can trap me into saying anything.

Scurrying around a twenty-foot cedar with red balls and silver stencil, I accidentally happen upon Jesse and his horse, which rears up on its back legs.

Jesse curses. "You're lucky you're Edgar's kin!"

I'm not sure what being related to Edgar has to do with anything, but I pull my jacket closed. Whatever Grammy said to him must have worked. Maybe Jesse and Edgar were friends or something.

After darting past an inflatable snowman, along with a slouchy Santa and his sleigh, at last, I come face-to-face with the trio of red, green, and blue Victorian houses. Here I am, at the foot of Babbling Brook Lane, where the homes' white fences breed nostalgia of quaint Memorial Day picnics and Halloween treats. Porches and windowsills look all festive, decked out in garlands and holly, but it's the blue craftsman after the trio that has the number I'm seeking.

House number 1229.

Do I remember coming here before? Do I remember Doctor Calhoun's mailbox with the fancy Y bracket and fluted base?

I rush down an immaculate rock path to a porch with a garland and miniature fir trees. A shiny white Mercedes sits like an effigy in the driveway. Right away, I can tell that the welcome mat looks way too clean.

As I reach for the knocker, the red ornaments on the squatty firs reflect my white-washed face. I take a deep breath. Lift the metal handle before I'm tempted to run—but no, no turning around today.

Though I release it harder than I intended, a gaggle of carolers muffles the noise. *Fa la la la la, la la la la.* They're almost horrifically merry.

I'm just about to grab the knocker again when Calhoun's heavy, oak door suddenly swings wide.

"Ms. Hardin." A tall, respectable-looking man with fancy business clothes flashes me marble-sized dimples in his thin cheeks. "To what do I owe the pleasure?"

His thick, Southern drawl and unprecedented sophistication nearly render me speechless while a whiff of tobacco mixed with peppermint nearly bowls me over. Still, I'm on a mission. Marching into his house, I assume the role that I can barge in anywhere I want, like *I'm* the police. He'll have some clues, if I'm lucky. An old card. A framed photograph of him and WT. Who knows? Maybe the two are old hunting buddies.

Or the good doctor has an old Christmas card from "Mr. and Mrs. Hardin." He *has* to have information that will help me sort through everything. Offer me protection from that FBI agent, at least.

Before me, in his living room, though, lies nothing but a simple set of chocolate-colored leather couches. A few short-haired throw rugs give a decidedly masculine vibe. Everything about the room is professional, sleek. No framed portraits. No Christmas cards hanging over the fireplace. Though there *is* a hefty gun rack with five or six shiny rifles. Best stay on the doctor's good side.

"I need you to tell me about WT." I squint past the wood-paneled wall to the back door.

With any luck, Calhoun's hiding WT back there. Maybe, all along, the two of them have been secretly waiting for me.

Calhoun peers down at me with this angelic level of patience, as if saying he has nothing to hide. His dimples flash again, and for the first time, I spot his fuzzy slippers. Hey, I wasn't too far off on my earlier dream. "While I'm honored that, after all this time, you have come to speak with me, perhaps we should leave our conversation for daytime hours. Call my office. Natalie would be more than happy to accommodate you with an appointment."

But I don't have time for social niceties. "You *know* he's missing. I was even stopped by the FBI!"

Doctor Calhoun's eyes widen infinitesimally before he rubs his chin with the back of this hand. "You, um, didn't say anything?"

I shake my head, grateful that he's not pushing me to talk to the feds, but still wanting to know what's happened with my life.

"You *are* my therapist, right?"

"Of course!" Calhoun glances at a side table next to the nearest of his couches. The surface of the table is empty, except for a miniature Bible and a hefty reading lamp. More peppermint and tobacco waft throughout the room, and the sleek, wood panel walls are filled with a terrifying number of framed diplomas.

Calhoun slips a little black book from the end table, along with an expensive-looking ballpoint pen. "What time would you like to come down to the office, Tansy?"

My stomach flips, and I stagger. He knows about Tansy?

Glancing up, Calhoun frowns at his mistake. "Oh, I'm sorry. I take it you're Gemma today."

I back up—way, way up—until I knock into yet another scraggly Christmas tree. Ornaments jangle at my neck, and one actually slips to stone floor with a terrible clang.

I've run my back up against the door. How is it that every time I'm close to answers about WT, another person knows too much about me?

"You *know?*" Never in my wildest dreams did I think he would know about Tansy.

"I am your therapist." He snaps his notebook closed. "Or, was. It's hard to say what your other half ever wanted from me. She never said, and it's been a very long time. But it's good that you've come to me."

My heart's fallen into quicksand. I'm seeing spots while a fistful of hot flashes burn up and down my legs. I thought Calhoun would be like Dwayne—vaguely aware of my peculiarities—but he seems to know *everything*. And I don't like feeling this vulnerable or out of touch. Or crazy.

I should ask how many people in this town know about Tansy, but the question is like hot steam—quick as it comes, it evaporates.

Calhoun's high cheekbones slacken. "Have you considered

that, maybe, *you're* the one person who might know the location of your fine WT?"

I straighten my jacket—a thigh-length peacoat I don't even remember putting on. "I thought ... you know ... since you're my therapist, you would know that I don't know where he is." Tears suddenly well in my eyes. "I haven't for a very long time."

"All right." Calhoun looks down his long nose. "I'll be honest with you. I only saw Tansy twice, but she refused to come in after our initial visit—and that time you wandered off to Boyd. The fact that you're here now speaks volumes, and I'm proud of the choice you've made today."

Oh, so he's the one who helped put me back together when I wandered off. But I don't see how Tansy even had the gumption to see a therapist after that. She's terrified of going upstairs, let alone anywhere outside our property. Maybe there was a time when she was comfortable leaving the house?

"You should call him." Calhoun pats my arm. "Invite him to return to Deep Creek."

But I don't have a phone. Or his number ... "If you knew something about my husband, you would tell me, right?"

Swiftly leading me to the door, Calhoun seems to be through with our visit. "I assure you, I would very much like to know his whereabouts. How about you schedule an appointment. I *would* like to touch base again. We can even continue the work I started with Tansy."

My nerves are so hot, I could swear they're being fileted. Can I trust him? I can't even trust Tansy. But he does seem to want to protect me from that agent, and he seems to believe me that I didn't murder WT. But I may not be able to get the money for his doctor fee.

I shuffle to the door, cheeks flushing. "I'm sorry for taking up your time."

"Call my office." Calhoun pats my arm for the second time. "Natalie should be able to squeeze you in as soon as Tuesday morning. Just keep doing what you're doing. For now, you can always lean on Dwayne."

14

*W*andering back home, I try to make sense of what Calhoun told me. He didn't automatically assume WT's dead. Plus, he says Tansy visited him, even used her name. My gut says she won't be too thrilled when she learns I visited him without setting up parameters for what she wanted me to say. She may have been cognizant of Dwayne telling me about Calhoun ... or she may have been MIA.

When I arrive on our porch, a white swatch of graffiti on the door has me pausing. Wide, white letters form a looping symbol I don't recognize. Thunder rumbles in the distance, and even the heavens seem to know I'm in deep.

The markings seem like something I might have seen before ... but where? I can't think. Or maybe it's a symbol I *shouldn't* recognize. Just a group of kids, painting doors to act out what they've seen on TV.

I lean against one of the pillars, grocery bags swinging. But the Doric column has been smashed to the right. I run my finger along the crack, the flakey plaster surprisingly sturdy. How could someone do this? Who would even do such a thing?

Tansy doesn't need to see the smashed-up porch light, or how the entire porch now slants sideways. Someone's taken the time to knock out the foundational braces. They must have attached a rope to a truck or something similar to get that kind of manpower. I should call the cops ... if that FBI agent and Jesse Beauchamp didn't already have it out for me.

Twisting the doorknob, I stick to the mission. Can't make any progress until I've recovered my memories.

I crack open the door, terrified I'll find even more destruction inside, but, apart from Tansy's random balls of yarn and freshly poured candles, nothing seems out of place.

What I do know is, the hallway reeks of paint.

Little green kitty footprints dot the wood floor, all the way to the kitchen—that'll be fun to clean—and I follow the trail, eager to set down the groceries.

I expect Tansy to come out the moment I set them on the counter, but she doesn't so much as hiccup when I pull out the chamomile tea.

I tap a fingernail on a soup can, trying to remember the last time I had something to eat. My stomach rumbles, so I grab the can opener and open it, letting out the nasty aroma of split peas.

While the soup boils on the stove, I put away all the cans in a neat little line.

Still, no Tansy.

I find her favorite bowl that matches her pink and green teacups and pour the hot liquid inside. It isn't until I'm settling into her favorite reading chair in the library, bowl and spoon in hand, that Tansy stirs from her lush, lavender bedding.

"They came," she says in this hushed voice.

Her consciousness scrambles in every which direction,

but she's stuck on a hamster wheel. Head spin-spin-spins—won't stop spinning.

Slowly, I set the soup on a coaster. "What's wrong, Tansy?" Not sure if she's seen the porch yet, but if she hasn't, I'm not about to goad the beast.

"They came," she repeats in her whisper voice.

The tourists? Or whoever did the vandalism and graffiti?

Tansy curls our legs beneath us, and the thin, green cushion sinks. Our position isn't all that comfortable. Before I even have time to wrap my mind around what's happening, she has us scrambling across the carpet. Ducking under the desk, she curls us into a ball—like we're twelve, playing hide and seek.

"They came, they came, they came." In our head, she nudges that wall of granite between us into its place, but there's still a crack. An infinitesimal crack so we can communicate.

It takes all my willpower to gain enough momentum to actually open my mouth to speak. "Who came?"

But our head's gone immobile against the oak sideboard of the desk.

With our arms, Tansy smothers our face. Our knees bend so that our chin's resting on top, and one arm's wrapped tightly around both our legs.

She rocks us back and forth.

"They came, they came ..."

I don't think this is a good time to bring up that I visited Calhoun, though she also hasn't blocked me out, which means she really does still need me.

Digging our nails into the underbelly of the desk, she screams, "THEY. CAME!"

I try to speak, but she's blocking me out and actual words become far too slippery. "*Who, Tansy?*"

All she can do is rock from side to side—like Jack the

Ripper himself climbed out of his grave. I try holding onto her the best I can while a cold sweat prickles from our arms, and she repeatedly knocks our head against the desk's side. Our heart's going to spiral straight out of our chest. Ears clog. Throat burns like sparking batteries.

"They came, they came, they came ..."

15

When I come to, I'm halfway across the yard, and in either hand, I'm carrying a "No Tres-passing" sign. The wind bites into my nose, and it seems Tansy's dressed me in that blush-colored peacoat I don't hate.

I don't want another repeat of where we hide under the desk, so I go along with whatever it is she wants. And from the looks of it, today it's more "No Trespassing" signs.

Marching to the fence, I become a soldier invading Normandy. A small family's just climbing out of a Volkswagen bug with a Mississippi license plate, cameras in tow, and I'm not in the mood for entertaining, so I yell, "Tour's over. *Silent Treatment Taxidermy* is just down the street."

The woman stares at my head—my hair. It seems I'm wearing a wide-brimmed hat the likes of which Daisy Buchanan would wear back in the day. I rip that off, spot the gigantic pink, plastic flower that's been duct-taped to the top, and only now notice the thirteen scarves I'm apparently wearing.

Slowly setting the signs on the grass, I wind off the

scarves, one by one, while the woman waves for her kids to get in the car and away from me.

Seems there's a large, dead vulture on the lawn, too. A legitimate Native American arrow protrudes from its side. Attached to the arrow is a slip of paper with Tansy's wonky handwriting.

"You're next," it says.

The graffiti people? I suppose this sends a message ... not entirely sure they'll care either way.

~

*T*he nice thing about living in a small town is Calhoun's office is only three blocks away from the square; I know this, because Francesca told me. After disposing of the vulture in a shallow hole next to the squirrel and magpie, I make my way to *The Hair Lounge*, and Francesca chats me up about the opening of the taco place. We discuss how gas prices are actually decent, and the rodeo in Fort Worth that's supposed to happen come spring. We don't talk about how there's a trio of glued seashells in my hair, or her husband, who I'm guessing still hasn't gotten back to her with his MMA advice.

By the time Francesca's finished with my hair and given my eyebrows a thorough tweeze, I thank her for making me mildly pretty. It's time to head to Calhoun's office—even if I don't have an appointment. But I still don't have a phone, and I'd rather show up on the off-chance there's an opening.

Calhoun's brick office is exactly one block from his house. More red ornaments pepper squatty firs, and patches of frost stretch across the grass in a thin cobweb that should be melted by lunchtime.

A petite blonde with shoulder-length hair and a tan jacket flashes me a movie star smile the moment I go inside. Natalie, Calhoun said was her name, turns her full body to face me. I feel like I should know her, but she's probably been trained to give special attention to every person she greets.

I grab the pen from the clipboard—both are decorated with cookie-cutter engravings of Texas' shape. I have to ignore the niggling in my gut that says I'm somehow "less than" for scribbling down my name. But long ago, Tansy read to me about what it means for us to have a condition like ours. Visiting a doctor is actually a great step for getting us healthy.

My handwriting's not all that legible. Part of me thinks maybe I should have written "Tansy," but I'd rather not draw undo attention to myself—especially since I don't have an appointment for the day.

"Thank you, Gemma," Natalie says in her chipper, soprano voice. "Doctor Calhoun will be with you shortly."

Unless she just read my name from the clipboard, looks like Natalie knows me. Plus, she didn't give me the third degree.

I turn on my heel before she can see the surprise in my eyes. No need to jinx this. Maybe something in this room will jog my memory.

Just like Calhoun's living room, the chairs are a dark chocolate brown, and the walls have the same sleek wood paneling. A TV hums in the corner where a newscaster recaps the wins of the high school football team. The whole room's so perfectly decked out with fancy bronze and silver Christmas décor, half of me wishes that Tansy and I went to the trouble of decorating. On the rustic, live edge coffee table lies a neat stack of magazines. I don't remember the last time I had the time to look at one, so I snatch one up and thumb through it while backing into a corner seat.

I wonder how many patients Doctor Calhoun sees.

Wonder what WT thought about Tansy coming here. Did WT know about Tansy?

A ticking Santa clock on the wall tells me it's precisely 4:15. I knew I should have made an appointment, but that would mean planning, and I never know if I'm going to come out of the ether in time.

The empty waiting room suggests either Calhoun doesn't see a lot of patients, or he only sees one at a time.

Wonder what Natalie's up to. Oh, but her station at the front desk is empty.

I hadn't realized she'd gotten up. I guess she's talking to Calhoun—seeing if he has time to see me.

Is it selfish to hope that WT's handsome? It would be terrible if he was as old and decrepit as the estate.

The slick pages show me *Hey, Sugar* is the first featured article in the magazine. The pale business owner gives a withering glare to the camera while her husband holds out his arms to a display of bright-colored treats.

The next article appears to be about the railroad, built in 1899.

Page eleven's an ad for cigarettes. It also reminds me to get my pap screen.

Page thirteen, though, right after an ad for a boot shop, has an image that latches onto my attention with nine-inch-long fangs. Just above the center of the right page is a man with his hands in his pockets and a close-lipped smile I can't *not* recognize.

He's wearing a blue pin-striped suit. A gold clip on a red skinny tie. A pocket square sits snugly in his breast pocket, perfectly complementing his tie. His hair's slicked back, but not in that "no personality, banker" kind of way." He's *handsome*, almost looks content, and his hazel eyes are directly on me.

The scruff on his chin hints at his lower thirties age, and on his wrist lies a watch—a silver watch ... he got from me.

As I stand, I knock into the coffee table, the entire room spinning. My hand quivers as I make out the blocky letters of the title:

CATTLE BARON FINDS OIL ON HARDIN ESTATE

A teeny white scar to the left of his lower lip nearly pulls me into the page. Those lips ... I kissed those lips, and that scar?

That scar ...

He cut himself while laughing at a joke I told him.

It's him.

Him.

WT.

remember.

I remember!

I remember how he loved to play cards. How he was the quietest man in the room, until you got him talking.

He was soft-spoken, yes, but intelligent. And patient! And ... always, *always* hard to read. I can see him even now, holding back his secrets in that picture on the page. On his shoulders, he holds the weight of the world, but he would never admit that he does or say it that way.

He's the epitome of class and understated conversations, and I *miss* him. I don't know how to explain it, but he made me feel understood. Safe. I'm glad I'm not already in a session with Calhoun, because impressions are coming faster than a movie reel, hurtling toward me at full speed.

I have to get outside.

Wrenching open the door, I hold the magazine between my teeth. Once I'm out in the open air, I bask in the cold. Yes, I remember how he looked when he said he closed a deal. What kind of deal? I don't remember. But that powerful look of satisfaction wasn't quite as charged as when he spent quiet hours alone with me.

Where was his office?

Cars zoom past, and I remember the feel of his scruff on my neck. The tender warmth of his whiskers. The *truck* he used to drive. A navy Dodge Ram—almost identical to the silver one right in front of me. Though his was a Longhorn Edition, stately letters printed on the tailgate.

A man walking alongside me on the sidewalk has WT's same light-brown hair, but it's missing the red tint WT's had when the sun hit it just right.

Plus, yes. As we continue walking along, I see that the man is walking a dog, and it seems like WT had a dog or his friends had a dog or ... Oil. The article said he found oil. And he was the heir to a cattle baron. He found oil on the estate. What was the date on the magazine? I flip it over. Last year, January. Did I already know him then? Why did I leave Calhoun's office? The doctor could corroborate facts. All of this. Anything.

Spinning around, I sprint back toward Calhoun's office as a man in a dark suit emerges from the doors I just vacated. Crewcut hair, pinched features ... the FBI agent!

Luckily, he's pulling out his phone and doesn't seem to have noticed me. He says something about Calhoun—and I think the police—but my stomach gurgles as he strides the opposite way from me.

Good. Good, good, good. Now I can talk to Calhoun about what I just remembered—without the pressure of the feds, taunting me.

I heave open the door, breathing in a sigh of relief.

By Natalie's vacant expression, though, I know leaving— even for just a moment—had been a mistake. "Oh, I'm sorry, Gemma." She's gathering a pile of scattered papers. "I thought you left for the day."

I release a breathy laugh. "Sorry." I gather my wits by leaning against the counter. "I'm ready to see Doctor Calhoun now, please."

But Natalie does this forced, crazy-eyed giggle, like she's afraid I'll bash her head into her desk for crossing me. "I'm sorry, but Doctor Calhoun had to leave for the day!"

"But ... before he said he would see me." Could this have something to do with the agent? My stomach squeezes for the tenth time, and on Natalie's desk, I accidentally knock over a wood-crafted Christmas tree. While I attempt it set it back up, my hands won't stop shaking.

"Look, Gemma. I'm *really* sorry." Natalie's doe eyes dart to the door where the agent just left. "Would you like to schedule another appointment?" She scrambles out of her roller chair toward a counter. "I can offer you some coffee. Or cookies!"

But this isn't a moment to be sidetracked. I point to my name on the clipboard. "I need to see Doctor Calhoun. Today."

"He might have another opening tomorrow!" Natalie scurries back to her chair and wheels across the tile to her computer. Her perfectly manicured fingers clickety-clack over the keyboard. "Oh." Her smile freezes in place. "I'm sorry, but it appears he doesn't have any other openings for three more weeks."

The Santa clock ticks so loud, holes are being drilled into my brain.

I'll grab the whole stack of magazines and shake them in her unhelpful face.

I *remember* him. I actually remember what WT looks like, and Doctor Calhoun—he will help me recollect everything.

Natalie rises from her chair. Accidentally knocks over the same wood-crafted Christmas tree. "Here." She frantically hands me a half-assembled plate of cookies. "Chocolate chip —your favorite, right?"

I push them back. Tear out of there before I do something questionable, even for Tansy.

17

William Thomas Hardin ran cattle and managed the money he gained from finding oil on his estate. He was born and raised in this town, and, for years, his family hosted parties at his home each and every Fourth of July.

Estimated to be worth tens of millions, my husband continued to build his business, while relying on a few key players, namely Dwayne. Dwayne took charge of the ranch and cattle side of the business. But as I linger on my bridge, I can't seem to push through my mental barriers to remember *any* other interactions between WT and me.

I want to know how we met. What our relationship looked like. I'm not mentioned in the article, which makes sense, since Grammy said we were married in February. But when was our first kiss? What did we do on our first date?

I can't seem to remember *any* of it. All I have is this ripped-open, gaping feeling in my gut, and it's weird, because it wasn't there before. Crazy as it sounds, I can feel it—I *know* he loved me.

Tansy must be hiding the details. Is this a power thing?

Maybe she's jealous of our relationship. Doesn't want to go down memory lane. I did see how messed up she got when we ran into Dwayne.

By the time I make it home, it's five minutes after six thirty. I deposit the trip's fourteen days' worth of groceries on the kitchen counter and march straight to the hallway mirror to hold up the magazine.

"I see him," I say. "I *see him,* Tansy!"

She takes exactly fourteen seconds to blink.

I shove the magazine into the mirror. "I see him, but I don't *remember* anything."

She runs our fingernail down the surface of the mirror. "I *told* you ... I've been holdin' onto our memories. For safe-keeping."

"Well, this is me telling you that I don't *want* to be safe!" It's like—it's like I can *still* feel the warmth of his scruff on my neck. See the way his naked back dipped in just above his jeans. "*Show* me."

Tansy smiles this spooky, Cheshire cat smile that I could smack off her face. "My needlepoint awaits."

"And I have a crater in the side of my head that's about to explode." I slap the table. "Explain!"

With our left index finger, Tansy scratches the mirror again. I'd overpower her, but maybe if I'm still for a moment, she'll eventually give in. Scratching a set of "Xs" and "Os" in the mirror, she simply says, "No, my little Loveday."

"What?"

"You think yourself clever, a detective, and Loveday was the greatest female detective of the Victorian age."

Anger practically boils from my veins. "Remember how scared you were before? When we crawled under the desk because somebody came over? I want to *help you* not be scared anymore. But I can't do that unless you talk to me!"

Tansy's face goes so pale, I'm afraid she's hyperventilating.

"You" —seemingly unsure, she breaks eye contact with me— "wouldn't like what you see."

"I don't care!" I slap our palm against the mirror, triggering a hairline fracture along the cool plane. Leaning in closer, I study Tansy's pupils to make sense of what she's hiding. "I need you to show me a memory."

"You won't like it," she says in her waif-like voice.

"What are you so scared of?" I knock my knuckles against the mirror. "And don't even *think* about making up something fake."

She purses our lips, seemingly resigned. "I'm not a magician. I can show you the past—who we were with the *illustrious* WT, but it will come with consequences. You don't remember how effortlessly successful he was, G!"

I gesture to the expensive crown molding and the crystal chandelier above our heads that's worth more money than most people see their whole lives. "You say that like it's a bad thing!" Leaning closer, I press my forehead into the glass and close my eyes.

There's a war waging on the other side. Tansy fiddles with the granite wall: to show me or not to show me? My gut says, she *really* doesn't want to show me.

Breath hitching, she grabs me by the scruff of my consciousness and lobs me to the darkest corner of her mind.

18

*T*ansy's mental world is so full of crisp color, it looks almost fake. In this dream—this memory—leaves are still fastened on the trees, and the holly bushes out front are so neatly manicured and trimmed, Hardin Mansion almost looks like a different place.

Periwinkle azaleas round out the flower beds; purple heart juxtapose Texas sage. A man in a simple brown sweater trims a rose bush, and he hums a country song I think I should recognize. WT—he's built like a bear, with wide shoulders and a chest that looks like he could prop up a car without even trying. His eyes are currently downcast, though, so it's hard to see his face.

He's examining flower after flower—meticulous hands trim dead pieces before the stems can become too unruly.

All at once, he glances up at me.

Neatly trimmed facial hair marks off a pleasant face. His kind eyes smile, and my entire world warms. I smile from where I sit on an herb-potted porch, reading. On my lap lies a book—The Baker Hotel Hauntings—and the trance between us flickers. Butterflies glide through the air while the heady perfume of the azaleas beg me to join him with his pruning.

Tansy abruptly pulls our hand from the mirror, severing our connection to the past—my one magical memory. "I decided to give you something to hold onto before ..." She purposely doesn't finish the sentence, alluding to something sinister that wasn't even there. She's lying to me!

"Bring me back!" I slap the mirror. "I'm sure the avalanche won't happen. Tansy, I've never felt more contented or peaceful in my life!"

Tansy cuts me a suspicious look with narrowed eyes. "You really do believe you can handle this." She spreads our lips into a smile that says she knows for certain otherwise.

I slap the mirror harder. "You haven't given me *any* reason to believe differently. Show me more."

She grinds together our molars. "If I left things up to you, we'd have at least sixteen other alters by the morning."

"That's not going to happen! Now, put me back inside!"

Tansy lifts our chin and frowns with this unexpected disdain. "If it were up to you, we would *only* be livin' in our memories." She slips on a pair of bracelets from my shorts pocket I didn't even know I was carrying. "You haven't figured out how to move on with our life."

I'm about ready to punch something. "How can I move on if I *don't even remember* what happened in the first place?"

Tansy has us break away from the mirror and practically floats toward the kitchen like our spirit's separated from our body. She passes an old blue vase, and I try to snatch it—maybe smash it to gain her attention—but she glides past, a ghost from Hollow's Eve.

"I'm sure you understand how I might be exhausted, G." She edges up to the stove that's covered with a milky layer of grease. "You're insisting on breakin' down the glories of what I've built. Remember our Third Rule? *Do Not Discuss Our History.*"

"But I've been accused of murder! How am I supposed to defend myself if I don't even remember what happened?"

She grabs the teapot from the stove with a practiced ferocity. "You should be thankin' me. I have given you a bright, happy memory. You would do well to show your appreciation, my sweet."

The buzzing in our throat tells me she's begun humming a minor-keyed version of the song WT hummed while pruning. She turns on the water, and I try to clamber up to stay awake, but, with a swift shake of the head, she sends me crashing down a craggy cliff I didn't even know I was on.

I squirm, spin to find my footing, but I'm falling through the chasm of her throat. She swallows, and I sink.

19

*A*fter all that's gone on, Grammy's the only person I know who can help me. There's Francesca, but I'd like to keep her separate from the drama in my life. Sure, I know a little bit about her personal life—and she, mine—but getting my hair done is the *one* time I almost forget anything's wrong. I pretend I'm not me for a second, and she makes me look like any other stranger I'd rather be.

So I do that, and it feels great. I go to *Grady Dean's* and load up the shopping cart with two dozen cans of soup and all the delightful packets of lemon chamomile tea.

Luckily, an ad at the back of WT's magazine tells me the location of the library. And the library—just around the corner from the grocery store—has computers. Computers mean search engines, and with a little digging into the local theater guilds ... I strike gold and find Grammy's name.

With her name, I'm able to look her up in the county tax records.

And her home address is right there.

I'm practically a private eye.

Now that I know that Grammy lives just south of the

cemetery, I know exactly where I'm going. If I had a car, it'd take me five minutes to drive. But I don't, so I walk, dropping off the cans on the porch along the way.

Taking a shortcut, I crunch over the neighbor's winterized grass and side-step all the fallen willows along the creek.

The sun's already going down by the time I reach Grammy's. I suppose it's only a few minutes before I'm supposed to return home to Tansy. But I purposely stride up Grammy's porch steps. Pass a pair of potted poinsettias and a red and yellow metal rooster with an open, chatty beak. It's the tire swing, though, that hooks its iron claws inside my brain.

"You'll do what you're told." On a tree branch, Edgar wrenches up the chain.

I nurse a black eye and a wrist that throbs from when he just shook me.

He heaves the chain higher. "Never. Again. Question me."

I don't know what I did or what he thought I saw, but I remember that the old me kept my eyes fastened on the horizon, hoping Grammy would come home and rescue me.

Now, though, a tractor weighs down the grass near an ice-frosted windmill that shudders in the wind, about thirty feet high. I clutch my shivering arms. Way to forget your coat, G.

Another cold snap warns me that maybe I don't want to go down memory lane. Maybe it's too dangerous, too icy. But I haven't come this far to tuck tail and run the minute things get scary. Plus, the good's mixed in with the bad in anybody's past.

Trudging up the remainder of the steps, I smile at the thought of having a real discussion with Grammy. Luckily, Tansy won't interfere. No way will she come out so far from home. There are perks to our arrangement. I'll admit it this time.

After I knock on the front door of an old '30s style house with broken shutters and a stone chimney, uneven footfalls greet me from the other side. Grammy emerges through the dim, her slight frame offset with the bright blaze of hope in her eyes.

"Gemma!" She raises her aged hand and waves for me to enter.

I peel open the screened door and find a shelf of books and a crooked antenna attached to a TV. Two forest green recliners hunch on either side of a table, and one boasts a mess of yarn not unlike Tansy's.

The TV stand's covered by a pile of remotes while Edgar catches up on his latest crime show and biography. Grammy silently knits, while I look for excuses to escape to my room for a moment of peace. I pour over books—on history. Edgar says reading fiction is a 'colossal' waste of time, so he lets me check out any nonfiction book I like. I study both the American and French Revolutions. He ensures that I know the wars he and his friends might have fought in, earning awards, accommodations, and the like.

I rebel by studying the Victorian Era. Prince Albert's Great Exhibit in the Crystal Palace becomes a huge inspiration of mine. Unable to help it, I pour over scientific wonders like the Koh-i-Noor, the world's largest diamond that was displayed there for weeks.

Grammy sews a prom dress that looks like something that would have been worn by the queen—full skirt, an exorbitant amount of lace. It even poofs up when I sit in the car with my date. Edgar, in the background, scowls, insisting that I wear something more American next time.

He buys me used books about all the Civil War generals, claiming there's a good reason why Buford and Hancock's names are crossed out with red ink. Is there something he wants me to decipher? I feel like he's indoctrinating me ...

A knitted project has come to be in my hands—a hat with a hole on top for me to slip my hair through and into a top-knot. It's perfect. Simple. The yarn has the perfect amount of flex when pulled tight.

"You were always so talented," I tell Grammy.

"*You* wouldn't learn," she teases me.

"Maybe I would have if you weren't such a bad teacher."

"Never did see a more hopeless student."

"Hey!"

Grammy smiles, sending a rush of happiness and warmth through me.

Suddenly, I remember the endless piles of books on my dresser, my bed, the floor—uneven piles encroaching on the doorway. Dog-eared pages meet dried-out highlighters. I forgot to cap them when I got sucked into an event in history. "I guess I was too busy reading."

Grammy taps the side of her temple. "A true savant, if you ask me."

I blush, knowing that's a lie. Still, I want to know more of the past. Did I play sports? Was I in band? Maybe I was the student body president. Heh-heh, wouldn't that be great.

No doubt sensing my questions, Grammy quickly says, "I just finished baking."

Without another explanation, she limps around the corner to a kitchen with chicken wallpaper and shelves with black and white cow figurines. There's a hominess about it, but it doesn't match her interests. From the sleek lines of her clothes, I'd expect more of a modern kitchen. This whole house is Edgar's domain.

Flour smears a gingham apron, cakes Grammy's long, skinny fingers. She teaches me how to roll out dough with a patience Job would find surprising. She uses a rolling pin, spreading dough counter-clockwise.

"Do it like this," she says, "to keep it from tearing."

She hands me the rolling pin, and it's a baton of hope after Edgar sucked the light out of life.

"You taught me how to bake!" I sound like a child, but it's

all coming back. So many things are coming back, and I'm not even nagging Tansy.

Grammy's pretty, thin lips quirk into a smile that reminds me of her actress days. "It didn't take you long to surpass your teacher."

I survey the deep country sink, the red painted apples on the tea towel hanging over its side. How many times did I wipe my hands on the thin fabric when I needed to return to my baking?

Grammy hands me a thick book—The History of Deep Creek —*a reward for our pie-baking enterprise.* "Read it," *she says.* "Read it to understand our history."

I read the first two sentences aloud, and she tells me to shush. Edgar will be home soon, and I should get the book out of sight. "Our little secret, my darling."

Instead of absorbing the subtleties of our past, though, I skip ahead and look to the tours and adventures to be found in the eastern part of the United States ...

An opaque flash of me teaching a group of people about old houses steals over my vision, and I blurt, "I became a tour guide!"

Grammy pats my hand before setting the table with a plate of peanut butter sandwich cookies. Numbed to all that I've already discovered, I sink into a curve-backed, wooden chair. When was the last time I ate something?

Only, my fingers don't know how to reach for the cookie. Instead, they curl under the chair as I remember something Tansy had said about WT. *You don't remember how effortlessly successful he was, G.* I suppose that means I had to work hard for the successes I got, while he inherited every one of his wins and station in life. But that downplays any effort he ever made.

"Did I have to come home," I ask Grammy, "from working—wherever I was—because I couldn't hack it?"

Grammy woofs a laugh. She raises her baby-blue coffee cup to her lips and takes a long, slow drink. Lowering it, she eventually says, "My dear, you came home to help me."

A long procession of trucks tail a pearly white limousine. Headlight burn bright. A choir of old women sing Rock of Ages. At the viewing, everyone says Edgar looks natural, even though his mustache is trimmed way too high.

"He ... had a heart attack," I recall faintly.

Grammy nods. "Even though he had a heart condition, nobody expected him to die a year under ninety."

Oh, I remember; at the time, she said I didn't need to come home, but it was her insistence that she could handle what was going on that convinced me to come back ASAP.

"I couldn't believe how quickly you showed up after I called you. Twelve hours later, you were on my doorstep." She holds out a cookie. "All bound and determined you were to work locally. You had a wonderful position in Williamsburg, but *my* Gemma gave that up. To help me."

Accepting the cookie, I remember that, too. Edgar was the reason why I left Grammy in the first place. But why didn't she leave him?

"How long ago did I come back from Virginia?" Oh, the death date on Edgar's grave is a couple of years ago, February. "Wait, what month is it?"

Frown lines frame Grammy's face. "February."

Oh, wow. How could it be February already? Okay ... "So, it's been about two years since Edgar died. How long ago was it that I first met WT?"

A far-off look settles over Grammy's eyes. "You meant to return to your job, but you refused to leave after you met him."

I try to think back to when that could be, but no more mental images surface. "You ... wanted me to leave?"

A flash of hurt skims across Grammy's face. "In all my

years, I have *never* wanted such a thing. But all too often, what we want and what we need become the two great opposites of our lives." Grammy taps her mug, finishing off her statement with understated authority.

Mulling over her words, I take a careful nibble of the cookie. The peanut butter is flavorful and sweet. Because of the salt. I remember Grammy saying a pinch of salt always enhances the flavor.

Accepting a glass of milk from her, I find the gumption to ask, "How did we meet, Grammy? WT and me."

Startled, her aged gaze drifts out the window, then back to me. "That, my dear, is something you would wish to remember for yourself."

"But Tansy won't let me ..." I feel like I'm four years old, complaining that my teacher's being mean. But it's how it is, and I'm loving how I can be honest with Grammy.

She catches my hand. "Go to your bridge. You were doing the ten o'clock tour in July."

I tear out of Grammy's house so fast, I nearly forget to say goodbye. An old wreath on the pantry door I think we made together reminds me, though, so I turn around and throw my arms around her boney shoulders.

"Thank you!"

Her frame melts in my embrace, and I'm out the door, nearly knocking into her metal rooster along the way.

My bridge is probably a full two miles from Grammy's. I tear past cedars and leafless oaks like the distance is only a hundred feet. Even the moon is fuller than I had expected, burnishing silver in the indigo sky.

When I make it to the bridge's red metal trusses, I grab the sun-bleached rails, trying to force my subconscious to another time—when oaks and willows staunchly hoarded their foliage. Cicadas roared. The scent of honeysuckle must have drifted through the air, pleading with me to try a taste.

A mess of people bunch together on the wooden planks of the bridge—on my right—and we're in various stages of being fully cooked in the summer heat. Sweat blends with adrenaline as groups of two and three tourists stand at rapt attention, hungry to be fed a story.

Almost like a hardy meal, and the main course is supposed to be supplied by me.

Taking a deep breath, I inhale the summer air. Taste the perspiration and humidity. "Goatman's Bridge hasn't always been this peaceful," *I say with great weight.* "In 1938, a certain African American goat farmer was murdered here by the local KKK."

A hush steals over the group. My words are poison, but I feel that I must tell the truth and expose what happened all those years ago in this place. While most of the tourists have probably already read about the Goatman online, each of them has booked the midnight tour to hear more specifics from a trusted source. I won't squander the responsibility.

"It is said that the Klansmen lynched the goat farmer." *I brush against the metal rail to find my footing.* "They hung him with a noose over the side of the bridge like it didn't matter to take a life. When the group checked the rope to confirm that he was dead, his body was nowhere—out of sight."

A pair of women in matching skull hoodies look to one another, jaws clamped. A younger girl clutching a notebook looks down, pain crinkling her blonde eye-lashed eyes.

"One version of the legend says the bridge is still haunted by the Goatman's wife," *I say.* "When the Klansmen finished with the goat farmer, they hunted down and killed the rest of his family."

A sharp gasp comes from one of the ladies in the hoodies while a college-aged kid folds his bulging arms. "Why?"

"Because." *I tread toward him, careful not to obscure the truth.* "They did not like the successes of the Goatman's business dealings."

Disgusted, the kid's jaw loosens, and he kicks one of the steel railings. He's feeling the way I felt when I first read about it. He sees the injustice. It's right that he should feel the pain.

"I realize this is a horrific point in our history." *My stomach twists.* "I almost didn't offer this tour because it's not a comfortable *topic for anybody. But if we don't shine a light on the past, we risk reliving the horrors of our ancestors' crimes."*

The discomfort of the group is so palpable, I wish I could scoop it up and place it in a jar for them to feel every time they're tempted to sweep something wrong under the rug. But we have to hold up a mirror to our history. It's how we sow the seeds of change.

"Has this tale been recorded in the county archives?" asks a sultry male voice.

The women in the skull hoodies turn to look at who's speaking. He's a few paces back, respectfully giving them space. Clad in a leather jacket and ripped blue jeans, he boasts the perfect amount of scruff and an especially kind face.

"I ..." What was his question? Oh, if the story's been recorded in the county archives. But I can't help noticing how still he is—how closely he's watching me. Like my answer really matters, but he doesn't even know me. "I would have to check ..." Most people don't ask about my sources, but I will do anything to help a fellow historian —especially one who looks ripped enough to be in the Highland games.

When the handsome stranger's gaze continues to bore into mine, I patch together some words. "I can call and ask. If you like."

He smiles, close-lipped. Mysterious. Fascinating. I doubt I'm the only girl who's fallen under his trance. I shouldn't let myself get side-tracked while the entire group waits.

Busying myself with details of other nearby hauntings, and a few hints about how some people believe that the Goatman haunts the bridge to this very day, I eventually reach the end of the tour and lead us back to the parking lot. The stranger makes a beeline for his motorcycle, which gleams black and metallic in the moonlight. Grabbing his helmet and slinging his leg over the bike, he raises two fingers from a closed fist and offers me a peace sign.

I almost give him one in return before my arm awkwardly thwacks the side of my leg.

"He's cute," one of the hoodie women says.

"I'd let ol' James Dean play Twenty Questions with me any day!"
Her friend laughs, toying with the strings of her hoodie.

With a gasp, I release the rails of the bridge, remembering how I did search the county records, but, apart from the Goatman story, I didn't see anything noteworthy. It was almost like the records had been scrubbed—or the court recorders had been lazy at the time. But I didn't know if I could believe in a conspiracy.

And now? As the wind tousles my hair, and the leaves shimmy like broken jewels against the grapevine, I know I have to get to the bottom of what happened.

Whatever it takes.

21

*E*ggplant and fuchsia-colored cupcakes salute me from the kitchen counter when I make it back to our place.

We don't have the ingredients. Tansy couldn't have made these.

Also, if Tansy were to bake, she'd make something like bran muffins infused with quinoa and split peas.

Icicle lights have been looped around the candle sconces on the walls almost like gingerbread icing, and with the curtains drawn and windows boarded up, they actually provide a healthy amount of light. Maybe Tansy deciphered my wish for Christmas decorations ... now that it's February. For all I know, I'll find a giant, inflatable snowman in the library.

"Hello, hello!" comes a far too chipper, female voice—a voice, I might add, that does not come from me. There's someone in the house? Who would bring cupcakes?

When I spin to see who it is, though, I plow right into Natalie. She's wearing that tan blazer again, her peaches and cream complexion a dermatologist's dream ad for curing acne.

"I was just coming to check up on my bestie!" The dimple in her chin is an exact replica of the dimple in left her cheek. "Hope you don't mind. I looked under the rock and found the key." She plucks up my hand and plops the freezing key into my palm. "After seeing you in the office, well ... you had me worried!"

Natalie raises her gaze to the ceiling, where another glob of Christmas lights have been wrapped around a Tiffany chandelier—next to a painting of a man with a healthy amount of chest hair and only one eye. His beard's on fire, and he's smoking a pipe.

Lowering her gaze, Natalie seems to accidentally set her sights on another one of Tansy's paintings—a headless woman standing in front of a fountain, holding a bouquet of dead roses. The woman's surrounded by the tallest of tombstones, which stretch like skyscrapers from a floor of red clay.

Natalie stares for a good fifteen seconds before lifting her hand to her forehead as if trying to think. "I didn't really believe your memories were gone until you acted like you didn't know me at the office yesterday."

I absorb her wavy locks and the fact that one of her eyebrows is partially shaved. So I *am* supposed to know her. Question is, how, exactly?

"You really must have forgotten all that happened," she prattles on, waving nonchalantly like we're old pals, visiting on a lunch date. "Otherwise, you would have reached out to me. You *do* know you don't have to be a stranger, even if I am the Sheriff's wife."

Oh, so she's married to Jesse Beauchamp. Wonderful human being. When Tansy learns I've broken *Rule Number 2: Don't let anyone in the house*, she is going to kill me.

Adjusting the headless woman painting so that it's somewhat less crooked, I try to come off as reasonably friendly.

"Hey, Natalie, have you been to *Hey, Sugar* lately?" Now

that she's here, we might as well discuss what she knows about my past—anything she can do to help me.

Natalie stares at me like I have three eyes.

"Okay ... when was the last time you came over?"

"Oh, not since WT ..." She glances furtively at the headless woman in the painting like WT suffered a similar fate. "I wanted to check on my bestie, is all. Don't you go and say *that's* a crime."

She fumbles with her jacket, suddenly acting anxious. Part of me wonders if she's being twitchy because she's thinking of Jesse. Natalie seems so open and honest, and Jesse is . . Jesse. It makes me wonder how well they knew each other before they got married. Makes me wonder if they have cute, beady-eyed children with matching police helmets and shaved hair on the sides.

Natalie surveys one of the Texas stars on the wall, which has also been draped in another mad frosting-like dollop of lights. Not sure what Tansy was up to, but thankfully, Natalie doesn't appear to be too peeved by the state of the place.

Trailing deeper into the hallway, she says, "Jesse mentioned that you were digging a hole round back." She catches sight of herself in Tansy's mirror and smooths her flawless, beach-blonde waves. "Everything all right?"

"Just some roadkill I had to take care of." I shrug like people bury roadkill all the time.

Right in front of a bust of someone with a grand mustache, who's now covered in bright coral seashells, Natalie stops to stare at me. Emotion simmers below the surface of her eyes.

"I *miss* you! Ever since, you know, WT went MIA, we never see you anymore." She leans in and drops her voice to a whisper. "And don't you worry—I know you didn't do anything." Straightening up, she resumes her normal chatter. "Think you'll start coming round again to the block parties?"

I want to ask her how she knows I'm innocent, when her gaze fixates on something about shin-height.

Preparing myself, I turn. Looks like Tansy's painted a raccoon that's been sawed in half, blood dripping down its middle a little too realistically. Is that ketchup or red paint? The painting's been nailed to the wall literally a foot from the floor.

Natalie spins away from the painting, giving her head a quick shake. She strolls deeper into the house, and I would have taken down that dress from the moose's antlers—and fishnet pantyhose—if I'd known we were having company.

Pretending she doesn't see the strewn clothes, Natalie drones on about the neighbors and an upcoming artichoke party. She refers to some expected improvements to be done to the grounds around the courthouse—courtesy of past funds from WT and his daddy—before delivering a final zinger: "Needless to say, if Edgar were still head of the city council, *no way* would they be bringing in a taco place."

Wait ... so WT and his father donated to keep up Deep Creek. And I almost trip over my next inquiry. "You knew Edgar?"

"Of course, silly. We've known each other ever since he took you in ... after your parents died."

Parents. I hadn't even gotten far enough to think about parents. What does that say about me?

"So then"—I accidentally bump into the table near where she was just standing—"what do you know about him—them—him?" I'm standing a little too close for comfort, but I've stumbled upon a new lead. Trying to appear cool, calm, and collected, I work moisture back into my mouth. "What was Edgar like?"

Natalie takes an awkward step back to give us a natural buffer. "Well, uh—hey! Maybe this is a perk of your amnesia!

You don't have to remember what he did to you *or* your grandma!"

Lifting a hand to ask her what she means, I accidentally bump into one of Tansy's teacups with a new candle poured inside. It clatters on the table but doesn't quite fall. "What does this have to do with Grammy?"

Natalie blanches. "Nothing, Gemma. Nothing!" She pats me on the arm way too cheerfully. "Why stir up old memories?" She practically gallops to the front door. "You asked me never to speak of it. To be honest, you're putting me in an awkward position, bestie."

Stopping just before the door, she leans in and kisses either side of my cheek. Not sure if this is something we used to do all the time.

"Don't be a stranger now!" She places her hand on the doorknob, shoulders pinned up, proving she knows she's leaving me high and dry. But her conscience must twinge, because, slowly, she turns back to me, stoic-faced. "Don't you worry yourself over the likes of Edgar or Jesse. All these rascals need is a little reminder that you're not wanting to stir the pot. You'll see."

She lifts her dimpled chin as she twists the knob, which gives a little squeak.

Regaining her composure, Natalie folds a hand over her stomach and adds, "Honestly, Gemma, you should consider yourself lucky that you *don't* remember. Ignorance is bliss, so they say."

No way is she going to leave things like that, so I lift my arm to block the door. "I'm sorry, Natalie. I need you to explain."

She opens her mouth. Closes it, eyes suddenly brimming with tears. Looking uncertainly to the door, then back to me, she lowers her head before admitting, "Edgar's the reason why your grandmother limps, all right?"

My chest constricts. "Why?"

Squeezing her eyes shut, Natalie whispers, "She was protecting you, and Edgar turned on her in his rage."

He ... hurt her when he meant to hurt me?

I feel like I'm falling further and further into a black hole that's lightyears from ending. "Why didn't she leave him?"

Natalie touches the back of my arm. "Because Anne's not your biological grandmother, sweetie. She and Edgar didn't marry until their late fifties."

My voice doesn't work. Grammy's not related by blood, and she stayed to protect me?

"Plus, she knew, with Edgar's connections, that no judge in Wise County would ever rule in her favor if she tried to take you away. So she stayed married to him to keep you safe."

Why didn't Grammy press charges? What exactly does Natalie know about WT? But her hand becomes an iron-clad manacle around my arm, squeezing it with surprising strength. "Sorry again about Zeb leaving when you came into the office the other day. That FBI agent took up a *ton* of his time. At least the feds finally left town ..."

"Oh, good." I can't help agreeing with her sense of relief.

"Glad that's behind us." Natalie exhales shakily. "You didn't, um, happen to talk to that agent, did you?"

Why does she want to know that? "No ..."

"Oh, good." She pats my arm way too cheerfully. "If you did, let's just say that Zeb and Jesse would be *furious*. Glad to know we're right as rain!"

22

"*I* need you to share another memory with me," I tell Tansy.

She takes another sip of her chamomile tea while we sit in front of the library fireplace. We're decked out in some baby-blue corset, her favorite copper necklace, and about thirty different jeweled rings.

"Something real. Something to help me understand what happened with Edgar and WT." The fire crackles as if clamoring in agreement while Tansy sets down her teacup.

Now that Natalie's shown a light on Edgar and Grammy's relationship, I *have* to understand who my husband was. He better not be like Edgar, is all I can say.

Quick as a viper, Tansy reels, "*Edgar was not a nice man.*"

"WT wasn't like that, was he?"

"*No ...*" Tansy's already testy mood sours. "*How is it that you were willin' to break Rule Number Two, G?*"

"Natalie let herself in." I tap the key in our skirt pocket. "She knows where we hide the key."

"*And my glowworm grotto! You haven't once noticed it. How is it that you do not appreciate the painstaking efforts to which I go to make you happy?"*

"Glowworm gro—oh. The lights." Leaning back, I try to get comfortable, but Tansy's corset's about as comfortable as sitting between two rakes. On the ceiling, the lights do sort of look like mystical glowworms dotting an evening sky. "It's thoughtful. Really, Tansy. I appreciate all the work you've gone to sprucing up the place." Studying the multitude of rings she's stuffed on our fingers, including a radish-sized ruby, I find the courage to say, "Now I need help putting together the pieces of what happened with Edgar and WT. Is there a connection? When I asked Natalie about it, she really freaked."

Tansy floats to the front of our consciousness, actually using our mouth to communicate this time. "I don't think you need me at all ... now that you have"—she waves a bejeweled hand in the air—'Grrrammy.'"

"Come on." I lower our hand. "Don't be like that. Grammy just suggested I go back to the bridge. I needed to sort out some personal things."

Tansy reels back so hard, the chair tips sideways. "If you were able to remember the bridge, then you *really* don't need me! I suppose you're all gung ho to go runnin' off to craft shows—and—and Bingo Nights."

"Tansy." I straighten the easy chair. "That's the last thing on my mind."

Once I've got us resettled, Tansy licks our lips, making us stare directly into the fire. She leans so far forward that our corset's about to burst into flames. An ember lands on our skirt, and I shake it off before we unintentionally cremate. But I can't anger her further—ember's going out anyway—so I grit my teeth and wait.

Sweat beads on our neck. Seriously, it's like we're roasting alive.

Gripping the heavy fabric of our skirt, Tansy coolly says, "Has it ever occurred to you that if you had been content with our life, we wouldn't have lost your 'precious' WT?"

What ... ? Okay, I'll pretend that doesn't at all sting. Still, she's giving me a sizable piece regarding our past. I can't push too hard. Must tread carefully.

Leaping from our chair, Tansy whooshes our skirts, suddenly becomes a lioness, stalking her prey. "You *liked* the idea of this small town. But it's never been enough for you, G. You've always needed adventure. To see things! WT was happy and content, but *you* had to go n' screw that up. You *pushed him.* The truth is, we lost our gentle husband, 'cause you couldn't find it within yourself to be happy."

Hammers are pounding in my head. I'm not even sure if I can handle what happened. But I can't live like this—cocooned and shielded from the truth. All *she* does is stay here, cooped up, like a potted plant all day.

Fists clenched, I open my mouth to tell her that I'm prepared to go thirty rounds to prove things need to change, when she droops our head and admits, "All right, all right, all right, I'll show you somethin' ... but this is the *last* time, my sweet."

I try not to smile at my victory.

"Also"—Tansy trills our hand in the air—"showin' you what happened is, in a word, exhausting. I need you to vow that after this, you shall willingly go away for three weeks."

"That's a full seven days longer!" But Tansy and I both know that she has no qualms with eating half a can of soup a day just to keep me inside. "Fine," I huff, retreating back to the cushioned chair. This better be worth it.

A small smile stretches over our lips as she grips the chair's arms and sits us back down to stare at the orange flames. "Once I share this with you, we shall *never* speak of it.

Do you hear me? You will see why he left. You will understand how it was *you* who drove him away."

23

*T*hey say that breakfast is the most important meal of the day, and outside in the garden, where the foxglove and azaleas bloom, I have quite the meal planned for myself and WT.

We've been cooped up in this town for months. Same food. Same people, same scenery. It's high time we spiced things up a little and got away. It's not that I'm unhappy, but I need adventure. It's times like these that I really miss the excitement, hustle, and bustle of Williamsburg and Washington, D.C.

Tapping my invitation on the table, I stare at the rustic cardstock and shabby chic lettering. To think what this promises—no preconceived misconceptions. No friends to complicate matters. Just him, me, and nature. It doesn't get any better than that.

We need this, more than I can say.

The screen door squeals as WT shoulders his way outside. I had thought about lighting candles, but the wind would just blow them out. It's daytime, besides. The pretty cherub statues and freshly pruned boxwoods provide plenty of ambiance. Not to mention the jasmine scent wafting plentifully from the Confederate ivy. WT will see that, while I'm comfortable here in our outdoor world, it's time to grow a little—stretch our wings.

Pulling out his chair on the grass, the love of my life leans down to kiss me. His beard's a little longer than usual, and I can already sense his serious mood when his tender lips meet mine.

"What are you doing out here?" His somber voice matches the sobriety of his amber tie. Reaching over, his fingers traipse along the bare skin just above my knee. I lean in, hungry for his touch, always.

When a bumblebee buzzes between us, I take my time sipping my orange juice, watching its pollen-covered body. "Oh, you know, just getting ideas ..."

WT raises his eyebrows with a conspiratorial glint in his eye.

I swat his arm. "Not that kind of idea."

"Too bad." He takes a quick swig of his juice. "I don't have to go into the office until 10:30 ..."

Tempted, but not about to be derailed, I hold out the card so that he can see his name. "For you."

WT's eyes light with humor as he accepts the card and rips it open. Is he going to be glad that I went to the effort, or will he silently think I'm being unappreciative of the comforts he provides? I know he hates to travel, but we've been married two months and haven't so much as left the county—not even for our honeymoon. I know work keeps him busy, but everyone needs a little balance in their lives.

As WT's warm, kind eyes scan my writing, though, his earlier humor fades. "You want to go on a trip."

"Just to Palo Duro. It's only a five hour drive."

Pushing back his chair, he rises to his feet. "What you don't understand, Gemma, is—" He catches sight of the hurt on my face, and he clamps his jaw shut. Rakes his fingers through his gelled hair and sinks back into his chair. Gently taking my hands in his, he says, "I'm sorry, but now isn't a good time."

But he's been saying that for ages. I suggested we go to Nashville after our wedding, and he wouldn't talk about it once. When I asked about San Antonio, he insisted he had an un-reschedulable meeting. But Palo Duro isn't that far, and it's supposed to be beautiful.

"We don't have to use any of your money," I explain. "I have my old camping tent, and Natalie said we can use her and Jesse's bikes."

Pain, sharp and fast, skims over WT's eyes. "You think this is about money?" His gaze traipses to the fence. The BMW he bought me is parked on the other side by the street. I insisted I was happy with my beater, but he wouldn't hear of it. He bought the Bimmer brand new and has it detailed every few weeks.

Burrowing my hands into the thick callouses of his palms, I say, "I don't know how to explain it, but this town ... WT, there's something wrong. And it's suffocating me."

"You go, then."

"But I want to go with you." I ball my hands into fists while we both pull away. "This could be really good for us."

I don't bring up the fact that there's something really creepy about his hired hand, Dwayne. He keeps lurking about whenever WT leaves. Not to mention the way the ladies at church have been acting. They stop talking the minute I approach them after services. It's not that I necessarily want to socialize, but ... I don't know. People have been acting so strangely. Not only have some of the locals been complaining about my Goatman's Bridge script, but someone draped a rebel flag over our mailbox, and I know that wasn't WT or me.

Leaning over, my husband raises his hand to caress the side of my face. Normally, I wouldn't let him do it without seeing a hint of a compromise, but he's got this strange, almost trapped look in his eyes. "You go ahead." In half a second, the look is gone. He skims his lips over my forehead, and I melt against my better instincts. "Take my truck, if you like."

24

*T*he worst part about losing consciousness is never knowing where I stand afterward with Tansy.

Sure, I know we made a deal. I know I agreed to be locked away for three weeks. But now I don't know if the cannibalistic Christmas short story she's left here on the kitchen table is simply an artistic expression of how she's feeling at the moment, or if it's more of a direct reflection of what she's prone to do in real life.

Jerusha and Hawkins have made a mess of their food. Kibble's mixed with water in their food tray. One look in their cupboard tells me I need to go to *Grady Dean's*. My stomach scrapes like I haven't eaten in years, and the gold-plaited mirror in the hall shows that my eyes couldn't be more bloodshot if I were a zombie.

Naturally, Tansy hasn't bothered with the laundry. But the last running clothes I wore didn't get all that sweaty. Wish I could dab on some concealer for the black circles under my eyes.

The only thing to do is grab my sneakers, and get out of

here before Tansy pops up and insists that I need to be locked up for three more weeks.

Time to take care of all the things. But it's time that I structured my day a bit differently.

Darting out the back door, I make a pit-stop in the garden —the table where I once sat with WT. It's a little hard to imagine the brittle foliage being in full bloom and the cherubs standing. It's even harder to imagine him—a man— living and breathing in this very spot, right in front of me.

He lived here. This was our home. How could I have forgotten him when he was such a full and integral part of my life? Yes, all right—I'm sure Tansy's the reason for the missing pieces, but why would she do it? Why would she slander the memories of the one person I was willing to be married to, pretty much the man of my dreams?

At least one of the cherubs needs to stand upright, so I stride over, lift the marble, and place it on its feet. Weather and erosion smear its features, and, as the wind picks up, leaves scatter in a whirl of mystery.

When I went to the bridge, I was able to dredge up more of my past. Maybe if I physically go to a key place, I'll be able to pull up another memory.

Yes, that's what I'll do.

I'll learn more through my senses. Ground myself with what I've already experienced via taste, touch, sound, smell, sight.

~

"Do you know anything about the Hardins?" I ask Francesca while she ties my hair into a Dutch braid.

I would go to one of the spots where WT and I spent time, but I'm not even sure where those spots are yet. Hence, reconnaissance. I know I said I didn't want to talk about my past too much with Francesca, but she's always been an excellent resource when I've been unsure of how to proceed. Plus, it feels good to come back here—despite Wanda—I spy her nametag, yippee!—being bent over her books at the front desk, scowling all the time.

Francesca glances up, her gorgeous, amber eyes almost jittery. "Isn't Hardin your last name?"

"Well, yes," I curb, doubting she wants to be bogged down with all the details. "My married name."

Chewing on her bottom lip, Francesca coaxes all my fine hairs into place before dousing me with half a bottle of "maximum hold" hairspray. It isn't until she's handing me a mirror to check the back of my hair that her shoulders loosen.

"Honey, I came to this town to get my husband and daughter back in my life." She lets go of a heavy-burdened laugh. "Even saved up for months to buy my daughter those checkered Vans all the kids like."

"That's a nice thing to do." I hold the mirror in wonder, deciding if I had kids, surely Tansy would tell me. "So ... how are your husband and daughter doing?"

"They"—she bites her lip again—"haven't gotten back to me." She scans the entire room, faltering when her gaze lands on Wanda, who's gone onto cataloging their entire file system. "I don't even know where they are, but I do know that a certain man with the last name of Hardin helped them get their place."

I nearly drop the mirror. "How do you know that?"

"That's what Tim—my husband—told my mama before they moved to Deep Creek." I'm just about to admit that I'm on the hunt for WT myself when Francesca uses the back of her hand to wipe the corners of her eyes. "In my past, let's just say I made a few mistakes." She laughs awkwardly. "Tim, uh, he got full custody. But I *had* to prove to him that I'm good now! Three hundred and sixty-two days clean."

Oh, wow. I never would have known she'd ever struggled with substance abuse. Pranks, yes, but nothing serious enough to disallow her custody of her own child. Still, she's obviously doing a whole lot better than me. I still don't even know if I murdered my own husband.

"I can't imagine the road you must have traveled." I lower my voice. "Looks like us girls have to stick together." I take her hand. "I'm sure it's only a matter of time before your family accepts the changes you've made."

An unruly tear courses down the side of Francesca's face. "I sure hope so, baby." Gently pulling away, she uses the back of her thumb to wipe the tear away.

Sensing she'll appreciate any and all information I have, I quickly explain, "I'm trying to locate Mr. Hardin myself ..."

"You mean your husband?" Francesca shakes her head, hoop earrings jangling. "Where do you think they ran off to?" But before I can say anything, her gaze falls to her work table to a framed picture of a little girl with an enormous smile, pink scrunchy, and a long, ebony braid. She's adorable. Maybe twelve.

"She's beautiful," I say.

More tears barrel down Francesca's cheeks. And now I feel like a total jerk for not noticing her daughter's picture before. And making her cry. "Her name's Delilah, and it's *killing* me, not hearing her voice."

"We'll find them." I promise, vowing to learn the connection between her husband and daughter and WT.

We have to—especially now that I know that this isn't just about me.

～

*L*uckily, I don't run into Ollie again at *Grady Dean's*. I imagine it's because I grab Tansy's cans in record time, and the store's jam-packed with a junior league baseball team. I do wish I knew what Francesca's husband's connection to WT means. Were they involved in some business deal that went south? Was WT also into MMA?

By the time I'm finished running my errands, it's 5 PM. I still have an hour and thirty minutes before I have to meet Tansy. Nothing is more important than regaining my memories, so I leave the groceries on the back porch before darting down the steps and heading to the first of the property's outbuildings. If WT never wanted to go anywhere, he and I would have spent some time together on the property.

And time means memories.

I zigzag through post oaks and voracious honey locusts, stepping lightly so any lingering tourists don't hear me. Ducking into an old, moss-covered shack, I spot a mess of potted plants just waiting to be found and babied. Looks like we're in a greenhouse, where a smashed terra cotta pot warns that it's either been ravaged by the wind—or somebody was having a bad day.

I kneel to pick up the pieces, and the terra cotta's cold as ice. The weight of the plaster and earthy smell instantly have me slipping down a rabbit hole.

"We have to go!" I hold the exact same pot and raise my voice. "WT, I'm drowning."

He wrenches the pot out of my hand and throws it so hard, it crashes to the ground, shattering. He looks like he wants to scream, but, instead, all he says is, "No." A muscle flickers along his jaw as he refuses to look into my eyes.

I try to pull down his chin. Force him to talk to me, but all he does is shake his head and back two steps away.

"You won't even tell me why!"

Bending down, he grabs another pot, and smashes it before spinning around and marching off into the night.

Dropping the pieces of the pot, I try to think what WT's outburst could mean. We were here, and I pushed him. Really pushed him, because something about this town didn't feel right. I wanted to go on a trip—a simple trip—and he wouldn't even entertain the idea.

I *have* to know what happened, so I back out of the greenhouse. Flee to the barn—supposing we have a barn—that *has* to be further back into the property. I trip over an overturned barrel. Tear around a pair of broken windows, and as I run, everything on our land skews, disproportionate and sickly. The elm trees are hollowed out cadavers, the trunks unusually dead and diseased. Tansy made me bury that squirrel and magpie, and now, after seeing WT's and my argument, I can't help wondering if maybe he had a violent streak. Did I hurt him when I thought he was about to hurt me?

The barn is more of a metal shed with scaffolding—an unfinished project with metal trusses and a woodpile on the side. The door sticks when I pull it open, and the entire room's airy and vacant, except for the sport utility vehicle at the back. A BMW. White. *"Go on an adventure," WT says with the sun shining behind him while he hands me the keys.*

"You should come, too."

He quietly shakes his head while his phone buzzes for the thirtieth time.

Pulling aside a mess of cobwebs, I make my way to the car, nervous that I'll remember something I *don't* want to see. What if I see myself accidentally knocking him out with one of those pots? Killing him, because he wouldn't listen to me?

Tansy said she took my memories because she needed to protect me, but what if I really do deserve to be locked up? What if I'm setting myself up for the avalanche, because I really can't handle the truth?

Giving a nice berth to the trunk—don't need to prematurely see any dead bodies—I drift over to the driver's side. Lift the handle. The heady aroma of leather hits me like a soft-handed punch as I sit, the chair's grooves hugging me with familiarity.

Feels like home. Comfortable. Pretty.

A dreamcatcher spins from the mirror as I place my hands on the steering wheel.

And I spiral.

Into the quicksand of yet another memory.

25

"*Drive!*" *WT whoops when he hops in the car.*

I grip the steering wheel, not sure if I've entered an alternate universe where we get to be Bonnie and Clyde.

"Don't just sit there, looking beautiful, woman," he roars, "DRIVE!"

His friends are on the sidewalk—on the square—and they're vultures swooping in, ready to feast. I can't make out their faces, but I do know that I've been begging to ditch this town for eons. He doesn't have to ask me twice.

With the courthouse in our rearview mirror, I peel out, rubber making glorious skid marks on the street. WT's friends shout something about carpetbaggers, and I laugh, because who even uses that term nowadays?

I've gone too fast to identify any faces or names, though we're finally off to Palo Duro. He called me to pick him up from work just before I headed out alone for the week.

We fly past a driveway lined with pampas grass and a clutch of red canna lilies. Elephant ears nod as we round the corner, and, after a few minutes, WT whoops after checking his side mirror.

Resting his hand on my knee, he says, voice thick, "I'm sorry."

I check my rearview mirror just to make sure nobody's following us. "About what?"

"You were right."

I can't help fighting back a smile as we speed past Harmon Park and the post office with its American flag and navy mailboxes. We wind our way through the outskirts of town—past Grammy's and the cemetery. It isn't until we're driving past a patch of prickly pears nestled against a magnolia's wide, stunning canopy that WT presses his fingertips to closed eyes.

"My colleagues ..." He rubs the scruff on his chin. "They don't know how to lay off at the right times."

"Why don't you remind them you're the boss? It's not every day you strike oil, then get a write-up in American Cowboy Magazine."

He gets this far-off look in his eyes. "I would, if they cared ..." He shakes his head. "Enough about this backward town. I forbid us from talking about them for the entire week."

"Forbid, huh?" I hit the turn signal to pass a tractor that's going about twenty. "Wait ... did you say a week?"

"Nothing short of a proper getaway." WT reclines his chair, threading his fingers together behind his head. "I'm the luckiest man in the world. The best historian on the planet has planned a romantic getaway for me."

I reach out to take his hand. Squeeze the warm callouses of his fingers and trace his simple, titanium ring. When he turns on the radio, Alison Krauss becomes an old friend, greeting us with her soothing storyteller voice.

26

*B*lue and green paint stripes the horsehair couch when I return home to Tansy. A bust on the mantel has new seashells glued to the hairline—and, oh boy—coral's sticking to the side of its head, like Tansy's created an elaborate crown for a mermaid.

Beyond that, it's stuffy as a grave. I cross the room to open a window.

Tansy, smarts, "Don't you *dare* open that window, missy. There are tourists outside!"

I hadn't noticed anyone out there, but that doesn't mean they're not there. I've been preoccupied.

Staring straight through the bright-red coral on WT's ancestor's head, I say, "I've made some progress." Avoiding the window, I wander across the parlor to the kitchen, and then on to the den. "I finally understand why you don't *want* me to have my memories. He went along." I pause before the rope pillars. "WT ended up going to Palo Duro with me."

Tansy folds our arms as we face the moose with a burgundy dress draped across the dozen or so antler points.

"Only because you were being as relentless and melodramatic as Anne Boleyn on execution day."

"Oh, so you're saying I should have been executed. Or trapped here the rest of my life."

"I'm *sayin'* you should have given up the game!"

I sweep out an arm. "So you wanted me to never speak out for what I wanted or cared about." Striding to the moose, I whip off the dress, stirring up enough dust to put the Dust Bowl to shame. "What you fail to recognize, Tansy, is how I now know the truth. WT *liked* adventuring! Which means, he couldn't have been upset about my need to travel." I tug a pair of shorts from a lamp. "You lied."

All at once, Tansy's blood's about to go on a full-on broil. "YOU. TOOK. HIM. AWAY." She tears off my sneakers, proving she's done talking.

Wait. Is this evidence that she existed even before WT and I got married?

"He was happy n' fine. Both you and I know, he could have been satisfied forever to never leave this place. But *you* had to go—and push n' push—to bloody well convince him to leave!" She flails our arms, doing a great imitation of one of those inflatable tube man signs. "Gemma, stayin' here was all I ever wanted, and you took that away!"

"But he was okay with going on the trip. It's not normal to stay boarded up in a house all the time."

Tansy sniffles. "Do you think I *care* about what other people think?"

I set the dress that's been tucked under our arm onto the coffee table. Now that I see it, Tansy's life could actually be so simple without me. Really, she would be a true agoraphobe, requisitioning people to bring her supplies. The girl doesn't even care about people's opinions. Doesn't waste time, worrying about the latest outfit or makeup or home design.

But living in a bubble means never stretching; never once growing.

"Tansy, we have to live in society."

"We don't *have* to do anythin'!" She digs our nails into the couch's fluted, wooden side. "Do you think I *like* bein' like this?" She collapses on the armrest. "I wish I wanted to go to parties. But they are exhausting. People stare, and I hate them! I hate them all, G!"

Hugging our arms close, I shush her like I'm holding an infant. "I know, I know. People can be harsh sometimes."

"All the time!"

"Or all the time." I spy the fire poker. Wish there was something I could do with it to convince her that it's time again to talk to Grammy. She would know what to do—what these new memories about WT mean. She'd be rational. Logical. Her point of view is exactly what Tansy and I need.

As the beginnings of a plan form in my head, I say, "Hey, Tansy, do you think we could maybe build a fire?" I force a shiver. "I'm freezing."

She slumps further into the armrest, obviously spent for the day. Sure, I could let her rest for a while, but all I can do is spare her a few seconds. . . before I change the paradigm.

One.

Two.

Five.

That's all the time I can spare. Doing my best to appear crestfallen, slowly, ever so slowly, I shuffle to my socked feet. Turning my body so that Tansy surely thinks I'm headed for the kindling, I trudge along, like I'm just as tuckered out as Tansy. Yawning to ham things up a bit, I wait three more seconds—before darting to the right.

The back door. It's about five or six steps ahead of me. Five or six steps to glorious freedom, and maybe even Grammy's peanut butter cookies.

But Tansy's never been slow on the uptake. Just as I pry open the door, she slams it shut with her fist, nearly nailing our fingers to the doorframe.

"Not this time!" she shrieks.

"But"—I wish I could think of something else she might listen to—"we need to talk things out with Grammy!"

I try to pry her fingers off the doorframe, but Tansy shoots me this disabling mental image of Edgar looming large and monstrous above me.

He's the wall of granite.

A pillar—an eternally solid stone of gray—just like his gray, gaunt face.

On instinct, I'm cowering.

Against my will, she has us back up, up, up—*all* the way to the armrest of the couch.

"I can't ever let you leave this house again, G."

"You can't keep me here!" I try to swipe for the door, but it's like moving through barbed wire, chained. "How would we eat?"

Tansy pretends to brush dust from off our shoulder. "Oh, I have my ways."

But there's no way she's going to lock me up permanently. From a side table, I reach for a scalloped and beaded lampshade, but the beads tangle in my fingers, and Tansy's grappling to be queen.

She seizes the neck of the lamp.

Lifts it.

Smashes it onto the arch of our foot so hard, I scream.

If I were still wearing shoes, the wound wouldn't cut so deep. But she kicked them off, and I wasn't even paying attention. Blood slips down the side of our foot, warm and watery.

"Stop—ruinin'—our—life!" Tansy kicks the broken glass

of the lamp again and again. Blood pools beneath our toes, and I can't help wondering if she's going to saw it off—in the name of making art come to life.

27

When I come to, my arm's so numb it feels like it's been disconnected from my body. My head's bent at an odd angle, and it looks like Tansy's tied me to the bed with duct tape.

Luckily, it's not a permanent solution, since my other hand is free. And I'm not even sure why Tansy relinquished control—except that my head's hotter than a furnace.

Pretty sure we're running a fever. Great.

Half-eaten bowls of spit pea soup line the comforter along with a scrap-metal, handmade toy guillotine. I'm wearing another Victorian dress—olive-colored, itchy—and, as ever, beads of sweat line my neck and chest. My entire body is shivering.

With a bit of elbow grease, I'm able to pull the duct tape from my wrist without dislocating anything. It doesn't make sense that Tansy would trap me here with only one tied hand, but since when has Tansy ever been sensible about anything?

Hobbling over to the mirror, I wipe away the dust to see how terrible I look today.

I brace myself for impact, and never have I had such large

bags under my eyes. I could have clumps of coal in there, and it would look the same. Dracula's cousin may need to move over, though, since I'm thinking I have a real chance at playing the original Vlad—if I can get that mustache to grow I saw hints of last week.

When I try resting my full weight on my foot, pain sears up and down my leg. I still can't believe Tansy kicked that lamp; I've never seen her so angry. At least it looks like she's wrapped our injured foot with bandages. Dirt soils the edges, and brown, dried blood stains our leg.

What I would give for a pair of crutches—or say I was confident that Tansy would get some for me. I could hop on over to the neighbor's to see if they have some, but I'd probably only make it about halfway down the stairs before Tansy pushes me out—for even longer this time.

Suddenly exhausted, I sink back into the bed, never more tempted to go back to sleep. Tired. So tired—not to the mention the fact that my entire body feels like it's crawling with fleas.

Okay, what are the clues I've been able to figure out? Tansy's upset that WT and I took off for Palo Duro, but did WT know about Tansy? If so, why would he even marry us? As a rich oil baron, he could have married anybody.

Really, I wish I could talk to Grammy.

Since I can't go anywhere, it looks like my memory search is limited to the estate. And while I can't go to Palo Duro to trigger what happened there ... maybe there's something I can do to bring Palo Duro to me.

Looking around the room, I canvass the empty desk, mahogany dresser, and another bust of one of WT's ancestors with coral glued to the side of the face. I know why Tansy likes seashells and coral—any crown really. She once said, "It helps me be queen of my own domain."

From the top of the dresser, an old vase catches my eye.

Orange and yellow dried flowers with jaunty, pointed tips yawn from the stems' grouping.

In contrast ...

The stems are a beautiful shade of summer green. Amidst walls of red rock, petrified wood, and sagebrush, WT suggests we go spelunking. When we find that our equipment is faulty, we grab Natalie and Jesse's bikes and set out for a trail ride.

At first, WT's all handlebars; very little pedaling. His earlier modes of transportation have always been a motorcycle, or a horse, sometimes, but here—here he puts his mind to a poor man's vehicle, and he rides with that boyish smile he reserves only for me.

"Is it even real?" I ask as we rest at the top of our path with our bikes parked amidst the sagebrush and red dirt that could be sawdust, it's so fine. Around us, the basin's a clay bowl, interspersed with the twisted feathers of mesquite trees.

"Real as you are." WT wraps me in his arms, pulling me close, smelling not so vaguely of sweat but so much love and unsurprising strength.

Before I know it, the sun is setting. He hands me a wildflower—a single Indian paintbrush—a torch of devotion and studded flames.

As the sun sets, he gets that understated, panicked look again in his eyes. "Are you glad you married me?"

How unusually vulnerable he's being. I kiss him hard and fast. "Of course. How could I ever feel differently?"

A shadow of pain flickers across his sun-kissed face as he lifts my fingers and kisses them, one by one. "I'm going to fight to be the man you deserve, Gemma Louise."

28

I remember his hands—how he would help me zip up dresses, slip on necklaces, cradle my hand like I was the only girl in the entire universe when we were dancing. I remember how he so crisply moved when he was putting on a tie, like he was negotiating a business transaction.

How he held the steering wheel with one hand and my hand in the other on Sunday drives.

I remember how he kissed me on our second date—he invited friends over for dinner and cards and dancing. The weather was perfect—September, before the leaves had started falling from the trees. I don't know how he did it, but he got Lewis Capaldi to come and play my favorite song. I can hear it in my head! "Someone you Loved." Capaldi's voice was so full and melodic and heartbreaking. It was like WT was saying, "I know I don't say much. And I can be hard to read, but you're it for me."

And yet, I'm not sure how to explain it. It was like this silent part of him was *begging* for me to understand something unspeakable. At least, something he couldn't speak about with me. But the way he held me ... I could feel this deep, resounding pain, wound up tightly like a spring. But I didn't know how to help. How to get him—the man I was falling for —to talk about what he obviously, so desperately, didn't want me to see was plaguing his mind?

So, we danced. The white twinkle lights hung from the horse stalls like fine jewelry, and the other dancers swayed around us as if we were collectively feeling the same thing.

It seems I've been hobbling around my bedroom, imitating the dance WT and I did that night. I suppose I got swept up in the moment. Didn't even realize I'd set the vase of flowers on the floor. But how could Tansy insist on shielding me from the truth when every memory makes me so happy?

They show me I'm loved. That I know who I am. If Tansy and I could work *together,* I'm sure there'd be no chance of the avalanche happening.

Maybe what Tansy needs to soften her stance is to see some of WT's belongings. She could be reminded of how happy we were together.

I hobble across the foot of the bed, careful not to knock into the settee. My ankle screams in protest, but there's something I need to do. Need to see.

Wrenching open the closet door, I step inside a tiny room that's smaller than builders make for houses nowadays. Though it is sufficient, with a healthy amount of clothes— mine on the left, WT's on the right.

While the clothes rack is newer—people used armoires and trunks back in the day—right away, there's WT's navy blazer. His salmon one. Green. I lift the green one to my nose and breathe in the cedar scent. I forgot he carried this with him—an echo from his truck's dashboard's wood inlay.

Sliding each garment across the rack, I take a moment to absorb the smooth and coarse textures, recollecting the way he looked in all of these. "Presidential," I would say, and he'd balk. Every time. It's not that he was old, or even clean shaven, but he had an understated, commanding presence *everybody* noticed in Deep Creek. Like Tansy said, he's the most beloved of all the town's residents. He couldn't help it. Everyone loved him and his quiet ways.

Reaching the back of the closet, I stop a little short, because a white stretch of fabric catches my eye. It must be one of his button-up shirts—except then it would be in the front with his other shirts. Maybe it's in the wrong place.

It's pretty far back. I have to hyperextend my arm to grasp the garment and lift it with the hanger, but, oh, it's not even a shirt. The hanger sags with impossible weight.

Heaving the garment nearer, I prepare to examine it closer. It must be my wedding dress—put on the wrong side. But something about the way the garment hangs doesn't feel right.

I take a step back. Accidentally knock over the flower vase. Holding up the robe, I find that it has a rope tie around the waist.

With the boards covering the windows, it's pretty hard to see, but taking a step sideways, I hold up the heavy garment in the creamy stream of light.

A red and white square-shaped cross marks the breast while a white, triangular-shaped hood drops to the floor.

I stoop to pick it up, my once-forgotten fever rushing over my head in a wave.

The hood is long. About three feet.

And there are cut-outs.

For eyes.

29

I drop the robe.

No. No, no, no, no.

This is a nightmare. I'm dreaming.

I wasn't married to a man who ...

He wouldn't *do* that. He wasn't that kind of a person.

A loud *crack* reverberates from my back as I collide with the bedpost. Something scampers from behind the curtain, and I fall back onto the bed as Jerusha in her tortoise-shell coat springs from the doorway. Her sweater catches on the side of the door, and she tugs on the threads, hissing while pulling herself free. All at once, she darts around the corner, reminding me of a spooked, deranged sphynx.

I gather the robe in my arms. Wad it up like a piece of garbage, because that's what it is. If I could, I would incinerate the thing. But I have to put it *somewhere*, so I barrel back into the closet. Stuff it into the farthest corner, wishing more than anything I never explored the space.

Swinging the door closed, I press my back into it, praying all of this is a dream. I shuffle toward the bed but don't have the heart to sit on it. I sink to the floor, pull my knees to my chest, Tansy's stupid gray-green skirts fluttering out around me. What I just saw—it can't be right. It's WT's Dad's or something.

WT and I, we were *happy*. He was kind and thoughtful, and I could *feel* his goodness in every part of me. But, apparently ... that was a lie?

Sure, we had a few arguments, but he also wanted to get away from this stupid town. But now I know his secret. *The* secret that was constantly plaguing his mind.

Is that what they *do* here in Deep Creek?

But Francesca's here ... she can't be. She has to get out. *Out*. I scramble up to warn her, when I'm hit by another terrible thought.

What if there's another robe in there?

No. No, no, no; *no* way.

I've become immobile. I can't get myself to move—can't even get myself to take a peek.

If there *is* another robe in that closet, it has to be somebody else's. Not mine. Not even Tansy's.

I inch up from the ground and creep toward the closet, knowing that I have to look inside that door a final time. But I don't want to. I'd rather pour acid in my eyes.

Holding out my arm, I wait for my other, dictatorial half to stop me cold, but she isn't here. Tansy's MIA. So I grab the brass handle of the door and give it a whirl. Steel myself to look inside.

One breath.

Three.

Okay, inside are WT's blazers.

Navy, salmon, green.

His other shirts and jackets are still in here, too, and way, way in the back is a wooden hanger that comes up empty. Oh, yeah, because I stashed the robe on the floor, brilliant me.

It's still there. Like a dead animal. But I'm not burying it for Tansy.

If Tansy or I were to have a robe of our own, I suppose it would be on my side of the closet. But since when have *they* had women in their ranks?

My side is stuffed with dresses and slacks and shirts and belts and sweaters and jackets and pencil skirts of polyester blends that have my hands shaking. Sweat beads like goose-flesh on my neck. Drips in rivulets down my spine.

What if I find one? What if I have a robe, just like WT's?

No wonder Francesca's been cagey.

I can't see the colors of any of my clothes. My eyes have gone watery. I think *maybe* I've set my sights on something ivory, but when I pull out the garment, it's a white, ruffled blouse with cute button-up sleeves.

I drop the blouse and hanger. Hands won't stop shaking. Must force myself further into the closet to make sure I don't miss anything.

There's a wedding dress, but it's in a plastic, sheer dry-cleaning bag. Little white embroidered flowers dot the snow-white fabric. Pretty.

Flipping to the end of the clothes, I hit some wooden slats. I've just reached the back wall of the closet. No more robes. *Thank you,* Tansy.

I do a final look-through before swinging the door closed, pushing my back into the door, and sinking to the ground. Without really thinking it through, I nudge my other half. *"Tansy ..."*

She doesn't so much as offer me a resounding sigh. She's probably ignoring me, because I pushed her too hard. We do have a fever, plus a wrecked foot. And she duct-taped me. So, what do I *do*? Tansy knew the robe was up here, just waiting for me to find it.

I still can't believe this is my life.

Actually, for the first time since all of this started, I get why Tansy's decided to lock herself away. The world is dark. Cruel—much crueler than any of us want to think.

Do I remember *what* WT did in that robe?

I remember ... a white blanket. Tulips in the back yard. Picnicking.

A white tablecloth on long, rectangular tables and billowing bedsheets.

My white wedding dress comes to mind, with those little embroidered flowers, and the skirts dollop, so elegant—like melted ice cream.

But now in those dollops, all I can see is the truth of that robe—how it stands for nothing but disgusting and nauseating hate.

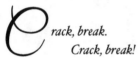*rack, break.*
        Crack, break!

Looks like we're in a cream Victorian gown, and Tansy's chopping a mangy carrot, gold bracelets clanking. I don't have a clue how long she's been going at it, but carrots, along with a mountain of potatoes and onions, are piled on the counters, a mile high.

Tansy must have gone to the root cellar. I didn't even know we had a root cellar. How long have I been out? Her fingers are moving so fast, I'm afraid a finger's going to get in the way.

Crack, break.
Crack, break!

"Do you see why I asked you to drop it?" Tansy grabs another carrot and annihilates the thing. "Now go away! I'd like a little more alone time, if you please." Except Tansy and I both know that a "little" alone time could mean up to a few weeks.

Actually ... between Tansy's diet and her tendency to

hoard things, I'd guess there's enough food here to keep her going for six months, at least.

"I don't need you," she says. *Crack! Break.* "I could go on for the better half of a year. Maybe, by then, you'd realize you crossed the line."

Crack, break!

Panic burrows through my chest like a restless king snake. I don't want to be locked away again. Time to smooth over her feelings.

"I'm sorry." For safety reasons, I try to take control of the knife, but it's like wading through water. "You and I both know, searching a closet in my own bedroom isn't a punishable crime."

"YOU WOULDN'T LET IT GO!" Tansy beheads another carrot before accidentally nicking our finger with the knife.

Blood pools on our fingertip, and she has us stomping over to the sink, bustle swooshing. The dishes and teacups in the cupboards shake in their boots, and I don't know if I should be shaking in mine.

Turning on the water, she sniffles, "Look"—the water blasts at full power—"I really didn't want it to be this way. We had a deal. You get the groceries, I tuck away all our secrets n' keep us safe. But now that I know that you've been diggin' around and goin' WAY past our formerly agreed-upon boundaries, I see now that I've been way too lenient. Fact of the matter is, I can't trust you, G."

"But I just investigated the room where you left me."

She growls something in French I don't recognize. This isn't just about the robe—as if that isn't enough. She's upset about something else. But knowing Tansy, she'll never say. So I watch and wait while she slowly turns off the water and dries our hands with the speed of an eighty-year-old woman.

Practically moving in reverse, she seizes the next carrot and resumes her chopping.

I don't interfere. I know better than to push her when she's angry. Instead, I allow a peaceful co-existence to settle between us. Kind of similar to when we watched the birds together through the skylight. How many cardinals did we see?

"I know you're still there." Tansy exhales. "You're about as cloak and dagger as a nine-pin bowlin' set on Broadway."

"Sorry ... but you know I have no control of when I go or stay. You're the one who always has me leave."

I expect her to shut me out this very moment, just to prove I'm right, but she merely continues her chopping. Which makes me wonder if she actually wants me here. Maybe she secretly wishes to talk about what's bothering her. It has to be quite the load, shielding me from so many things.

"Your grandmother stopped by," she says mulishly. She didn't say "our" grandmother. That's good to know. Hmm. "She wanted you to know that Jesse Beauchamp's not goin' to be botherin' you anymore. Except how can she promise that? Jesse Beauchamp's the 'Sheriff' and Grammy is 'Grammy.'"

"Don't you have faith in her?"

Tansy snatches up a potato, which has more eyes than the peacocks at the exotic zoo in Boyd. "Jesse Beauchamp is the devil himself. She's an outsider, so he'll put her in prison just to get her outta the way."

I try to relax, but I can't help stiffening our grasp around the knife. It didn't occur to me that Grammy would still be considered an outsider, but I suppose she wasn't raised here if she met Edgar in her fifties. "We have to help her!"

Tansy grabs another carrot, and I force myself to take a few deep breaths. I have to consider what I found upstairs. Think rationally.

Maybe Jesse has plans to plant WT's murder on me. That's saying WT's dead, but Tansy says he's still alive ...

A freezer-cold chill scurries up the back of my neck, and part of me fears that, any second, WT's going to jump out from behind one of the pillars and strangle me. He'll force me into one of his robes. Swear that I agreed to *all of this* since the beginning. He'll remind me of some field trip he took me on where he revealed the inner-workings of the Klan—there, I said it—and, somehow, I hate to go there but somehow ... he brainwashed me?

Tansy's fingers are moving so fast I'm sure to lose a pinky.

"*Shhh.*" I hush her within our mind. If I could, I'd set my hands on her shoulders and tenderly read to her from her favorite Shakespearean play. *Macbeth.* Or *Titus Andronicus*, possibly. "*We* have *to work together, ladybird. It will be okay.*"

Sensing my sincerity, Tansy eventually calms, shoulders loosening. Still, she doesn't set down her knife. Instead, she has us tightening our fist around the wooden handle and forces us to do this synchronized chop for five minutes straight. It almost feels good. Therapeutic—if it weren't for the fact that we have a *Klan* robe upstairs, in the very room I shared with WT.

This is the longest I've ever been a silent bystander while Tansy's been awake. It actually shows me that she can focus on a job without any extra dramatics, as surprising as that can be.

At long last, and only after our fingers have numb, Tansy sets down the knife. Wiping our hands on the tea towel, she says, "It's time you saw my favorite place."

*T*ansy pauses before a closet, a little door between the front entry and the stairs to the left. When she twists the handle to let us in, an entire bedroom with a bed and desk and curtains lures me inside. Floral curtains, floral wallpaper, floral crown molding. It's definitely a feminine room, and spread out on all the surfaces, are teeny-tiny glass figurines.

A unicorn.

A dog, bear, cat. Too many to keep track of, but they're *beautiful*, tinted ballet slipper pink.

As we limp inside, I find the ones on the desk are tinted blue, like cotton candy. A beautiful collection of birds of all sizes.

Straightening a crooked giraffe on the bedside table, Tansy appraises the entire room like she's manning an antique shop. "There." She pets the brittle giraffe with great fondness. "That's right."

She has us straighten the velvet shade of a lantern, too, and a rose-embroidered kerchief folded in half on a chest of drawers to the right of the doorway. In all my time with her,

I've never seen Tansy be so calm. So orderly. It's even less musty in here—as if the dust has been absorbed by the glass figurines.

"I bring you to this room," Tansy says with a lilting hum in her voice, "to show you how fragile we can be. The deer are always the first to go." She gestures to a collection of glass deer lying at the foot of the bed, with broken antlers and legs. "Then the cranes." She gestures vaguely at the broken neck of a solitary crane. A pillow cushions its head, and Tansy has us perching on the bed's side.

After having us sit and stare in wonder at the crane for what feels like hours, she whispers, "Well, what do you think?"

I don't want to say the wrong thing. If I say they're pretty, she'll assume I have sticky fingers and hide them away from me. If I say they *aren't* pretty, she'll accuse me of having no taste. So I remain quiet, a silent bystander as she pets the fragile, broken head of the crane.

Pulling in our legs under our massive cream skirts, she says, "We are fragile, G. We *wish* to do the right thing—but the world is plagued with monsters. Everything is so much better if we stay inside."

I'd like to push her to elaborate. But, instead, she plucks up the crane and cradles it in our palm with the devotion of a nun attending a convocation ceremony.

"Seven months ago," she says, "we saw something truly terrible." She pets the rock-hard back of the crane. "Something no one should ever see. Some people are equipped to handle such happenstances. Others ... well, they're already vulnerable, because of how they were raised."

I think of Edgar, but don't say a word. I don't know the extent of what he did to us—or what Grammy did to defend me—but I can't deny the twisted feeling I get every time I think of him, down to the daunting, gray mustache on his face.

But Tansy's saying we saw something later ... something to do with the Klan? Something to do with WT? "It's how you and I more fully split—whatever we saw, right?"

Tansy peers closer at the crane's tiny, oval-shaped eyes. "That's right."

"But what if you're wrong in assuming that I'm unable to handle what happened?" I hate to think that I'm as fragile as a bunch of glass figurines.

Tansy grinds our teeth. "*You* forget that you asked me to be the bearer of secrets."

I wish I could go back in time. See whatever I need to see in a quick, matter-of-fact memory, then give it back to her if it's too painful. That wouldn't be too greedy, right?

I also wish I knew if it was smart to keep digging. But if it has something to do with the robe, I have to know for Francesca. I have to keep her safe.

Setting the crane back on the pillow, Tansy cups our hands on our lap with a melancholy grace. I'm not sure which thread to unravel, so I start with an easy question. "Why are you so afraid of everyone outside?"

Somewhat lost in thought, she stares at our heavy skirt's pleats. I almost think she hasn't heard me, when, after a moment, she shifts our gaze a little to the right. "Half the town believes we killed our husband. The other half believes we killed him, but we qualify for an insanity plea."

Wait ... "*Everyone* thinks we killed WT?"

Tansy snaps our head up with a startled thought. "Your friend, Francesca, doesn't, I believe."

And, I'm assuming, Calhoun and Dwayne. But Tansy knows about Francesca? How? A paring knife has begun hacking apart our insides. "So what's stopping them from locking us up?"

"I told you. WT's still alive. There's never been a body." Smoothing out our skirt, she adds, "Plus, Jesse Beauchamp and Zeb Calhoun struck a deal. You—we—get to stay outta prison as long as we stay tucked up in here, where Jesse can keep an eye on us and check in"—she trills our fingers in the air—"from time to time. In exchange, Calhoun gets to try n' continue to examine us from afar when you go out every two weeks."

"So you know that I visited Calhoun?" To think I'd thought I might have been sneaky. "He said that you had gone to visit him before. And that he helped us after I went to Boyd."

Tansy's voice deepens in warning. "Even the innocent have to make a deal or two with the devil in order to survive."

"But Calhoun doesn't seem all that bad ..." What exactly is she saying?

Tansy shoots me a warning look. "Let's just pray that he continues to be that way."

"What does that mean?"

Quick as a whip, Tansy pushes me onto the windowsill of our conscious mind. There must be something I can do to convince her to explain, but the ledge is wet, slippery. I do know that basically the whole town thinks I'm a killer, and Calhoun and Jesse are in league, but does that mean they're also in the Klan? "Tansy, wai—"

"Don't want to overload you." With a pitying smile, she shoves me off the ledge, and I drop into an unending black space.

32

When I come to, I'm sprawled across the horsehair couch in the parlor, draped in a red and black dress covered in lace. Satin opera gloves house my fingers, and Hawkins is sprawled on my stomach, fast asleep.

I move an inch, and he locks his yellow eyes on me. Digging his paws into my stomach, he jumps off, his dainty claws catching the lace.

Black feathers have been strewn across the rug and hardwood almost like rose petals, lovingly placed. A cooked ... turkey? ... lies on a silver platter on the coffee table with perfectly browned skin and healthy amounts of pepper and parsley.

But Tansy couldn't have bought that; she doesn't go to town.

Unless ...

Black feathers. That isn't a turkey.

A note on the coffee table has Tansy's loopy writing where she's written, "Bon Appétit!" Two wine glasses perch next to the platter, though one of the glasses has already been drained. Wonder what it is. Beet juice? I wouldn't put it past

Tansy to have found some beets in the root cellar and decided to play barmaid.

On a nearby chair lay my running clothes, folded in a neat pile, my sneakers on the rug just beneath.

I stand from the couch, knowing I have to find Francesca, whatever it takes. I should also make some time to stop by Grammy's. Wonder what the chances are that she's really figured out how to handle Jesse.

On the way to *The Hair Lounge,* I think what it must be like for Francesca to move here, completely clueless as to what people are capable of in Deep Creek. Though she's probably felt a degree of discrimination everywhere. I *hate* that she's had to deal with such hatred and ignorance. People can be so self-serving and ugly.

By the time I make it to the salon, the line's out the front door and sprawled halfway down the street. The sharp hair chemical fumes draw me closer, and I veer around a self-standing chalkboard that says, "Half off eyebrow sculpting."

Usually, Francesca's stationed at the counter, but *Hey, Sugar* lady's already standing at the front of the store, clutching her phone rigidly. "What are *you* doing here?" Tobacco wafts off her tunic, and, when she smiles, it seems she only has time to sometimes brush her teeth.

A scuffle breaks out from the door, and her husband emerges, big, brown mustache bouncing. The moment he sets his sights on me, his eyes narrow to slits while a pair of teens and an eighty-year old woman suddenly march through the door, barring the way.

I've got to get Francesca out of here—something about this doesn't feel right.

Hey, Sugar lady draws closer to me as more people crowd in around us like sardines. A few murmurs break out across the group, but I can't make out what they're saying.

"You do realize how your choice in friends is problematic

for us in Deep Creek." *Hey, Sugar* lady's breath is a biological weapon, making it very hard to concentrate. "Not that it matters, now that she ... "

Goosebumps rise on the backs of my arms. What's going on? Something's on the floor behind her and—that better not be ...

My heart catches in my throat as I stagger to the right. Maybe it's Jessica—or one of Francesca's other colleagues—but, no, a beautiful, buxom form is just lying there like someone's busted a knee.

Gorgeous, umber skin has never looked so flawless—except for the gaping hole that's now in her hairline.

Blood pools onto my sneakers. And Francesca ... she doesn't blink.

No. No ... I bite my tongue. Blink past the white spots floating in front of my eyes. I've got to get her—hold her—but someone's holding me back while I scream, "Someone lift her to a chair or something!"

A fat piece of porcelain lies on the tile—almost like it's the missing piece of Francesca's head, but that isn't the right material, and it's covered in bright-red food coloring.

"Who did this?" I'm choking as the customer chairs spin about me.

"Does anyone know how much it's going to cost me to replace that sink?" Wanda asks blandly.

"Such a terrible accident," the eighty-year-old woman says, holding onto those two scraggly teens.

"Not to mention the stain," one of the teens agrees.

I round on the trio, tears burning in my eyes. "What is *wrong* with you?" I lift a shaking hand to my friend. "She's ... someone's ..." Why can't they see what I'm seeing?

"Truly, a terrible, terrible accident," the eighty-year-old woman says again, and how can she believe that? That's not how Francesca died!

"She was *murdered*," I say, staring down the woman.

The woman's white hair whooshes back as she flinches with fright.

But *Hey, Sugar* lady narrows her eyes at me like I belong in a padded room with a straitjacket and chains.

"Please, you have to listen to me." My voice hitches, and I spin to explain this to everybody. "*They* did this." I think of the Klan robe hanging in my closet. "I have proof! If you see it, I know you'll believe!"

"Oh, sure." *Hey, Sugar* lady rolls her eyes. "The 'untouchable' Gemma Coldiron Hardin. You still haven't even confessed to what you did to WT."

The eighty-year-old woman seems to have recovered from her fear. Her slight shoulders are bunching up as she jabs a crooked finger in my face. "Murderer!"

But she has to see that Francesca's been the target. A target of the worst possible hate crime.

Only, the old woman's teen escorts are closing in on me like they're about to eat me for lunch. *Hey, Sugar* lady's husband dials on his phone, like he's calling the police.

He should call the police. But the only police I know in this town is Jesse.

The bell on the door chimes, and speak of the devil. A stocky man in a police uniform shuffles in, and Jesse rolls back his shoulders while he rearranges the wad of chew in his left cheek.

Setting me in the crosshairs of his gaze, Jesse narrows his eyes, and I already know I'm in trouble.

I have to get out.

I have to get out.

"It was an accident," Wanda says.

33

*W*hen I return home, Francesca's blood splotches my shoes—giant, angry scratch marks from hungry beasts. Sure, I'm smearing blood on the rug in the parlor, but I don't care. She's dead.

Dead.

How could I be clueless enough to let Francesca die?

The only thing that makes sense is that *someone* in the Klan did it. Tears burn sharp as razors in my eyes. How could I put her in danger? How could I be so oblivious to what was going on in Deep Creek?

I pound the back of a parlor chair. "She's dead!" Vulture feathers fly up from the breeze of my swing. "She's dead ..." And they called it an accident, of all things.

Francesca and I were friends, and I didn't even know her last name. Who is going to do my hair from now on? And how is *that* one of the first questions that crosses my mind? She said her husband and daughter got a house because of WT, but now they're missing and she's dead.

I shouldn't have ever asked Francesca to do my hair. I

probably shouldn't have ever confided to her that Hardin is my last name.

Spinning, I grab the first thing that I come into contact with—a metal and brass canon paperweight. I don't know what I'm doing, but I toss it to the Civil War-era bone china where it chips away a good quarter of a plate.

That didn't do enough damage, so I grab an empty teacup and hurl it into the fireplace.

The saucer goes next as pure, raw rage washes over me in a tidal wave. To think that the Klan is *here,* and I just let Tansy hole us up and blindly take over the reins.

A candlestick joins the saucer in the fireplace, and my hands tremble while I remember how that isn't a candlestick but a girandole—another stupid fact from all the tours I did in D.C.

I'm just about to grab a framed self portrait of Tansy with one of her cats, when my other half flops up from her frilly, mental bed, fully awake. "You need not let out your frustrations on my artwork, G."

I grab the portrait anyway.

She snarls, and I guess it really is important to her, so I let her set it back on the mantel where it clatters, nearly falling

"They killed her," I say, sinking onto the coffee table next to the roast vulture meat.

What gets me is, I don't even know if Francesca *tried* to tell me about the Klan. She told me people here aren't what they seem, but I was too busy obsessing over my own issues to see what she was saying. Did she even have any other clients? How could I not notice?

Perching on the edge of her bed, Tansy mimics the way I'm sitting. In quiet solidarity, she doesn't say a single word while she waits for me to steady my breathing. Mattress springs coil as she leans forward, and I get the impression that she wants to give me a hug, but she holds back. Not exactly sure how that would work, anyway.

Groaning, Tansy says, "I knew it was only a matter of time before we saw a casualty from The Knights."

The ... ? "Don't you *dare* call them that." There's nothing about them that even remotely warrants them being called "knights."

"Sorry." Tansy mentally tucks her legs up beneath her skirts. "That's just their name. Ironic, isn't it? The 'True Knights' of Deep Creek."

I'm going to puke. Give me a sword, and I'll impale something. My hands feel so broken and useless—anything I touch dies.

Tansy purrs, "We can call them 'the Klan,' if you like ..."

All of this is so crazy. She's crazy. I pull at our hair. "I don't *want* to call them anything!"

"Yes, Gemma, I understand that. But this"—she gestures about the disordered room—"is our reality. Despicable hate groups and antiquated secret societies. Why else do you think I prefer to hide?"

I *really* wouldn't mind hurling her precious portrait into the fireplace. "Tansy, *we* have nothing to fear. We. Are. White."

"People of other ethnicities are not the only ones who have reason to fear, G. *Anyone* could die who crosses the big names."

I think of how Jesse arrived at the exact moment when I tried to convince the town that Francesca was murdered. How deathly calm he looked. Scary. How he would like nothing better than to lock me away.

"You and I both know that the color of Francesca's skin is the reason why she died. I *saw* the robe. That's what they do. They hurt innocent, *good* people—no matter who you or I are. Unless there's something you're not telling me."

In a futile attempt at comfort, Tansy pats the closest of our two knees. "No, no. You're right."

"Yet you're not even surprised that it's happened. I can't *believe* I didn't run to Francesca the minute I found that robe."

Tansy settles one of our hands on the table. "Handling such matters is not our responsibility. It's why we need to stay here, safe—"

"WE SHOULD HAVE TRIED TO WARN HER IF WE THOUGHT MURDER WAS EVEN A POSSIBLITY!" I punch the platter on the table, nearly sending the roasted vulture flying. Pacing over the rug, I say, "This is what they do." I hate this detached, numb feeling crawling over our body. "Just sit around for innocent people to move in—and harass and possibly *kill* them." I hunch over, ready to lose whatever food Tansy last ate.

Lifting our hands, Tansy presses them into the skin on our forehead and rubs them all the way down our face. "Look, we're in no position to take down the Klan. I would like to. Stopping them would be a fabulous idea, but we already have a target on our backs, what with how they think you killed WT."

"But I didn't *do* that!" I snatch a horseshoe bookend from the fireplace mantel and toss it into a tabletop clock tower. They both fly back and smash into a curio cabinet, making a terrible clang. Though maybe, considering what WT might have done, maybe getting him out of the picture is somewhat … justified? No. No, no, no. That's not who I am. I don't kill people. I would never take anybody's life.

"Ah, but you're afraid of *the avalanche!*" I trill my fingers in the air, mocking Tansy's self-absorbed worry. "Heaven forbid we ever stand up for something."

Tansy mentally scoots back. "Look, G, I'm sorry." Reaching up, she seizes our left fist and forces it down with our right. "Would you like me to play you some music?" She nods to a stringed instrument in the corner. "I've been givin' myself harp lessons and think I may have *finally* mastered *La bohème*."

I'll head-butt her into the wall if it means she'll stop living in a fantasy. But I guess it would be stupid to knock her out right when she's in a sympathetic enough mood to share more about our history. "Is Calhoun one of the leaders?"

Startled, Tansy lifts our chin, half-nodding.

"Beauchamp?"

Cracking an eye half-closed, she nods a second time.

"And where, exactly, on the totem pole is WT?"

She lifts our head higher, higher—all the way toward the ceiling.

"So you're saying he's at the top."

"I'm not *sayin'* anything, G. *You* have to figure out these things."

A loud *BOOM* outside the door tells me that an agitated tourist—or townsperson—has come to play. And they're bearing weapons. Great.

I dig our hands again into our hair. "They killed Francesca to teach *me* a lesson. They're acting like"—I fight back a gag —"reserving our town for only white people is a matter of principle or something." I had no idea they'd follow me home. They're probably the same people who left the graffiti.

A brick or a rock bounces off the board covering the window in the very room where Tansy and I are standing, and we stagger a step back.

"GOLD DIGGER!" a crazed woman roars, her husky voice sounding an awful lot like *Hey, Sugar* lady's.

"Conspiracy theorist!" her husband wails. "Pointin' fingers at *everybody* else when *you're* the only murderer in Deep Creek!"

Glass shatters from a window somewhere in the house, and someone just spouted off a racial slur I will *never* repeat.

Tansy winces. "Evil does have a way of catching on where it's invited."

"I didn't invite them!"

"I'm just sayin' it spreads like wildfire, my sweet."

All I know is, I hate him. I *hate* WT. *How* could I have ever had feelings for a person who inspires so much hate?

"YA BETTER TURN YOURSELF IN!" Olly Joliffe's oily voice screams as someone out there lobs a rock through what must be one of the half-moon stained glass windows in the library. Whoops and catcalls curl from every direction.

"Beauchamp's been keepin' your cell empty!"

A gravelly voice roars, "You should be livin' up to the Hardin legacy!"

"If Edgar saw how you turned out, he'd be rollin' in his grave!"

More shouts ricochet from the walls while another gunshot rocks the very foundation of the estate.

Tansy marches to a cupboard and pulls out an old, rusted pile of padlocks and chains.

"Where did you get those?"

"WT's great-granddaddy." Tansy sounds way too cheerful. "He used them on his slaves."

I fight back another gag when she pulls a second pile of chains from another cupboard. I gave plenty of tours of plantation homes back east, but I never had to handle chains.

"I can deadbolt the front door," Tansy says, "but I need *you* to climb up to the second floor. Don't want anybody else slippin' in through the upstairs window, like Dwayne."

I can feel the blood leaving my face. "Tansy, how many members of the Klan live in this town?"

She kicks the curio cabinet closed before giving our head

a firm shake. "It's hard to say. These townies really like their secrets, don't they?"

I do not think Tansy's and my definition of "townies" is the same.

"You have to remember, WT was *very* popular with the rich and poor, alike. They look up to him, one of the many reasons bein' that he was always generous with his money."

"'Gold digger,'" I whisper, mortified.

Tansy's nodding. "They feel like you stole him from them, G."

"But what does this have to do with Francesca? Are her husband and daughter holed up somewhere with him?"

Tansy shakes our head. "That I cannot say."

Spinning around, she has us survey all the boarded-up windows, the window glass that's now resting next to a broken wineglass—and I hate this powerless feeling that she's once again muzzling me. I would do *anything* to go out there, guns blazing.

Sensing my anger, Tansy says, "I'm afraid some people are willin' to do *anythin'* to hold onto their backward beliefs."

Another gunshot booms in the air, this time in the back yard. Tansy and I tear off for the hallway.

"Do not fear, my love." She bear hugs the chains. "I have gathered enough food to keep us afloat for a very long time."

34

*W*e've been locked up for I don't even know how many days.

It wouldn't feel so long if Tansy would let me disappear, but she's scared. We all know she likes having me in reserve just in case. She says my joints hurt less when it comes to cleaning up glass and finding new homes for the bricks our neighbors threw inside.

When the chores are done, we *still* have to live Tansy's version of an idyllic life. Her idea of dinner is eating a parsnip whole, and her "exercise" consists of lifting paperweights like dumbbells between creative projects.

It kills me, hiding in here while Klan members have duped the town into believing that Francesca's death was an accident. And I hate knowing that Francesca's little girl could be held hostage somewhere. I should call the police. But from what Tansy said, it sounds like Jesse Beauchamp's just as much a part of the Klan as WT.

In the meantime, Tansy's content living her blind, idyllic life. I don't even want to think about the kind of pushback she'll give me if I insist on going out. So, I weather these nineteenth-century shawls and petticoats. Ignore the piles of necklaces, bracelets, and broaches she's so fond of wearing. She's even pinned up our hair with a crown of dried flowers and feathers. I wish our dress was at least a different color. Canary-yellow washes out our face.

I wonder what the townspeople have decided now that they can't get inside the house. Would they burn it down? I suppose they wouldn't want to harm the home of their precious WT. So maybe they put up roadblocks until they can get Jesse to take me away. Jesse seems like he'd love nothing more than to bring me in, but Tansy said Calhoun made him agree to some sort of arrangement because of Tansy's and my eccentricities.

What I really want to know is why Calhoun doesn't lock me up, ASAP. Is it because I'm Edgar's granddaughter? Some sort of twisted way of honoring his bloodline?

Honestly, I have no idea what to think. For now, I have to sit in the library and look at some gigantic aquarium Tansy's drawn, chockfull of plants and randomly ripped apart arms and legs.

"Does everything you paint have to be so ... murdery?"

Tansy sticks out her tongue, sassing me. "Better for me to paint it than for us to see it in real life."

"So you're saying that painting is your therapy. I don't ever dream of killing people, Tansy."

"It's not that I dream of killing them." She dips her paintbrush into her favorite color—chartreus mixed with pollen and other "natural oddities." "It's just what the muse prompts. I pick up a paintbrush, and before I know it, I'm drawing guys falling off of roofs and lions eating people alive."

I keep my gaze centered on Tansy's green well of paint. Maybe she really did kill WT and has yet to admit it. "You certainly have a morbid sense of creativity."

She heaves an almost pleasurable sigh. "Fear has a way of making me pay attention. Keeps me awake."

I open my mouth to ask about dinner, when a scuffing noise from the French doors has us turning.

Dwayne, in a plaid shirt and Wranglers, comes marching in, spurs jingling. He pauses just past the doorway—obviously waiting for a welcoming reaction from Tansy or me—but Tansy flat-out ignores him, dipping her brush in the green paint.

"*Don't be rude*," I internally say, but she doesn't even bat an eyelash. I'd say hello—maybe ask Dwayne if he knows if any of those townspeople are still outside—but Tansy keeps my tongue under lock and key.

"You need to find another place to live," Dwayne says. His spurs jangle as he crosses the floor to warm his hands at the fire.

Dwayne glances back, but when Tansy refuses to look up, he turns around and slips a pair of bolt cutters into the back pocket of his jeans. Oh, so that's how he got in. But I thought we chained the doors from the inside.

Nonchalantly, Dwayne goes back to warming his hands, betrayal flashing in his muddy eyes. He takes his time clearing his throat. "You know this place isn't safe."

Clearly unimpressed, Tansy rolls our eyes so hard, I'm afraid they're going to get stuck that way. "We are quite capable of takin' care of ourselves, Dwayne."

He spins around, spurs clinking. "Just who do you mean by 'we'?"

Tansy has us dab a yellowish hue of paint into her masterpiece, obviously buying time. I think she's going to ignore him altogether when she huffs, "Are you goin' to tell me why you're here, or are you goin' to keep hanging around like a lost puppy?"

Dwayne balls his hands into fists. Pulls his cowboy hat off

his head before stuffing it back on his head and marching directly in front of Tansy. "*Everyone* is sayin' that you killed him. That you're claimin' that hairdresser was murdered. That you're cra—" He holds up a hand. "I know you're not. Crazy. Gemma, I need you to tell me what happened. *Talk to me.*"

Tansy suddenly lurches forward, paint dripping from her paintbrush, gaudy bracelets jangling. "You get outta here, Dwayne Bone! I never wanna see your face!"

Hurt, sharp as a cutlass, flashes across Dwayne's eyes. While I'm not exactly sure how he's gotten under Tansy's skin, I do know that our heart is thundering in our chest, it's hotter than a sauna in here, and we're seeing spots—the boy's gotten us into quite the tizzy.

The tip of Dwayne's nose darkens. "I have been *waitin'* for you to come to me."

Tansy digs our fingernails into our palms, obviously trying to restrain herself. Heat surges up and down our chest while the corset strains against our ribcage. She scratches the silk bodice, clearly distracted while the wheels in our head spin in a melee.

Suddenly seizing our wrist, Dwayne tugs us toward him. Our skirt brushes into him like he's Rhett Butler and we're Scarlet O'Hara having our feud of the week. I think she's going to slap him when, as if on a slip of paper, Tansy discreetly slips me a memory.

He brands the cattle, sweat glistening off his bare chest beneath the blistering summer sky. She knows she shouldn't stare, but she can't tear her eyes off him while he bales hay.

She offers him a chicken salad sandwich. He graciously accepts without any idea that it isn't me. In the garden, he watches her dance to a funny mashup of bluegrass and jazz, and she's dressed in one of those old-timey dresses with a modern flair of lace cut-outs. He chews his sandwich like a peeper, silently watching.

Snipping the connection, Tansy flings us back to the present by saying, "Dwayne." There's the slightest of quivers in her voice. "I want you good an' gone. I need you well and good outta my life!"

It seems we've grabbed a girandole. Tansy and I have raised it high above our head, and while I'm not entirely sure *why* she feels the need to club him, it does occur to me that he could be a member of the Klan. Maybe she didn't know he was tied to them before she developed feelings.

Tansy pulls back our arm to clock him upside the head. Dwayne ducks, but we do succeed in smacking him on the shoulder. Not sure whether to be scared or electrified.

A million daggers shine in Dwayne's eyes. "*Three* days. You need to stop playin' your games and come to me in the next three days." When Tansy doesn't retort, he adds, "I don't know exactly what it is, but I reckon Calhoun and Beauchamp are plannin' something. Pretty sure Calhoun's about to go back on the deal he made."

The deal? To not lock me up? Why might that have changed?

No doubt sensing the fear coming off Tansy and me, Dwayne's tone softens. "Despite everything goin' on, despite everything with WT ... you n' me both know what we have is real."

He waits for a hint of validation, but Tansy doesn't so much as quirk our lips in response. He presses his lips together in frustration, turns to the French doors, and leaves.

35

I watch Dwayne go, spurs jangling the entire way. To think that he really expects her—me—to join him. And Calhoun and Beauchamp changed their plans? What does that mean?

"How did he even get in? We chained the house from the inside!"

Tansy shrugs, causing her dozen or so necklaces to clang against our clavicle. "He's keeper of the grounds. Master of gettin' in wherever he tries."

I fight back a shudder. "We should go find the door or window he crawled through and secure it with double the chains."

Limp as a ragdoll, Tansy perches on the arm of the reading chair. "Soon enough, my sweet."

She's tired. So worn out, she's relinquishing control to me. Feeling the buzz of wanting to repair the lock—I content myself with padding to another room. Maybe Tansy will let me fix the door or window in a little bit. Besides, it's been eons since we left the library.

There's not a lot of firewood left, but I suppose the broken chair in the den will do nicely.

Sure enough, in the back corner of the house is the old dining room chair with only three legs. I break it apart and steeple three pieces of wood in the fireplace. Of course, I would offer to go chop wood, but I'm not going to jinx the fact that Tansy actually let me leave the library.

When she still hasn't said a word for another full hour, I settle down for a heart-to-heart on the stone hearth.

"Do you want to talk about it?" I gently nudge her where she sits beneath her bed's canopy.

Last thing I want is to come across as pushy. Strange as it is, I can't help feeling bad for Tansy. I got to be married to a man I loved—even if he likely deserves to be locked away for the rest of his life—while Tansy was alone. I had no idea she had such strong feelings for Dwayne.

"He *is* pretty cute ..." I nudge her again, marveling at how he could ever think that Tansy and I are one and the same. If he knew about our condition, he'd probably run for the hills. Poor Tansy.

Pulling on another tufted quilt, I try to keep us warm. The temperature outside must be dropping. The fire's already starting to die down, and I guess we forgot to pay the gas bill. For all I know, it's March by now. I suppose I could feed the fire with more chairs ... or a grandfather clock. . . if I wanted to feel even more terrible about my life's choices.

"How long ago did it start?" I nudge Tansy for the third time.

Grabbing the fire poker, I tuck a loose chair leg between the flames. Of course, we could talk about the fact that we live in the worst town in the history of forever—but I'd rather settle on something light.

Tansy groans. "Won't you please let me be?"

"Hey, you're the one who's chosen not to banish me. You

could make me go any second you like. Though, if you don't want this fire going out, I should probably stay."

"It was all a big, fat, *stupid* mistake." Tansy curls our fingers in our lap, the knots in our stomach twisting. "I knew WT only had feelings for you, so I watched and waited and took somethin' that could be mine."

A fresh wave of sympathy tolls through me. "Maybe we could find a way to include Dwayne in our life ..."

This bitter, high-pitched laugh tears from Tansy. "Says the girl who was oblivious to him in the first place."

I set the fire poker on the hearth. "Hey, I'm trying to be nice. You obviously have feelings for him, and I know how difficult love can be. Plus, it's not my fault that you've always been in the driver's seat."

"You *know* that's not true."

"Actually?" I grab the iron poker again. "All I ever know is what *you* tell me, Tansy."

She's silent for a long time, so silent that the only noise between us is the crackle and hiss of the fire. Listless, our eyes trace a makeshift outline of a mockingbird in the venetian flames. In some ways, I wish this was the only thing we had to worry about in life. Find warmth. Roast hot dogs and s'mores. Listen to Ludovico Einaudi.

Tansy's knees pop as she heaves us up, blankets and all, from the fireplace. Moving like an ages-old ogre, she has us settle into a wing-back chair pointed toward a boarded-up window. Surprisingly, this rectangular window's not broken at all, though it's smaller and less decorative than the stained-glass ones in the library.

Sinking into the velvet tufts puckering from the frame, Tansy holds our blankets close. She puffs a perfect, cloudy circle of white.

"I'll tell you some things you'd like to know," she says, teeth chattering.

"Well, now, I'm on the edge of my seat. What do you want in return?"

"Ab-so-lutely nothin'."

My breath hitches. I can't help wondering if she's being honest with me. Could it be possible that Tansy's really going to be truthful about our past?

I nod, not wanting to break the spell.

"Before I tell you, I need you to tell me the truth." Steepling our fingers, she says, "I need you ... to explain why you want to leave."

This isn't a topic I was expecting. "It's ... who I am."

She shakes our head, bobby-pins loosening. "While I understand that, I, as a person, took on your artistic qualities —your flair for drama n' history—I need to know *exactly* what you are hopin' for, adventure-wise."

My throat goes Gobi desert dry. Why in the world is this important to her? "I suppose it's just like you said. I want to see the world. Staying in here all day makes my skin crawl. I wasn't built to be locked up in such a tiny space."

"Hmm."

"That's all I get? Hmm?"

"*Hmm*."

"Okay ..." I wish I knew why she wanted to discuss that, but we're not getting any younger or warmer, so I knock the arm of the chair to get her to start talking. "I think it's only fair now that you explain why *you* never want to leave."

Tansy smooths the lace bodice of her yellow dress. Which now has a bit of soot on it, thanks to me. "I suppose, it has somethin' to do with when we were younger—a little girl, to be precise. But I need you to brace yourself for this one. Are you ready, G?"

I nod, simultaneously wondering why she thinks I need to be ready.

She rearranges her bracelets, obviously stalling for time.

"We accidentally happened upon somethin' we shouldn't have seen."

Well now, that's not vague. But her warning tone just about hits me like a whack-a-mole, and I'm reeling. "Are you about to tell me the reason why I created you in the first place?"

Tansy stares unblinking into the fire. "I suppose I am, G."

I can barely form words. I know I've said I want answers, but I really don't know if I'm ready. I mean, why is she willing to tell me *now*, after all this time? What if we accidentally bring on the avalanche, because, even if she's ready, I'm not?

Bringing a shaky hand to our forehead, Tansy says, "I'm *tired* of keepin' all this to myself. It's a monumental task, dearest. It's why I have to paint. But I'm tired of harborin' all the secrets, and I am *tired* of you not trustin' me. I think it will be easier if you understand why I am who I am. You need to truly know exactly why leaving our home isn't safe."

"Okay."

Shifting in the chair, Tansy asks, "Are you ready?"

I give a half-nod. "Ready."

Sucking in a shaky breath, she clasps her necklace with her hand, fist tight. "We saw a man. In the cellar. We must have just turned five. We weren't supposed to see what happened to him, but Edgar—he killed him. He was the man who was responsible for our parents dying."

Parents. What kind of a person am I? I haven't even thought about their existence since my discussion earlier with Natalie.

"The man was a drunk driver. Felt terrible about the accident. He even sent money. But since Edgar's a devil of the tallest order, he kidnapped him. Murdered him. And we stumbled upon the body."

A flash of the image I saw as a little girl suddenly hits me square in the eyes. *A corpse. In a dank cellar. Throat slit; severed arms and legs.*

Automatically, I close my eyes. My stomach churns. Any second, I'll be dry heaving.

"It's why I paint." Tansy's voice becomes bleak. "It's how I deal with it. G, I ... no matter what I do, I cannot get that image outta my mind. Thankfully, Grammy never saw the body. But she suspected Edgar had somethin' to do with the guy's disappearance. It was in the papers and everythin'."

"Tansy ..." I think back to my recently discovered memory. The cellar was dark, so it was hard to make out the details. "What was the man's race?"

She closes her eyes. Barely breathes. "He was from Israel."

I about rip off our necklace.

"He was Jewish, G."

Bile and sickness roll through my stomach in caustic waves. "Edgar killed him like that because ... he ..."

"Edgar was a White Supremacist, yes. As unconscionable as one can be. But as you know, the devil wears many faces in Deep Creek."

I tense to rip off the arm of the chair—feed it to the fire. Anything to get these callous, disgusting, *demonic* people to stop hurting people. To think I'm *related* to him. That I have his DNA.

"The world is evil," Tansy whispers as the fire goes out. "It is why I can never leave."

36

*C*ar doors slam, immediately waking Tansy and me. I've no clue how much time has passed since the last time we talked. I don't even know if it's been three days.

"Who do you think it is?" I ask Tansy, yawning. "Tourists?"

Oh, but that's an awful lot of car doors slamming.

Tansy pauses to listen to the soft chants curling from outside. Another language? In my mind, I can see the letters in the margins of the history books Edgar leant me. There were always symbols. Greek symbols. "The holy language," he would say. Something inside me says that graffiti symbol on the outside of our door is also Greek.

"Are they even real?" I ask Tansy. I mean the Klan. Do they honestly go to peoples' homes and chant foreign languages to scare them into submission? "What do you think they want?"

I'm right with her when we grip the bottom ledge of our plush seat.

Tansy leans forward, then backward in a full-body wave. "All the evidence, probably."

"Evidence ... of WT's death? Or Francesca's!"

She pushes back our chair with a clatter.

"But we can't give that!"

Tearing off for the stairs, Tansy has us grab the rail and limp, step by step, up the staircase. Through one of the boarded-up windows in the hallway, an orange flame passes by, and I could be wrong, but I'm pretty sure that was a torch.

"We *can't* give them the robe, Tansy." I clutch the rail, horrified that she's even entertaining the idea.

"I'm sorry, my love, but it is the only way."

"But it's the only evidence we have!" I kick the wall of the stairs to get her to listen to me.

Tansy pulls us up the stairs, higher and higher. "You saw that torch. They mean to smoke us out. No way am I lettin' go of the estate."

Fear and horror ring through my limbs in a cyclone through my body. "But we *can't* do it!" Against my will, she's made sure that our feet have found the top of the staircase. "Tansy, you don't understand. I'm not willing to turn my back on the *only* person who's ever treated me with decency in Deep Creek."

"I'm sorry, G." We've reached the closet and Tansy tugs on the brass handle. "But it's the only way." She tugs on the handle again, but it's useless; the door won't budge.

"Did you lock it?" I ask, feeling slightly satisfied.

"Arrrrgh!" Tansy screams. "I thought it best to keep you from revisitin'!"

More shouts ricochet off the walls outside. Glass shatters —one of the stained-glass windows in the library probably— and Tansy's right—the Klan's going to smoke us out if we don't do something—and quickly.

But I can't betray Francesca by turning in the *one* proof I have of how she died.

"I can't. I won't." I shake my head rapidly as a slight

breeze has us turning. The open window proves how Dwayne first got inside. There's a platform just outside the window. Something teases my mind ... like WT and I used to go out there to watch the stars at night. Not that I care at this point.

Tansy backs us away from the door, and I have no idea what she's doing until she purposely marches us across the hall, past an enormous chest and gourd-shaped canteens.

Pausing before a wall of frontier-time pieces—a leather saddle, and a sugar cane knife—she lays our eyes on a hefty-sized tomahawk with a black and brown handle and more geometric Greek symbols on the curved blade.

Wrenching it from the wall, Tansy marches us back to the closet, Amazon warrior-style. I hate that this is the choice she believes she gets to make.

"No!" I try to wrench the tomahawk out of her grasp. "There has to be another way!"

The blade cuts my inner arm with a slight sting.

"There isn't!" she shrieks before heaving the tomahawk and slicing it through the door with the meaty side of the blade.

The wide end catches at an odd angle, but with an extra amount of gusto, we heave it out with our combined strength. I think about fighting her some more on this, but last thing I need is to give myself an accidental beheading.

With about ten or so swings, we end up doing enough damage to make a hole big enough for us to climb through and we ditch the blade. I'm tempted to tuck tail and run now —but almost on impulse, I'm following her lead. Ducking past all the clothes—WT's shirts and pants—and going along while she finds the robe. It's still balled up on the floor in the farthest corner.

"Are you *sure* there isn't anything else we can give them to buy us more time?" The lump in my throat about doubles in size. She has us grab the robe while both of us end up gagging.

"They'll do anythin'"—she dry heaves—"to get the existence and inner-workings of the Klan under lock n' key." Stepping out of the closet, Tansy has us hold out the garment like it's covered in fleas. "You n' I know, their worst nightmare is being discovered on the outside."

I trip on the fabric as we bumble toward the window. "But we should give it to the police."

Tansy guffaws. "You mean, like Jesse?"

"We'll take a picture of it, then."

"With all our *fine* digital cameras?" The chanting's rising in a crescendo, and our pulse quickens to ramming speed. "There isn't time!"

Corset constricting, Tansy stomps us over to the window. We grip the lip of the window with one hand while holding the robe beneath our elbow, and I can't believe I'm not fighting her on this. I should be fighting!

But I hold back—because they do want to smoke us out, and Jesse would only make the robe disappear anyway.

Heaving, we eventually lift the window open and, much faster than expected, guilt hooks me with its iron claws as we push out the screen.

Below us on the lawn is a throng of ten or so men in white-hooded costumes I never wanted to see. They remind me of a bunch of demented Oompa-Loompas, trying on doctors coats and dunce caps for size.

Bile rises again from my throat. How could any of them ever want to join this sick and twisted secret society?

Tansy shoves the robe through—and the milky fabric falls to one of the holly bushes like a parachute from Be'er Shachath, or "pit of corruption"—tour guide thing.

One of the men steps up to the bushes to retrieve the robe. Gently, he lifts it up like he's performing a sacred ceremony. He looks like he belongs in a medieval time period video game with his idiotic, wide, white sleeves. More torches wave at us amidst the waning moonlight. One of the men lowers his torch to set fire to a bush, but a second, taller man knocks the first man's shoulder, causing him to drop the torch to the rocky pathway.

A deathly silence steals over the group as the tall one says something in a low tone and directs the group to leave.

Something tells me they'll be coming back. How are we supposed to be ready? How are we *ever* supposed to get justice for what happened to Francesca now?

Turning to Tansy, I have to ask, "Is one of them WT?"

Tansy shakes her head. "*Non, mon cherie.* Plus, dear one, it is time to visit the basement. You have finally proved you are ready."

37

"*B*efore I take you where we need to go," Tansy says, "I need to show you another memory."

I'd rather get right to it, but no way am I turning down more information at this point. I help her take a few animated steps down the stairs, past all the metal sconces on the walls, toward the hallway.

At the bottom, though, I cannot deny that Tansy's stalling. She wrings our hands and clutches her necklace again, breathing louder than a howler monkey. "The second time we saw WT was at the grocery store. You already saw how we met him on the bridge?"

I nod.

She hobble-steps down the hall, favoring the sturdier of her bad knees. "He was buyin' dog food at the cash register, and we didn't know whether to duck or come right out and say that our mission to research the county records had gone ka-blooey."

Tansy leans on the table, taking a breather to explain things. "We didn't want him to dismiss us outright, so we chose a third option. Walked *right* past him, just barely grazin' our arm against his. 'William,' we said, noddin' formally. 'Course, we didn't in fact know that was his first name, but it seemed likely. If he *was* interested in talkin' to us, he would correct us ... or pretend we were right. Didn't take him long to say in his gravelly voice, 'What did you call me?'

"It was a question we would have asked if we were in his place, but mysteriousness, G, was on our side. We had only returned to town for Edgar's funeral a few weeks before, and, after askin' round town about who he was, we reckoned he wanted to get to know a pretty face."

Tansy knocks the table with our knuckles, having regained some of her energy. "So we walked on to the produce section—shoppin' for pomegranates and celery."

"He asked us out for that night!" I remember suddenly. An image of WT awkwardly holding a grapefruit in his palm flashes like a searchlight in my mind.

Tansy nods, shoulders tensing. "When he picked us up—"

"He was wearing a three-piece suit, a Rolex, and—his red skinny tie!" And, yes, I can't *believe* I'm remembering. But I shouldn't be happy. He was part of the KKK.

"We didn't want to admit that this would be our fanciest date." Tansy lays out another hint for me. "The most spectacular thing we'd ever done was go to a movie—"

"And he took us to Bass Hall to see *Cirque du Soleil*." Oh, I hate to admit it, but that was one heck of a date.

Never more forlorn, Tansy suddenly pauses before her raccoon panting and studies the "ketchup" that has long dried. "You really are remembering."

"Tansy ..." I wish I could find the right words, but it's hard to express exactly what I'm feeling. "Please don't be angry with me, but what if—and I know this is crazy—but what if WT really was a nice guy?"

She tightens our lips. Not the takeaway she wanted.

"I know, I know. I'm probably wrong, but I have seen half

a dozen memories already, and I may be remembering them wrong, but he seemed so gentle and ni—"

"He wasn't!" Tansy shrieks as she spins away from the paintings. Our footsteps have definitely grown louder, and Jerusha, with her fuzzy black tail, darts around the corner to avoid us in the nick of time.

"I know the idea's insane, but from what I can remember, he really did seem torn. I mean, he wanted to go to Palo Duro and—"

"I'm warnin' you, G." Beside the Texas bluebonnet artwork, Tansy clenches our teeth. "You need to understand how evil he was, so you don't question the choices we had to make."

I swallow the lump in my throat. "Tansy, what are you saying?"

Running the backs of our nails along the cool surface of the mirror, she says, "Sometimes it's worth scarin' ourselves to protect the heart of things."

"Okay ... not sure what that means."

Tansy pats the coat rack where I left her feather boa. "Let's think about our date, back when you thought he was such a *nice* guy. Do you remember what he kept in his coat packet?"

A white swath of fabric floats to my side of our mind. "A handkerchief!"

"And, *oh*, how we loved that *white* handkerchief."

I almost add how, when we listened to music in the car, WT tapped the steering wheel. And, once again, I'm reminded of his smell—that cedar smell from his truck's dashboard's cedar inlay.

Lost in the moment, I find that Tansy and I both have to close our eyes. We remember how the actors were draped in bright melons of color—yellows and pinks. While WT played with the lace on my skirt, I made sure not to move, because I didn't want him to stop all night. When we hit intermission, instead of getting up, WT leaned closer, and brushed his lips along my ear. Fire erupted along my skin, and it was all I could do not to dissolve into a puddle. At the ankle, I wound my leg around his lower leg. For the remainder of the performance, I couldn't concentrate.

When the play was over, he ran his finger down one of my ringlets, a warm geyser shimmering through my entire body.

"And, oooh, did WT know how to bake," Tansy says. "He made homemade glazed donuts and tiramisu and the most *killer* soufflés."

"He gave us a tour of the house!" I hold out the crook of our arm, reenacting the way he led me down the hallway.

"Showed us the parlor," Tansy agrees. "Not a pillow or carpet fiber outta place."

"It was the *library*"—I spin for the French doors—"that we could tell was his domain."

"The books were helter-skelter, an' a dozen or so papers were heaped upon his fancy desk o' mahogany."

"But what we really liked was the pie safe." We pause before a free-standing cabinet I hadn't noticed lately. Wrenching open the honey doors, I try to remember the pies I once placed in here to keep safe. WT didn't even know what it was ... but I explained that it was just a cabinet that kept the pies safe from impatient children and flies.

"Show me the grounds?" Tansy and I say together, recalling how we asked WT to show us the main floor of the house, but he didn't dare take me upstairs. *I am traditional in relationships*, he said, and I couldn't believe it, because so was I. And we kissed, our lips turning to butter, his and my arms becoming a blur of muscle and heat.

"Tansy." I have to pry open our mouth to force her to talk to me. "I need you to tell me the truth. Is WT dead or alive?"

She rests one of our free hands on the shelf in the pie safe. "I don't think you really wanna know, G."

"If WT *is* alive, where would he go? What makes you assume that he went away?"

"Maybe the Klan killed him," Tansy taunts me. "Maybe he didn't live up to their expectations, and they finished him off for good. Decided to plant it on you n' me."

I have us stop before the basement door, hesitating. "What if he's not actually a Klan member? What if someone stashed the robe in our closet to make him look guilty?"

The little hairs on the back of our neck stand on end as Tansy warns, "Or *maybe* you need to stop flappin' that yapper of yours and start listenin' to me!"

"Sorry ... sorry." I lick our lips, trying to be patient, but not exactly being successful. "Okay." I square our shoulders, doing my best not to feel weighed down by her restrictive corset and jewelry. "I'm ready."

38

*S*taring at the basement door, I get the feeling that there's something on the other side I really don't want to see.

I don't want to go down there.

I've never been down there.

Not while I've been awake.

"This way," Tansy says while reaching for the doorknob with bumps and grooves and an asymmetrical design.

"Are you sure you don't want to just tell me what's down there?" I don't want to be in any windowless rooms. Claustrophobia's a real thing. "What about the avalanche?"

Annoyed, Tansy grits our teeth. "I'm here to *protect* you. And while the avalanche is always a risk, I don't see how it can happen if we face the truth of what happened together. This is the final piece."

An unexpected bout of paranoia shoots up the back of my neck and throbs at the base of my skull. "Why did you just stop to show me those beautiful memories?"

"Because"—Tansy strangles the doorknob with a

surprising strength—"the sweeter the love, the more acutely the betrayal stings."

Lead burrows and solidifies in our veins. I don't want to keep trudging down more steps. What if her plan is to lead me down there to lock me up? Or ... she's got WT's head in a freezer. A person can't paint violent images without thinking about committing the crimes at some point.

Golf clubs. She's taking me downstairs to show me golf clubs. Old tennis rackets. Steven F. Austin's mummified remains.

As if she's the queen of pied pipers, Tansy leads me down the stairway. Not only is it blacker than space, but it smells of rot and mildew; quite literally like something died.

We're about three-quarters of the way down when the mother of Charlie horses cramps up my foot. I tense to lift it up while Tansy says, "A little further, G." She pries our foot from the ledge of the next step and leads us deeper and deeper into the cave.

What if, for some outlandish reason, she's got Grammy down here, hooked up to an IV?

We take three more steps before Tansy slaps our hands together. "Good! Good, good, good. Are you ready for this? 'twill change your life!"

My throat's closing up. Dizzy spots are floating in front of my eyes. "Tansy ..." My gut twists into the mother of all grapevines.

I can't look. Cannot breathe. Honestly, it feels like I've been bound and gagged and thrown into a dryer. Can't get out, even if I tried.

Tansy raises our arm and tugs an overhead chain. I don't want to be in here. Don't want to see. With a shaky arm, I raise my hand to shield our eyes.

You know, I don't know what I expected. Tennis rackets really would have been the best thing. But it seems we're in a room packed full of antlers from deer heads—a labyrinth of bone chutes, crisscrossing in a corn maze. About thirty.

Actually, they kind of remind me of Snow White—how the animals were drawn to her. Maybe another version of Snow White needs to be based on Tansy and me.

While Tansy leads us around the first set of antlers, we pass a huge stuffed beaver with cinnamon fur, along with his kiddies.

We stumble on something in the dark toward a waist-high black mound, though I don't know what it is. Our eyes are still adjusting.

"You'll have to excuse the odor." Tansy has us sniffing. It smells like a locker room—gym socks, football pads, cleats. "To preserve things the way we needed, I've had to experiment with biology."

Before I know it, we're staring face-to-face with a large, horizontal planter box filled with a human shape. It's human, but not. A huge pile of sludge with a head lies connected to eroded shoulders and ribs, all the fat and muscle missing. The person's form is tar-dipped—like plastic wrap has been stretched over a skeletal frame.

"See?" Tansy slaps our hands together proudly. "I was paying attention when you were givin' all those tours in Washington, D.C. Bog bodies! Oh, G, their literal and bona fide existence really is rivetin'."

My heart's become suspended between two impossibly high beams. Without meaning to, I suddenly see what Tansy's saying—I remember the real and true definition of bog bodies.

Really, really old remains," I tell a group of middle schoolers. Around us stands the stately walls and fine collections of the Museum of Natural History. The tour's long, but it's my favorite. So many fascinating artifacts from human history. Pointing to the sleeping, statuesque man who looks like he's been dipped in a blackish-brown ore, I say, "The first bog bodies were discovered in Ireland, Finland, and Norway. True scientific wonders. The scientific composition of the bogs has a way of preserving the corpses. True, the skin has darkened and the fat and muscle have eroded, but these people are preserved in almost perfect condition. And this"—I smile brightly at the girls and boys—"is why science is so fascinating."

My neck spasms. Knees are giving out. I'm not prepared for this. Why is this *here*? How has Tansy created a bog body?

Through the punch in my gut, I have to ask, "Is it him? WT?"

Moisture drips from the shadows. The unholy stench of the bog rushes around the antlers while Tansy gives me the world's most patronizing sigh. "Gemma Louise Coldiron Hardin. What do *you* think?"

When she has us step closer, I survey the leathery, brown skin that's too shriveled to be recognized. My late husband's once beautiful auburn hair has taken on a sickly, radish sheen. I'm guessing it's from the chemicals of the soil. His clothes have somehow melted into his skin, like he was once made of wax. And his face—his once tranquil face—has stretched into a grimace with a twisted mouth and missing nose ... like he's nothing more than a prop for Halloween.

The pile around him is a slick, disgusting pile of sludge, and this used to be my husband. The man I actually chose to marry.

Tansy stretches out her hand to retrieve something small, titanium, and round—

"*No.*" I stop her.

She's reaching for his wedding ring, and I can't help it. Unwelcome tears are welling in my eyes. I want it to be somebody else. Anybody else. Or we're visiting a haunted house or something. But on WT's wrist is the Rolex he always wore, and *I remember* giving that to him over breakfast on his birthday. *Pancakes, orange juice, sausage links.*

Yes, he was part of a terrible hate group. But did he really deserve to die? I don't *actually* remember his involvement, so it's hard for me not to mourn what I see in my memories. There's our time together, dancing. Palo Duro. *Cirque du Soleil*, even our fights. Maybe—and I know I'm being ridiculous for hoping—but *maybe* he was surrounded by these men, yes, but he didn't agree with Klan life. Maybe he tried to stop them? Stop them from what they were doing.

Lifting his ring into the amber light, Tansy has us squint at the band's laser-thin engraving. *A perfect fit*, the interior says. I put that engraving there. It described our connection —the unexpected and complete fit of our souls and bodies.

When I sink to the ground and lift my hands to cover our face, Tansy croons, "Now you shall hear how the grubby brute died."

39

"I thought you said he was still alive!" Sheer, raw terror fills my voice.

"I know I said that, G, but he can't hurt us or anyone else anymore!" Tansy makes us stand and pace around her experiment of a bog body. Maggots or some other insect crunch below our boots. "No one can. We just need to stay home, keep up our weekly routine. Everythin' will be all right!"

"Everything ... are you insane? Tansy, you turned our husband into a *bog body*."

"Months ago"—Tansy bats my accusation away—"we had quite the quarrel with the love of your life." She leans forward and traipses our fingers along the silt that's now become his chest. "Actually, what do *you* think happened?"

I try not to tremor. "You killed him."

"Gemma, dear Gemma, has it ever occurred to you that I only do that which you need of me?"

My stomach flips. When I take a few steps back, my shoulders knock into the cool wall of cement, and I fight the urge to quietly slip back into our mind.

"You're the one who regularly steps back ..." Tansy prompts, knowingly.

"But I would never be okay with murder." I don't like the uncertainty in my voice.

"I suppose you could say that we *both* loved WT." Tansy runs our hands down the side of what used to be WT's face, but it's now sticky and gooey. "But at the time, you and I were still not fully divided. And I still had my eye on Dwayne."

"Tell me what happened, Tansy."

"Are you sure you can handle it? If you're feelin' unstable, you n' I both know how the aval—"

"JUST TELL ME!"

Rocking back on our heels, Tansy smiles like the cat that ate the canary. "You want me to trigger your memory? Well, if you're sure ..." In half a flash, she has us spinning around and flying through the basement, arms extended, past the deer heads, past the cinnamon-furred beaver family.

Unable to contain her excitement, she has us hobble up the basement stairs two at a time. Before I know it, we're in the main hall, catching our breath at the raccoon painting. She smears the gritty "ketchup" to cover more of the fur on the canvas before lurching deeper into the hallway. Holding fast to the banister, we scramble up the next staircase. Up, up, to the third floor we go, as if a cast's being closed over our entire body.

From the moment we reach the top, I think maybe Tansy's going to let us rest, but she has us round the corner so that we're facing *another* door with long, rectangular panels and a doorknob that's been smashed to the side.

Reaching out, Tansy twists the knob. Hinges groan, and the door squeaks open to yet another stairway.

This one's about half the width of the stairs that led to the basement, a third of the size of the one that led to the second story. The cramped quarters magnify the dust, and the walls close in around us like we're in a coffin, being buried alive.

We climb—our breath and boots the only sound, smacking the wooden stairs like timpani.

Stair after stair. Shins on fire, burning.

Oh, we're headed for the cupola—the high tower of the house all the tourists drool over.

When Tansy and I reach the top, rubber comprises both our legs. The walls are as cold as air conditioning. Little white clouds puff from our breath, and the banister embeds little splinters into my fingers, though they're too cold and numb to feel anything.

Raising our hand, Tansy shoves open the cupola—a stained glass window large enough for us to crawl through to get outside. I can't believe this. She really wants us to go out there.

"Tansy ..."

But she's too busy smooshing our bustle through the narrow opening.

Before I know it, we're shimmying along the edge of the roof, sweat covering our palms as we grip the decorative wrought-iron railing. A tinge of mist swirls through the air, and everything smells like rust. Mold seems to coat my skin and teeth.

Shortly out of breath, Tansy says, "Beautiful, aren't they?" She's addressing the trio of turkey vultures that are swooping low from the sky. We shimmy farther, farther—along the perimeter of the roof to the south corner toward town. This is madness. How did I ever let her take me up here? We're going to slip and fall, break our necks surely.

"Tansy ..." I swallow down the fear with my final warning.

While the wind blows straight through our dress, she cries, "I needed to see if you could remember where *it* happened. Our crime."

My arms and legs freeze.

"You're so convinced that you are the honorable one." Tansy tsks her tongue. "But what the blazes do you think I've been doin' all this time? I took what Edgar did so you didn't *have* to bear the memory. Do you remember when WT followed us out here? When he wanted to know what we were doin'?"

I shake my head just as a hot vision flashes into my mind. *WT, in his salmon blazar, slips one leg after the other through the cupola to reach me. The wind rustles his slicked-back hair, and he settles on the ledge on the roof just to our right.*

We've just finished breakfast. We saw ... something. Something I can't remember. Something WT swore he would explain.

Staring into the distance, Tansy has us hold ourselves in her Tansy way. Spine bent, shoulders hunched—like she doesn't know whether she's going to recite a poem or bite the head off something.

"Gemma, what are you doi—" WT takes a step back and stuffs his hands in his pockets. "Tansy."

"Hello, sweet cheeks. Just takin' in the view. So glad you came."

Not letting her out of his sight, WT takes a few steps closer while still maintaining a safe distance. "What are you doing up here?"

Behind her mass of skirts, Tansy hides a rope—a hefty one, all wound up, and plenty strong enough to hold just about anything. "I have somethin' to tell you. Wanted to do it up here to avoid pryin' eyes."

WT's face goes wan; he becomes silent as the grave.

"I suppose you're not goin' to say you're sorry," Tansy says, fingers tightening around the rope.

"If you will let me speak to Gemma, I will say to her whatever it is I have to say."

"I mean, your little club *may be secretive, but I had no idea that you still killed people. Tell me, William, how do you sleep at night?"*

"Tansy, that's not ..."

She tightens her grip on the rope at her back. "As the wife of a

'True Knight,' I do have to say that I'm intrigued with the artistry of which you've played your double life."

WT staggers, clutching the rail as his face pales and his eyes bulge wide.

"The effects of the foxglove are starting to take effect, sweetling." When Tansy smiles, she flashes way too much teeth.

Fear splits like an open wound in WT's eyes while Tansy strides forward and loops the rope over his neck. "The foxglove your mother planted is gorgeous, really. Much prettier than all those animals your father slice n' diced. When G didn't know how to handle your indiscretions, I told her I would take care of it, easy peasy."

"Gemm—" WT gags, clutching his neck. "Come—back—to m—"

"The thing is" —Tansy tightens the noose around his neck—"your wife is incapable of havin' a relationship with a man who lies."

"Gem—ma!" Frantic, WT pulls on the rope, but his eyes are bloodshot, and his skin's covered in a sweaty sheen. He tries to tug the rope down. Tansy blocks his movements with our hand. "She'll" —his face is turning purple—"be furious—when—she sees—"

Tansy leads him toward the edge of the roof, rope clinched in her hand tight. "I find it poetic how there are two of you and two of me. The town prince, so generous and charming, and the racist who would rather kill people than change his family's legacy."

He's foaming at the mouth, spasming.

"So, too, there's the adventurous, law-abiding Gemma, who would never hurt a soul." She holds up her hand and slips off a diamond wedding ring. "Then there's the reclusive, law-breakin' Tansy." She tosses the ring at WT, and it bounces off him, rolling across the roof and dropping over the side. "I never wanted to kill you, darling, but who's goin' to protect G, if not me?" Tugging him toward the edge, she adds, "I'm willin' to take the law into my hands when 'the law' in this town means nothin'."

While WT stares into oblivion at the now fallen ring, Tansy slowly loops the rope around the decorative holes of the wrought-iron rails. He slips and staggers as he struggles to crawl to get away.

His foot slips on the rail. Tansy catches his leg, but his shoe snags on the arrow tips and plummets after the ring—eighty or so feet.

I don't know if I can watch.

I don't even know what outcome I want, if he lives or dies.

Taking a good, long look at my husband, Tansy slowly pats him on the shoulder. "I'm doin' this for the both of us. Now I'll never need to leave your gorgeous estate, and you'll never have to tell G about your family history."

In a swift move, Tansy reaches out, shoves him off the roof. And the rope zips down, dragging WT out of sight.

40

"*Y*ou *poisoned* him ... and pushed him off ..." I rub my thumb over my ring finger where I once wore my wedding ring. "How could you ever do that, Tansy?"

"Well, doll, you asked me to."

"No ..." I'm putting two and two together as an angry raven swoops low from the sky. "I never would have asked that. Yes, *you* decided to kill him, but what gave you the right?"

"THIS ISN'T ABOUT RIGHTS!" Tansy licks our lips, trying to regain her composure. "You saw what he was. He killed people. Remember Edgar? He was exactly like that. He deserved to die."

As the crisp wind whips our hair, for the first time in a great, long while, I feel like I can truly think. "I'm not okay with WT being part of the Klan, and for that, yes, he should have paid. But, Tansy, it wasn't up to us. We should have taken him to the poli—"

She holds up a hand, about to complain.

"I *know* about Jesse, but he's not the only police. There

are plenty of other cops in the world. Feds—" I think of the agent who came to town, and wishing I'd talked to him. Then Francesca could still be alive. "State Troopers, even. But *you* took matters into your own hands. We ..." I grip the wrought-iron rail, head swimming. "We could go to prison. It's only a matter of time before Calhoun or Jesse Beauchamp find his body."

"We can move it!"

"Tansy, you *killed* him, and then you kept it from me." Through another gale of wind, I scoot us toward the cupola to go back inside. "I have to go."

Tansy suddenly seizes control of our limbs and tries to pull us back. "No, you have to understand. You asked me to take care of what we saw, and I did. You should be *thankin'* me!"

A ripple of anger shoots through me. "I don't know what we saw or if WT was as evil as Edgar—but I *never* would have asked you to 'take care of it' that way."

Tansy opens our mouth to argue, but I clamp it shut. "We aren't murderers, Tansy."

I've scooted a lot faster than I thought I could, but, against all odds, I'm already in front of the stained glass of the cupola. Lifting our legs, I start to climb back inside.

"We beat him!" Tansy bends us backward, throwing us precariously off balance. We're going to fall to our deaths if she doesn't work with me. I grapple for the cool wooden side of the window. "I know I originally said that WT was still alive," Tansy begs, "but he's gone, G. Think of Francesca! We just need to lie low. Stay home. Keep up with our weekly routine."

How dare she throw Francesca's death in my face? "I want justice just as much as you, but I never would have asked you to kill him." Another fit of anger surges through my chest. "I need to get out ..."

I know it makes sense that she did it because of his involvement with the Klan, but I can only think about how she used our hands—*my* hands—to kill a husband for which I only have fond memories. I *hate* it, but it's true. I loved him, and I can't recall ever seeing him hurt anybody.

I don't even remember leaving the roof; my shins won't stop throbbing. I flee down the two sets of stairs, hand squeaking against the handrail the entire way.

Once outside, I wander for hours. Past *The Hair Lounge*. The courthouse. *Hey, Sugar*. Construction of the new taco place.

Suppose WT was a murderer and led a dual life. When you find yourself living in a corrupt town, could there be something to be said for being a vigilante? Tansy did a service. Right? His death could almost be considered merciful, considering what the families of his victims would like to do in payback, assuming he did horrific things.

When I make it to the post office, I don't even know how I got from point A to point B. The only thing I can think to do is run—but of course I'm not in my running clothes or shoes. Stupid corset, bustle, and jewelry.

Kicking off Tansy's antique boots, I fling off her necklaces and bracelets. And run. I run so hard, I almost forget what Tansy just showed me. Cool sweat washes over my face. I push harder, faster, Tansy's canary yellow dress billowing out like wings around me.

How can evil like this still exist? Here, in the town where I grew up and got married.

I need to vomit. Disappear for a while. See Grammy.

Truthfully, I should have run to her as soon as I saw the bridge memory. She told Tansy that she had successfully stopped Jesse from bullying me, but what exactly did she do? Like Tansy said, Grammy's an outsider. She can't have power over him or authority.

Picking up speed, I tear past an auto glass repair shop and a gas station with a dime-sized eatery. The scent of freshly crisped corn dogs wafts through the warming air, and I turn to go in to pilfer some food—no pockets in this dress, no money. Guess I could have bartered with the jewelry I just threw away.

For all I know, everybody in this town is part of the Klan. The man in the tan coveralls pumping his gas. The gas station owner. What's to stop them *all* from taking out someone else? From killing any person of another ethnicity?

I don't know why I was so resistant to seeing the evil in WT's face. Tansy showed me the kinds of things Klansmen do, specifically what Edgar did to that guy who accidentally killed my parents. *No one* deserves to die that way.

As I pause in the gas station parking lot, the sun stretches its arms in meaty fists of pink. I've enjoyed the sunset for all of three seconds when a throng of people at the end of the road has my heart jumping. I squint to see who they are when a semi-truck rumbles past, blocking my line of sight. I duck into the convenience store. At least I have the option of hiding in plain sight.

As more cars rumble past, I very nearly run into a ground pyramid corn dog sign. But I square my shoulders and right my footing.

Maybe I can ask to borrow the store attendant's phone— if I knew how to get ahold of Grammy. I'll just wait a few minutes in here while the mob passes.

Hopefully they won't break into the mansion and find the bog body.

I still can't believe Tansy was able to mimic the conditions of a real Mesolithic period bog body. How in the world did she do it? In the summer, it never would have worked. But it's been unusually cold this winter and now, early spring, so, if she had the right ingredients, I see how it could work ... for a time.

I'm just standing in front of the candy display, running over every scenario of how she must have created the bog body, when a firm hand grasps my bicep.

I turn to find a stoic face—covered in scruff, and massive shoulders, about twice my width, the perfect height.

My breath hitches.

It's him.

Him.

WT.

41

*B*ut I saw his body. In one of Tansy's memories, I watched him die.

It takes everything I have not to let out a rip-roar of a scream. He's *here*. Not dead. How could he be alive?

On autopilot, I wrench my arm out of the Klan leader's grasp. "You're part of *them*." What I want to know is, how did Tansy lie to me?

The shop owner—a bald, portly man with a fist-sized birthmark on his face—eyes us from behind a rack of cell phone chargers. I still think I might be seeing ghosts when WT, with his calm and confident demeanor, gently murmurs, "Come with me."

Part of me wants to summon Tansy. Either she's mistaken when she thought she finished him off, or she outright lied to me. I'm thinking the latter. That doesn't help in any way.

Still, Francesca and who knows how many other people are dead. Because of *him*. Their precious King of Deep Creek. Oh, how the people mourned his loss. They were practically foaming at the mouth to kill me.

Still unable to fully grasp the moment, I let my husband

lead me to a row of tables on the far-right side of the store while a tired-looking couple wanders in to pay for gas. The woman's gaze lingers on my yellow dress, but, luckily, the shop owner says something, pulling her attention away from me.

"Sit." WT stands there in his stupid green plaid shirt like he has the right to bark orders all day.

I lift my chin, daring him to try.

He hands me a bottled water, and I don't remember the last time I drank, so I rip it out of his hands and guzzle it. I'm exhausted, so I crash into his offered seat.

The truth is—and I try to keep myself from noticing—he's as rugged and handsome as that rosebush pruning memory.

No, I'll choose to remember how he looked when Tansy's rope zipped him off the roof. How's that for fantasizing?

I still can't believe he's here.

He's supposed to be a pile of sludge, silty goo, and sphagnum—Tansy's scientific experiment of a bog body. But here he is, in the flesh. Tansy has some serious explaining to do. What other lies has she told me?

Baseball cap pulled low, WT sinks into his folding chair across from me. While he impassively studies my face, I can't help staring back at his longer-than-usual scruff and oval-shaped face. He looks tired. Thinner than usual. He probably hasn't been sleeping well or eaten a decent meal in weeks.

"I assume you have a million questions," he says in his subdued, baritone voice. Who in the world was that bog body? "It's been torture not being with you."

He tries to take my hand, but in a knee-jerk reaction, I pull away. I want to trust him—my stupid, romantic instincts say I can trust him—but, obviously, my instincts are fried.

With the customers gone, the store owner eyes us while restocking the gum and candy. Either he doesn't know who

WT is, or he wants to see how things play out before he does anything.

Absorbing WT's longer-than-usual beard and auburn, medium-length hair, I don't know whether to laugh or punch him in the face. *Did* he hurt Francesca or Tim or Delilah? I hold onto the brittle ledge of the table to stop myself from doing anything too hasty.

"Why are you here?"

WT's pupils enlarge as he stares at me for a full five seconds. "Gem—" He extends his hand again, and I flinch back so hard my chair rocks back.

Blanching, WT rubs his bloodshot eyes. He casts a militaristic glance over his shoulder. "I need you to trust me."

What I want to know is, how does one prepare for this? For their hate group leader husband to rise from the dead? I'd give anything for Grammy to be in this room, coaching me.

"I—" somehow I have the wherewithal to weigh my words very carefully—"didn't even know you were alive."

The sound of several heavy boxes crashing to the floor tells us the store owner misplaced something. Bending over in the aisle, he grumbles about not being able to find any good help nowadays.

Not wanting to get off track, I adjust the lace on Tansy's frilly sleeves. Not what I would have wanted to wear when facing him, but there's nothing to do but make the most of it at this point. "Tansy showed me your body."

WT's eyes widen in surprise. Groaning, he scrubs his face with his left hand, which, of course, is missing his wedding ring. I suppose Tansy took it. But when? Why?

"I'm not sure whose body you saw," he says, "but as you can see, that wasn't me."

Catching my eye, he tilts his head to the side to show a horizontal scar on his neck that looks like Edgar slit his throat with a knife. But that wasn't Edgar. Tansy. No, she hung him with a rope ... so maybe WT cut *himself* while trying to break free?

The upper skin on his neck is layered; puckered pink. I doubt it will ever fully heal. I don't know whether to be glad or terrified.

"I understand why you did what you did," WT says. "You asked Tansy to take control. Take care of me. But a long time has passed since then. There are things I need to explain."

But I can't trust anything he says. All I can do is regard him like an infected animal. A coyote with rabies. I won't be so dumb as to be lured by his charm. I peel out of my chair and back up until the small of my back presses into the fountain drink machine.

"Stay. Away. From me."

A fresh wave of pain flashes over WT's eyes. "Gemma, I've come to set things right."

"What, the way you 'helped' Francesca? Who else have you 'helped,' WT?"

His jaw slackens as his brow furrows. "Who's Francesca?"

"You *killed* her! You and your friends ..."

Maintaining eye contact, WT sets his jaw but still says nothing.

Taking a step toward him, I smooth the front of my skirt. "You or your friends smashed her head into a sink. Though now I suppose you're going to tell me how that robe isn't even yours."

I hadn't meant to raise my voice, but it's grown loud enough that the store owner is muttering something. I'm just about done with people lying to me.

Leaning in, WT plants one hand on a knee. "We need to get out of here."

But there's no way I'm going anywhere with him. He's been lying low until he can, I don't know, kill me off or something.

Thankfully, Tansy's taught me how to be resourceful, how to defend oneself if need be. The toaster oven on the counter could be a charming weapon, but it's attached to a cord, and the cord's plugged in, out of sight.

I need something that can *truly* make a mess of things ...

Thinking fast, I slump my shoulders and let my skirts drag on the floor as I inch toward the fridge full of drinks. Lacing my voice with this false sense of helplessness, I say, "All right." I choke up—actual tears and everything. "But first, I need you to hold me."

I'll let him think I've given up. That he's far too much of a temptation. I'm still madly in love with him and willing to do whatever he likes.

Avoiding any and all eye contact, I try not to sound too pathetic as Tansy's corset constricts my airway. "Please?"

Gradually—clearly not trusting me—WT rises from the table. Shifts his feet. I can tell that he wants to help but he's being cautious. Smart boy.

"I'm ... sorr—" My voice breaks off, and I successfully don't finish whatever it is I'm sure he wants me to say.

I wait for him to draw nearer. And he does—oh, he does —one fatty bootstep after the other.

He's fully within reach, but I need him to think that I'm ready to collapse in his arms. Be the Damsel in Distress I'm sure he's always wanted me to be.

He's only half an arm's-length away. I could reach out and kiss him if I wanted to, but Gemma Louise Coldiron wasn't born with a last name like that to be weak.

Seizing the door of the beer fridge, I slam it straight into his right shoulder, catching him so off-guard he doesn't make a noise.

I've only hit him once, so I swing the door closed before whacking him again.

The thrill of getting the upper hand rushes down my

shoulders. WT staggers, but he still hasn't fallen, so I reach into the freezer and grab a beer bottle. Heaving it, I smash it straight into his face.

He staggers again, but, unfortunately, he's still awake.

So I grab the fridge door and smash it into him so hard that the glass shatters on impact, bursting into a million diamonds around his scalp and knees.

Fully covered in glass, WT twists and falls into the cotton candy. I think he's finally going to come after me, when he steps forward, and his boot lands on the fallen beer bottle. He flips onto his back, smacking his head on the cold concrete.

He's out.

By sheer, dumb luck, he's out. And I'm off, scot-free!

Grabbing the revolver in his belt—figured he'd be carrying —I gather my skirts and tear after the store owner before he tries calling the police. Feeling very "Annie Oakley," I level the revolver straight at the guy's face. *Pumpkins, shot gun shells with nothing but white-tufted buffalo grass for company.* Ah, looks like I'm recalling shooting lessons with Grammy.

"Car!" I bellow, re-grounding myself next to the gum display. "Where's your car?" I spy the owner's nametag. "Marty."

Marty shakes his head, a generous amount of neck skin flapping.

I cock the revolver, proving this isn't your ordinary day when Marty holds up his hands.

"All right, all right!" He clutches the counter like a scared weasel. "In the back. P-please! Just don't kill me."

I tower over him, partially wanting to freeze-frame the moment. Scrapbook a black and white Wanted poster where I'm holding a rifle with a swath of tassels and a cigar between my teeth.

"Gemma Louise Coldy," the Wanted poster says.

Well. It's the best I can do at this time.

Looping my pointer finger through the trigger guard, I give the revolver a little whirl. And it spins too fast, bringing me to the end of my outlaw days.

Smoothing out the front of my puckered bodice, I find my cool. I find my grit. "Now, Marty. Give me your keys."

$\mathcal{G}$rammy's house is exactly as I remember it, except the icicles are gone on the windmill, and it's missing a few blades. New potted petunias have been upended on her porch, and mud coats the stairs in heavy streaks.

Discretely, I shut the driver's side door of Marty's banged-up Dodge Dynasty. Picking my way across the rocks, I wish I had my sneakers since bits of glass from the gas station have embedded in my feet.

The porch steps groan in protest as I tiptoe my way toward the front door, trying to avoid the mud but not entirely succeeding. A shotput-sized ball descends on my throat. Did those people I saw earlier come here? I hope I'm being paranoid.

Peeling open the screen door, I half-expect Grammy to come out with a plateful of peanut butter cookies. But all I get in response is the lonely squeak of the floorboards as I step inside.

Her knitting projects lie in mish-mashed piles on the wobbly table where all the TV remotes used to be. The smell of cinnamon hangs heavily in the air; she must have already eaten her oatmeal this morning.

When I tread toward her knitting chair, I can't help but notice something that looks a lot like oatmeal has been spilled on the recliner's arm and side. On the hardwood, too —raisins and walnuts rest on bits of porcelain like Francesca's sink.

My heartrate thrums faster.

If her oatmeal's here, where's Grammy?

A rumpled form on the rug about Grammy's size makes my knees give way.

She must have taken a fall.

A terrible fall.

Paprika hair covers a lifeless face.

I need to check her pulse. Check her pulse. She has to be okay.

Blood pulsing in my ears, I take the three or so steps to reach her and kneel at her side. She lies so still, she could be a sleeping bag full of straw, but on her head, just like Francesca's, is a crater where her perfectly round skull used to be.

Blood drips from her ear to her nose in a straight line.

Grammy.

My heart seizes.

No, no, no. *Not Grammy*.

She can't be dead. I take her freezing fingers in mine. "Gra —" I break off with a sob. The people on the road … they *were* coming from here. I could have stopped them if I hadn't been such a coward and decided to hide.

I cradle Grammy's head in the pleats of my lap, and it's cold—too stiff and weak. Will my memories always be limited to the precious few we shared around the table and in the cemetery? I can't accept that. We've been robbed of our time.

How could the Klan do this? How could they be so callous and violent and so ugly?

I try to keep it together, but another sob wracks my body. Air—it's gone. I can't believe they would attack a frail woman like Grammy.

Almost like it's coming from a source I don't recognize, a crystal-clear image floats into my mind. *Arms outstretched, and in a slim, stately dress, Grammy delivers a soliloquy from Rachel Lynde in Anne of Green Gables. She tells Marilla she's doing a mighty foolish thing. The theater is packed. Everyone hangs on every gossipy word she says.*

Weeks later, Grammy takes me hiking around Possum Kingdom Lake. We pose before a sunset for a picture with the perfect lighting.

She takes me down to Fort Worth with its welcoming skyline. We stroll amidst the crowds past a spice shop beneath a spray of icicle lights. She introduces me to a makeup artist. Tells me that he kept her the same age for nearly a decade. We stop to buy peanut butter. She insists there's more flavor in the crunchy kind.

Edgar accuses me of not sweeping the front porch fast enough. His gray hair flops up as he gets closer—closer—close enough to slap me. Grammy stands between us, receiving his punishment. Never complains.

Limping across the porch, she wraps me in her arms and takes me out for a girls' lunch at Sweetie Pie Ribeye's. After the entrée, we finish with butter pecan ice cream. I ask her why she married Edgar. She says, after performing for so long, she just wanted her own love story. Unfortunately, she met the wrong man and jumped headfirst and blind into the wedding. Then she inherited a granddaughter she never knew could be more precious than life.

One day, we take in a cat that shows up on our doorstep. We feed him until he gets plump, about six months. We call him Humphrey Bogart. Grammy tends the chickens. Feeds the birds, instilling an unnatural love for all winged creatures in a now dissociated part of me.

Grammy.

She was nurturing, loving, an unfortunate romantic; fierce, kind. From what I can tell, she never knew what Edgar did to the man who killed my parents, but she did *everything* she could to protect me.

I don't know how long I sit on the floor and hold her, but much later, heavy bootsteps ascend the porch steps. I'm too tired to see who it could be.

The screen door pops open. Remotes on the nearby cabinet clatter as the person's footsteps shake the floor as he tears after me. It could be WT. He's finally putting on his Klan leader hat, come to finish me off, but I don't care. Grammy's dead. Just like Francesca.

Against my better judgment, I look up to find a fresh cut now graces the side of WT's face. He just got that from me. I suppose the revolver I stole from him is beside me on the floor—didn't realize I brought it with me. I should pick it up, point it at him, but my arms are heavier than lead. He's not looking at the gun anyway.

Sinking to the ground, WT washes pale as a sheet. He swings his fist. Knocks over a lamp and Grammy's beautiful pile of yarn.

"NO!" he screams.

He pounds the wall. Like that will make her come back to life.

Before shoving over a few other lamps and the cabinet holding all of Edgar's remotes—lovely—WT finally calms down enough to kneel next to me. After a few deep breaths, he reaches out for me, simultaneously pinning down my skirts with his knees.

I slap him hard. Shove him off.

He grabs me again, and I slap him even harder across the face.

My hand burns, but, still, he doesn't hit me back. Instead,

his face sags, and somehow he's secured me in his arms, his brutish hands cradling my back along with my dress' silk tufts and lace.

I don't know how or why I do it, but for the tiniest of moments, I do let him hold me. After all, I could reach for the gun and shoot him before he even admits to killing Francesca or Grammy. My bones have turned to mush. I barely feel alive.

I don't know why I notice this, but my face fits perfectly in the nape of his neck, his skin several degrees warmer than mine. I try not to smell the cedar wafting off his skin, drawing my mind into a blank.

Quick as a cat, I shove him off.

It takes catching sight of Grammy's smashed-in skull for reality to sink in for real this time. She's *dead*. She's not coming back. No more trips to Fort Worth, no more impromptu luncheons at *Sweetie Pie Ribeye's*.

Heart flopped over, I stagger over to the screen door while WT says something. I should have grabbed the gun, but I can't even bring myself to touch it now. Not that it matters. Not after all the death I've seen.

He shouts something else—something about them framing it as an accident—but I can't do this again. I'm about to lose my mind. Right as I hit the exit, I stumble straight into Natalie's petite frame. She's clutching a basket of poppy seed muffins and has the most clueless grin on her face.

Why is she here? I elbow past her, Tansy's ridiculous skirts whooshing.

Shocked, Natalie drops her muffins. I should apologize, but all I can do is run.

Grind the breading of the muffins into the porch with my bare feet.

43

*D*eep Creek's population is exactly 439. Or, that's what it was. Now we're down to 437. Guess I shouldn't have ever thought I could beat the Klan. Grammy stood up to Jesse Beauchamp, and he had her killed last night. What did she say to him? If she lived here for years, why did it take her until now to stand up to the local police?

Once again, my status quo is to walk around town blind. There's no way I'm ready to head home and face Tansy—especially with that bog body. I wonder who it is. Wonder why she insisted it was WT. To convince me to never leave the house? I don't even care at this point. Of course, if the person was from this town, we're down to 436. Population's dropping like flies.

Regardless, I keep walking. Even if I'm in Tansy's stupid dress, blood smeared on the bodice's lace. I couldn't stand out more if I wore blinking Christmas tree lights.

I'll walk to the next town. Rent an apartment with the whole thirty dollars I stashed away. I knew I should've kept that jewelry. Though the last time I wandered off, I had a seizure. I'm really good at being an independent lady.

I don't know how many hours pass before I find my way back to the bridge. My bridge that I thought was magical when I first met WT. Not that the history behind the tour was magical. That made me sick, even back then. But at the time, that's all it was. History. Where else is the Klan running around and terrorizing anyone different from them? They can get me any minute. Kill me for the same reason they killed Grammy. Makes me wonder if they even know WT's still alive.

As I sit on the edge of the bridge while the sun goes down, I come up with a solution for what to do next with my life. I'll tell Tansy I'll go away for a couple of years. Let her live it up in the house, making any random statements of art she likes. Then, after her time is up, we'll see how the town's shaped up. By then, maybe somebody else will have stepped in and found justice for all those who've been wronged by this filthy place.

The worst sound ever comes in the form of WT's boots scuffing along the wooden planks. I don't even bother to look up as he settles his barrel-chested body next to me. Why did he even bother to come back? Does he *want* me to string him up, this time above the creek?

Part of me still argues that maybe he's guilty of killing Grammy. But no matter how good an actor he is, there's no faking that reaction.

I'm so confused.

I'm about ready to break.

In the distance, a train blares its brassy horn at the exact time WT murmurs, "She was a good woman." What makes him think he deserves to talk about her? He looks at his hands. "Anne was unfailingly patient with me."

Anne. I knew it, but I'd forgotten that was her name. I curl my fingers into my palms. He isn't worthy of using her name. I'm not sure I can trust myself not to push him off the bridge—in a fateful twist of the Goatman reenactment, naturally.

"I'm going to help you bury her." WT stares at the newly leafed black willows with their scraggly bark and thin leaves.

He's waiting for me to speak up. Say something, but all I can think about is how both Francesca and Grammy had head wounds on the sides of their temples, almost like someone took a hammer to their skulls just above the eyes.

I can't get it out of my head.

Wait ... WT just said that he would help me bury Grammy? "No." I slice my hand through the air. "No way. Grammy gets a *proper* funeral at the church—" I was going to say *where she and Edgar were married*, but I'm sure he knows as well as I do that Grammy wouldn't want to be laid to rest anywhere *near* Edgar's grave.

"I already have her in the back of my truck." WT stands and strides toward his vehicle like he's been chosen by God's good prophet to handle her body.

"You're not touching her." My skirt rustles as I jump to my feet. Slivers embed in my heels, along with the glass. Feels great.

WT ducks his head as he peels open the driver's door to his truck, his plaid shirt unusually crinkled with rolled sleeves. "Gemma, either I can take her alone, or you can come with me."

That's it. I'm literally ducking my head and tearing across the bridge, feet pounding wood. Time to take him down. It's all I can think.

All at once, my palms collide with his chest—fifteen-pound anvils hit a turbine. My arm swipes the broad side of his beard, and I'm shoving him so hard, my wrist pops back painfully. Ooh, it's a reminder of when Edgar hurt my wrist all those years ago. Some injuries never go away.

I should have grabbed the gun when I was at Grammy's.

Why was I so stupid in leaving it behind? He probably has it in the back waistband of his pants like before. I plow my head into WT's stomach. Reach for the gun, but it isn't there, so I push him like I'll bury him beneath concrete.

Wrapping two impossibly strong arms around me, WT grunts while I launch a fist into his meaty side. I don't care that he groans while I pound my fists into his stomach. Or that my knuckles go sore. This will teach him what pain truly feels like.

He's still standing. Part of me wants him to fight back, so I raise my hand, and pop him straight in the eye.

He staggers. I think he's finally going to beat me to a pulp or pull his revolver from its secret location on me, but, instead, he gently says, "They get their hands on her, and they *will* desecrate her body."

I flinch. Is that what they did to Francesca's body?

"Calhoun and Beauchamp—they control what happens in the funeral home. They've always controlled the Joliffes."

Joliffes. Olly. *Grady Dean's.*

I curl my arm to take another swing—WT's eye is already looking deliciously red and puffy—but he catches my hand and firmly yet gently lowers it. "Gemma. Let me help you bury her with whatever dignity we can. Please."

But I can't handle this. Tears are threatening to blaze a trail from my eyes. "How *dare* you act like you get to handle her body?"

Holding out his hands, he says, "You're right. Tansy *did* have a good reason for wanting me to die, but"—his beard ripples in a shivery gust of wind—"we need to talk about this later. If they find your grandmother, you *will* never forgive me."

I don't know whether to gut-punch him or wrestle him to the ground for the gun and actually pull the trigger this time.

How does he feel like he can still be involved in my life? How does he think he deserves that?

But Grammy ... Grammy's body has to take precedence over any of my needs.

Wrenching open the shotgun side of the truck, I growl, "Take me to the cemetery."

WT pauses at the hood of his truck. "We can't take her there. I'm sorry." Visions of burying Grammy next to the squirrel and the magpie plague my mind while WT hurdles inside the truck. "I have a place."

44

"You don't have to help me dig." WT grabs a shovel from the truck bed, then another. "But it'll be faster that way."

I try not to stare at the red, white, and blue Texas quilt he's lain over Grammy. She used to pull that over her legs when she came over to watch a movie. *Casablanca.* She cried every single time. I still can't believe she stayed married to Edgar after he made her limp for the rest of her life.

She stayed to protect me.

Leading me to a meadow of bluebonnets and a pair of twisted mesquite trees, WT pauses before a cluster of Indian paintbrush. The orange pop of color reminds me of when he gave the same flowers to me. When a bumblebee buzzes past my ear, I shake away the memory.

After picking what looks to be a random spot and digging for about five minutes, WT says, "My mother is buried here."

I glance around to find a simple, wooden cross near an oil rig with its metal head in the ground—a giant, metallic woodpecker gone to sleep.

"I was five," he says. "She wasn't caught up in the politics of this place, but she did have an affinity for liquor and marriages. My pa was her last of five."

I don't know why he's telling me this, but I stare at the rig, absorbing every single detail he says.

"Cirrhosis of the liver." He leans on his shovel. "That's how she died. From there on out, Pa was in charge of raising me." He returns to his digging, heaving the clay-like soil as if that little introduction is all one needs to understand his family.

But he can't stop at that. I draw closer while still giving him a wide berth of space. Dig like this is a normal way to spend our time. I don't know if I believe everything he says, but ... hearing about his past somehow dulls the pain.

"Calhoun and Beauchamp don't know about this place." He bats away the bee. "Years ago, when Pa struck oil here, he moved my mother's body to the cemetery. Didn't want to knock into her, so to speak. But the oil soon dried up." He digs again, disrupting the brown-red clay. "We thought, for years, that was the last of it. Turns out, we had more oil closer to home." He nods to the rig across the field. "That rig should've gotten moved, but I kept it here. Ma always said oil rigs made her feel safe. So, I eventually brought her back to her final resting place."

I'm not sure why he's telling me about how he keeps moving his mother's body, but, if he's telling the truth, I suppose he did it out of love. Duty. Besides, I'm not entirely sure how an oil rig could make anyone feel safe—except for the dividends one would see ...

Ah. Smart lady.

"So if we bury Grammy here"—I nod to the hole we've been digging—"they won't touch her?"

WT gives me a hard nod, and I'm not entirely sure why I feel like he's being honest with me. Maybe it's because he's not pulling a "snake oil salesman," as Grammy used to call Edgar anytime he upsold a customer at his auto shop.

He was a mechanic. Oh, I remember. Yay.

Without another word, WT and I slip our shovels into the ground and dig until our arms are sore and the grave's a good four or five feet deep. The clouds are welling up and drizzle on us like syrup on pancakes. Blisters coat my hands. I'm a little glad that Grammy can lie next to someone else who didn't fit in at Deep Creek.

Truthfully, I wish I could talk to WT about the pies Grammy taught me how to bake. *The Encyclopedia of Italian History she gifts me.*

Taking me round back, she shows me how to hold a shotgun—just in case. We use pumpkins and empty coffee cans as targets, but Edgar is always near, watching. She scraps the guns and ships me off for my very first internship in Washington, D.C.

I write her letters, and she responds—always slipping in a few extra dollar bills when Edgar isn't looking.

Oh, why did I leave her? I could have—should have—protected her. Beat Edgar somehow. Beat all the Klan in Deep Creek.

Before I know we're doing it, WT and I are already lowering Grammy into the humble grave. I hate that this is what's come of our lives. The Texas quilt is far too thin. She should be protected in a coffin. Guards should be stationed about to scare off coyotes.

Fighting back the tears, I grab my shovel to get back to work—can't think about any of this—when WT's thick fingers block my hand.

"I can do the rest," he says.

I laugh, because if he thinks I'm not going to do my part, he's crazier than Tansy.

Unloading the loose soil onto Grammy's slight frame becomes therapy. She always loved gardening. *She grows gladio-*

*las, daffodils. Her smile is enormous when they burst through the soil
for the first time in spring.*

Ah, but Grammy was supposed to tell me what to do
next. She was supposed to help me know how to deal with
the corruption of this place.

Suddenly dropping his shovel to the ground, WT barks,
"Get in the truck."

I glare back, not in the mood for his barking.

He clutches my arm. "Gemma, get in the truck *now*.
Someone's driving up. It could be Calhoun or one of his
cronies."

I shake him off. Sure, I'll listen, but in my own time.

WT throws me on the ground, my skirts whooshing.
Without any shape or form of propriety, he slams his body on
top of mine. His thick torso becomes a blanket of armor I
didn't expect. He smells like the clay of the soil, and, *no*, his
body does not feel good as the vehicle rumbles by.

By the time we look up, a Tesla, of all things, is cruising
around a bend in the road, '70s disco music blaring. WT
continues lying there, though, and I try not to notice the
safety I feel with his warm chest heaving against my neckline.
Or the heat now pouring from my chest and face.

When the Tesla's well and good out of sight, WT rolls off,
and I hate how I'm immediately left feeling ridiculous and
empty. Knowing what I know, I don't understand how he can
affect me this way. But I *will* kick this weakness. Once I see
the complete picture of what's happened, it will be easy.

When WT holds out a hand to help me stand, I push off
from the ground. Shake the dust from my skirts, ignoring him
the exact same way Tansy ignored Dwayne.

Taking the hint, he stoops to pick up the first of the two
shovels and stands it against the weathered trunk of a
mesquite tree. Scooping up the second, he seems to mull over

a thought before finally saying, "I'm not great at eulogies, but we could say some words. If you want. About your Grammy."

I straighten my dress. Pretend he's nowhere nearby before stuffing my hands into my skirts and quietly recalling the day she taught me how to make cornbread muffins—and how to shoot a bullseye.

45

*I*t's nothing fancy, but WT finds us a motel, keeping the curtains closed and door dead-bolted, I suppose to keep us safe. Luckily, he's also gotten us sand-wiches, and I'm thinking he would have finished me off before he bought them if he truly wanted to kill me. Though he does deposit his revolver on the end table as if inviting me to grab it any time I like.

My fingers itch to grab it. Anything to fill the void. It's almost pretty, with its engraved brass scrollwork. Surely an antique.

The turkey club's delicious. I do my best to pace myself between bites. When WT hands me a cream soda and salt and vinegar potato chips, I get déjà vu, because we ate the same snacks while watching *Casablanca* with Grammy. While he sits next to me on the bed, I do my best not to make any sudden movements. I don't even open my chips. That would be too noisy.

Stomach growls.

He doesn't say a word when I give up my vow of silence and open the chips. They look too good not to eat.

Rubbing his thumb on his ring finger, WT hunches his shoulders, obviously thinking deeply about something. Makes me wonder what he could be thinking about—if there's really a good and evil side of him like Tansy said on the roof. I suppose that makes sense—why, regarding him, she and I feel so differently.

I've just downed the last of the cream soda—fizz sizzles on my tongue like a dream—when WT takes the bottle and sets it on the bedside table next to the revolver with somber grace.

I don't mean for it to happen, but my eyes slide to every movement he makes. How relaxed and confident he looks in that plaid shirt with his rolled sleeves. He's rarely dressed so casual. Really, he seems almost *too* likable, with his unassuming presence. What I want to know is, how he was involved in Francesca's murder. Grammy's.

"How is she treating you?" WT asks, staring at his clasped hands before raising his hazel eye to look at me.

I try not to notice the answers that seem to be lurking there, the sheer intensity. Lowering my gaze, I stare at his finger where his ring used to be. Maybe Tansy stole it before she hung him from the roof? Also, he must have a *killer* metabolism if he was able to survive the foxglove poisoning. "Tansy doesn't get out much nowadays."

WT's gaze drifts to my lap—no, my hands. Seems I've been picking at a hangnail. It's bleeding.

"Did she ever tell you how we met?" His voice is so soft, it's hard to imagine him threatening to hurt anybody.

"On the bridge?"

"No." He fixes his gaze on my chin. "Tansy and me."

I never considered the fact that WT and Tansy would need to meet. But, I suppose, even Kay had to learn who the real Michael Corleone was eventually.

While he gestures to a pillow to my left, laughter, of all

things shines in his eyes. "Why don't you rest for a while and let me tell you about it."

I don't *think* his intention is to take advantage of me. What's crazy is, it's the first time he's suggested that I do something without flat-out ordering me. My turkey coma is starting to settle in, and since he's finally popping open his own cream soda, I take that as a sign that he's not going to do anything sketchy. A bit of rest might do me some good. I'm sure I could sleep for weeks.

As I lay down, not exactly comfortable with the corset's stiff boning, I do find a way to settle in on my side.

WT shifts to face me. "I had just gotten home from a fourteen-hour workday. Headed straight to the library. I must have been in there for hours before I heard something in the parlor, so I went out to check on the cause of the noise."

He takes a swig of his cream soda, arm muscles beneath his shirt bulging. "It was funny, see, because you and I"—he gestures between us—"had only been on one date. I'd brought you to the house after we saw *Cirque Du Soleil* and Tansy ... well, she was on her hands and knees, days later, hiding the fact that she'd collected all my late great-grandmother's jewelry. She claimed that she'd been there for hours. Wanted to see Hardin Mansion with her own eyes. I thought it was bold—cute, even—in an unnerving way. Still, having her in the picture was more than I bargained for, so I tried to break things off with you." His chest heaves. "But you were impossible to get out of my mind."

Running his hands through his hair, he stares at the worn carpet while bracing his elbows on his knees. "Tansy was very convincing. She reminded me that you were raised by Edgar, and he was never kind. She promised that she would only come out once or twice a year—when you needed protection —and, knowing what I know about Edgar, I gradually put together that she was a survival tactic *you* created in order to survive."

WT rises to his feet, pacing with even greater agitation as he builds on his story. "I figured I could handle her. You know, since she's a self-proclaimed homebody. I thought she was keeping her word in not coming out until I saw her dancing in the garden with Dwayne. At first I thought it was you." He knocks his leg with a fist. "I was *livid*. But then I saw the way she moved, heard her higher, more Southern voice, and I knew it was her."

"But Dwayne doesn't know about Tansy."

A muscle flickers along WT's jaw. "He believes he makes you 'more alive.'"

My stomach churns. It's a lot of information all at once, but I have to know one thing. "WT ... before Tansy strung you up on the cupola, what did I see?"

He turns his back. Places his fists shoulder-width apart on the dresser. Doesn't say anything.

"Tansy says she finally took over when I saw something terrible. It's why I let her be in charge. It has something to do with the Klan. Please tell me."

His shirt stretches across his back as he leans further into the dresser. "We will get to that. I promise, Gemma." Slowly, he turns to lock his troubled eyes on me. "First, you need to know how the True Knights came to be a part of my life."

"Stop calling them that."

He nods, seeming to understand my aversion to the name. Nerves pinch my stomach as I try to find a comfortable position to think. I still don't know if I can trust him, and, against my better instincts, I still only see kindness in his eyes.

Sinking onto the foot of my bed, WT says, "You have to understand, I was raised in this filth. Inducted into the Klan right after Ma died."

"I thought you said she died when you were five."

WT bites the inside of his cheek. "Deep Creek is one of the few Klans that builds from the ground up. They feed their bull to kids, indoctrinating entire families."

"No ..."

"There's an old photograph in my desk—back home—if you want to see my induction ceremony." He scrubs his hand over his face, highlighting the crow's feet around his eyes. "For some reason, Anne's always looked out for me. Both you and I know she's never loved Edgar, but she married him on a whim and only stayed with him to protect you. She believed she would eventually find a way to take down the Klan. That, and she thought she could talk my father into changing his ways. God rest her soul, next to marrying Edgar, that was the most foolish thing she ever tried.

"Three years ago"—he pounds his fist into his lap—"Pa died. A year or so before Edgar. Even though Anne tried to get me out of this mess, this town has always seen me as a sort of future king." He holds up his hands before I can say a word. "Not for anything I did. If it wasn't for my money, they never would have looked at me twice. But my ancestors— along with the Beauchamps, Coldirons, and Calhouns— founded Deep Creek. Ever since my parents died, the whole town's been waiting for me to take my 'rightful place.' Then, when I married you, everyone got swept up with the idea that you were a 'princess' of sorts—the last of the Coldirons."

My stomach twists into knots. "So they *liked* Edgar because of the sick things he did?"

WT nods, then shakes his head. "It's a bit more compli-cated than that. It's a sense of pride, family pride. It's not what Edgar did per se, but that he kept the "family tradi-tions" in the name of White Supremacy. That's why they never touched you. You've always had immunity, being the last Coldiron. Doubly after marrying me."

A rat feels like it's gnawing on every inch of my insides. To think that I thought WT's and my marriage was created out of love—but, instead, it was a safety net for evil I never wanted to be a part of in the first place.

"Needless to say, striking oil was the worst thing that could have happened. Once news got out, Beauchamp and Calhoun believed it was my 'duty' to fund more of the Klan's activities."

I push past the shock of my "status." "You refused?"

WT shakes his head, which is another sock to the gut. "Not openly. I knew, to make them stop, I needed to continue to infiltrate their ranks until the time was right. It's why I felt like I couldn't go to Palo Duro with you. They were watching my every move. But I sort of blew a gasket when things got tense and needed a break. Then, the night you showed up at headquarters, I was actually planning to burn down the place."

Headquarters ... I'm not sure what that means.

"But you saw us with a pair of prisoners, and—"

"You killed them." I'm not sure how I know this, but I know it, clear as day.

"I was trying to help them escape. But Calhoun—he ... let's just say that it got messy."

I still don't know what he's talking about. "What do you mean?" The pit in my stomach widens, and I don't know how much more of this I can take.

"After Tansy did what she did to me"—he evades my question—"I decided to leave town and lie low until I could get the feds involved. Figure out how you and I could be together, for good this time."

He still hasn't answered my question, but I have to trust that we'll get to what I saw eventually.

"How do I know I can trust you?" I scan the cowboy paintings on the walls, wishing I could sort through all of this with Grammy. "You've been gone for months."

WT knocks his hand against his leg twice. "Anne encouraged me to stay away. She wanted me to keep reporting, supplying the feds with information and names. I believe you met one of my contacts—Agent Spence."

"Crew cut, squirrel face?"

WT bites back a smile. "He's been looking into ... all the Klan's activities."

"I thought he wanted to verify that I killed you."

He cracks a small smile at that. "Good thing I'm still alive. I hate that I was gone for so long, but Anne insisted that what you had seen that day had set you back, and that Tansy was now in charge most of the time."

I lean back against my headboard, letting all his explanations sink in. "I went to Calhoun's office."

WT's face washes blank. "He's been waiting for you to come to him for months. All he cares about is gaining access to the Hardin money. That and keeping a lid on everything that happens in Deep Creek."

So Calhoun never cared about helping me find WT. I hate that I fell for his ploy.

Sitting up further on the mattress, I say, "They have to answer for what they did to Francesca and Grammy."

"Wait ... is Francesca—"

"Delilah's mother. Tim's wife. You helped them get a place."

Realization, sharp and hot, suddenly transforms WT's face. "And ... the two of you were friends?"

An image of Francesca gathering up her twenty hair products to save me from my hair travesty flashes through my mind. "The best."

WT clamps down on his lip. Covers his face. "I ... didn't realize that. I didn't even realize she was in the picture. I'm sorry."

That would be because Francesca had lost custody of

Delilah. I guess it makes sense he wouldn't have known abou her, though it still sucks that she isn't alive.

"The town believes her death was an accident," I say between gritted teeth.

"That's what they do." WT chews on the inside of his cheek. "That's what they'll say about Anne, too. That she had a stroke or something. But we can *right* this. I've been working on this for some time."

"What exactly do you have in mind?"

A flash of resignation flares across WT's eyes. "We finish what I started that night."

"Burn down headquarters?"

He bows his head in agreement, but it can't be that easy.

"I don't even know who Tansy killed." I fiddle with the silk flowers on the front of Tansy's dress.

"Hopefully somebody who had it coming."

We grow silent for a while, and before I know it's happened, he's scooted closer to me on the edge of the bed. He isn't proud or defensive or even all-knowing. He's simply *here*, and from his calm demeanor, I can't help believing that everything he's said is true. Is this why Tansy claimed that corpse in our basement is him? She didn't want me falling for him again, after all this time?

Stretching out his hand, WT slips a piece of hair behind my ear, his touch feather light. His cedar smell washes over my skin, and his voice comes out husky. "Do you know why I fell in love with you, Gemma Louise?"

Every word I know has now been encoded in Japanese.

"You weren't willing to keep quiet about Goatman's Bridge. *No one* talks about that place. I don't know if you ever learned this, but the Klan used to do an annual ritual there to *celebrate* what happened to the Goatman in the '30s."

"No."

"It's why I suggested you look in the county records. Until

the '80s, the disappearances of tourists—people from all around the world—always used to happen on the same date. My pa's generation always covered it up. I wanted to see if you could uncover the conspiracy."

"But I was too focused on all the other details." My shoulders sag. "Like more historical sites."

WT's once focused eyes soften as he looks into mine. "Which made me fall in love with you even more. Understanding the past helps us know how to beat the enemy."

"But they don't do the 'ritual' anymore?"

"Calhoun and Beauchamp were gearing up to resurrect the old ways that night."

I lean back, horrified. But is he telling the truth? It *sounds* like he wants to take down the Klan ... but he could be lying. I could be overlooking his weaknesses just because of our history.

I lick my lips, trying to reconcile what I want with what's right. Maybe I'll gauge his reaction after I give him a peek into my current life. "Tansy keeps me very weak."

Leaning in, WT places his elbows on his knees. "The Gemma Louise I know has *never* been weak."

"She only lets me out every fourteen days."

A flash of hurt, then sadness rims his eyes.

"The town said I killed you. I didn't even remember who you were."

WT presses his fist to his lips—clearly hurt by what I'm saying—but he stops himself from responding.

"They were going to lock me up, but Tansy says Calhoun convinced everybody that I only needed to be watched. And that I qualified for an insanity plea."

A tendon flickers along WT's neck. "Calhoun tried drawing me out. He wasn't sure if I was really dead or alive. But one of his men spotted me a few towns over, and after Agent Spence left, I knew it was time to come back and make things right." Raising a cupped hand to his forehead as if making a vow, he says, "Once all this is over, we're ditching this filthy place."

My heart swells a little prematurely at the idea. "Tansy would never let me."

WT leans over, gently laying a hand on my face. I should push him off, but his touch is warm. Tender. Oddly inviting. "*You* used to be the one in control. Put her in her place."

Not ready for his advice, I shove him off. "People with my condition tend to get agitated if things don't go as planned. Tansy's already agitated. I—we—risk gaining another alter."

A dimple appears above WT's nose, showing how deeply he's concentrating. I expect him to curse—he's going to lose it—but instead, he leans forward with this unnerving, love-filled look in his eyes.

"That's not going to happen—" His voice cuts off while he runs the side of his thumb along the side of my face. Everything tremors beneath his touch. My lips, my face, and I can't help it; I can't help hanging onto any shred of hope he offers me.

"Are you ready to face her?" He takes my hand. I don't know if I should accept it, but, for the moment, I don't pull away.

46

While WT and I hide behind one of the massive, untrimmed hollies, Natalie emerges from the mansion, casserole dish in hand like an oversized ticket to a play.

Jesse Beauchamp's police truck's sitting in front of the house on the street, too.

Tansy will be thrilled about the company.

"What's her deal?" I whisper to WT, referring to Natalie.

"Apart from parties and social calls, she's never been much of a leader. I know she regrets marrying Jesse. She's never had the bandwidth to stand up to the Klan. Though she means well."

"Does she know you're here?"

"She saw me at your grandmother's. I think she's trying to find her voice in her marriage. But she doesn't like stirring up things ..."

To be sure, as Natalie scrambles through the gate—guess I forgot to lock that when I left after seeing the bog body—her expression reminds me of a spooked rabbit.

"So she's my best friend?"

"More like a friend in a small town when there aren't a lot of options."

Part of me worries that Jesse's in there, giving Tansy the third degree ... but I know that he can't be talking to her. Tansy's in me.

At any rate, he'll soon be heading out to his vehicle. WT must read my mind, because he takes my hand and leads me back to the greenhouse, my heartbeat getting jittery.

It's all so surreal, being around him after not even knowing he existed. I don't know how to explain it, but no matter what I do, I can't help feeling drawn to his every word, every movement he makes. *Please* let him be honest. He claims he wants to take down the Klan ... but what if, just like Tansy, he's spinning some elaborate trap?

I don't think he's as vindictive as that.

Too bad we can't just talk with Tansy in the greenhouse, but no way is she coming out before I go in the house. Somehow, I have to make her see reason while proving that I'm still combatting the possibility of other alters.

The man upstairs must know we need something encouraging, because a spray of shell pink evening primroses wave to me from the doorway. Brown-eyed Susans intermingle with the pinks, and their brief visits are my favorite part of Texas in the spring.

Softening, I turn to WT. It's not like we can go barging in there when Jesse's inside the mansion anyway. "How come we never met until I came back from D.C.?"

The dimple above WT's nose reemerges, implying how deeply he's focusing. "Edgar was infamous for his temper. My pa avoided him when it came to social calls and business dealings. That, and he sent me away to boarding school when I was eleven."

"But how could we not have *ever* met? There aren't even five hundred people in this town."

"I saw you a few times, but Edgar kept you and Anne on a tight leash."

I bristle—not exactly something one wants to hear. But it's true.

"Sorry ... that's nothing against you or Anne. That was just Edgar's way. Then, after boarding school, I went straight to Vanderbilt. Didn't come back until you had already left for D.C."

"But how could Grammy have had *any* influence over you when our families were in different social circles, and you were away most of the time?"

WT checks the chamber in his revolver, handling the weapon with a natural confidence and ease. "While I didn't see her much, your grandmother had a way of making the most of her time."

Grammy catches wind of Edgar breaking one of his employees' kneecaps for being late. I spot her at the kitchen table, secretly writing out a check for the man's medical bills. Afterward, she brings over chicken divan with Natalie.

"Anne sent me article after article about how the Klan uses propaganda to twist ideals, much like the Nazis. Then she introduced me to a professor from the Congo. He changed my life." A twig snaps beneath WT's boot as he draws nearer. "I may have been brainwashed as a kid, but it made me sick, even then. I was only too happy to have someone there to help me root that filth out of my life."

I don't know how it's happened, but his chest is suddenly only two inches from mine. His breath is awash with mint, and I can just *feel* his itch to grab and hold me.

Leaning in closer, WT stretches out his hand. His index finger traces the skin on my wrist, and sparklers flicker and ignite. How am I supposed to be rational when his touch makes it so hard to think?

When he rests his hand on the small of my back, I know

it's something he does as we cook. When we go to church. When we're watching the fireworks on the Fourth.

This moment ... I foolishly don't want it to end. Soon, we're going to stalk inside that house and face Tansy. She'll break the spell. Finally reveal why I can't be with WT.

"Gemma." His voice and breath are smooth as ribbons. He trails his hand down the side of my cheek, and I swallow the bulge of nerves in my throat. Brushing his thumb across my upper lip, he looks at me like I'm the most precious thing in life.

But I have to break the spell. "Aren't you mad you were almost murdered by my other half?"

WT laughs. "As I recall, Tansy was only doing what she thought was right."

"So, she didn't know your allegiances weren't aligned with the Klan's." I have to verify this, but from around the corner of the house, Jesse is suddenly marching to his police truck, phone to his ear, saying something about a body being in the basement.

I stiffen as WT gently cups my elbow with his palm. "He's probably only telling Calhoun. Remember, Beauchamp's not your typical police."

Slipping into his car, Jesse guns the accelerator and flips a U-ey without waiting for anybody to join him at the scene of the crime. Okay. Yes. WT's probably right.

By the time the dust's settled on the road, I have to ask WT a final question. "What if Tansy stops us from fighting the Klan?"

I've gripped his arm without meaning to, so I pull away.

WT's eyes soften with sadness. "She deserves the chance to show that she's on board. Plus, I think it's *you* who wants to convince her to stop hiding."

It's true. But how can I convince her to listen to me this time?

47

*I*n the parlor, we try to reach Tansy. Flies buzz over the roasted vulture, and WT doesn't say a word about how the once-cozy room now smells like an abandoned KFC.

When we try the easy chair in the library, I have WT hand me a knitting project—another outfit for Jerusha or Hawkins—but Tansy doesn't even come out to rave about the symmetry of the stitching.

Next, the kitchen. The open cupboards and thrown away cupcakes tell me Jesse wasn't amused when he found them while searching the place.

After the kitchen, WT and I even try the basement. We tiptoe around Tansy's bog body experiment, and WT doesn't even comment when he spots his Rolex on the cadaver. But still ... no Tansy.

"Maybe we shouldn't worry about getting her on board," I say after we've gone back upstairs and I've planted myself in front of the mirror in the hallway. The blood and dirt I got on Tansy's dress now makes it look more brown than yellow, and the lace on the neckline's so ripped, I doubt it will be able to be saved. "Maybe she'll understand that it's time to take responsibility."

WT pulls the basement door closed behind him. "If that's what you want ..."

"Ah, but she could spring up at the *worst* possible moment. For all I know, she could come marching out, insisting it's time to reenact Romeo and Juliet's death scene."

WT waggles his eyebrows. "Just as long as we get to consummate the marriage."

I flinch. How could he feel comfortable enough to say such a thing? But of course. He remembers everything about what it was like to be married, while I haven't gotten past our first date.

"I ..." don't know how to face him. Not to mention how my throat's gone dry. "I need to change."

WT's arms plunge a little too heavily at his sides. "Gemma—I don't know what I was thinking. I'm sorry." Staring at a broken teacup Jesse or someone must have knocked to the ground, WT digs his hands in his hair again, shaking his head.

I grab the stair rail and mount the stairs, not sure what to say. Yes, his remorse feels genuine, but it's yet another reminder of what I've lost from my memories.

"I'll call my contacts," WT says gruffly. "Let them know we're on our way."

Pausing halfway up the stairs, I have to ask, "You mean Agent Spence ... and his other friends at the FBI?"

WT nods.

"They're okay with us burning down the place?"

"Well, it *is* my land ..."

I give him a light-hearted laugh. "Well, of course it is, my liege."

Drawing closer with two quick steps, WT stammers, "Gemma ..."

I look down, never more lost as to what to say.

"I told them, after we finish with this, they can do with me what they like."

A warm flurry flutters through me. "But I thought you said you never hurt anybody."

"I haven't but ..." He braces a hand on the hall table. "I also didn't stop something that you'll soon be remembering." A muscle feathers along his jaw. "You also need to know that I *swore* to them that you have nothing to do with any of this."

I actually want to give him a hug—the slightest part of me. The other part—my more skeptic side—tells me to run upstairs, get away from him, and tuck myself out of sight.

When I make it to the master bedroom, I find a pair of khaki pants and a sweater that actually make me feel like me. Both fit quite well, if a bit baggy. I pull my hair into a messy bun before splashing cold water on my face. More than anything, I'd love to decompress in the shower, but WT's waiting downstairs—no need to provide him with the opportunity of accidentally peeping on me.

I'm just grabbing a plush towel to pat my face dry when Tansy comes prowling out of my subconscious like she's Queen Latifah, strutting with all her glitz and glam down the runway.

Grabbing a bottle of perfume, she gives me a healthy spritz. "You got a *lotta* nerve, bringin' him here, G."

I force her to set the bottle down. "*You* told me he died."

"So what if I did?" She regains control of the perfume and spritzes our wrists and neck about three hundred more times.

"Tansy"—I force her to slam the bottle down—"how can I trust you? You lied!"

My other half's eyes narrow to slits—until she spots a flashy box of jewelry. "It needed to be done. You wanted to go gallivantin' around, who knows where, and I needed to convince you to stay home, locked up n' safe!"

It takes everything I have not to punch our reflection in the face. "You *do* realize people out there have died."

Like a hobgoblin who can only think of shiny objects, Tansy reaches for the jewelry box on the counter with its rose gold trim, sparkling in the dappled light.

But we don't need *any* distractions, so I try turning us toward the door. "How can you ever be content, holing up in this place?"

Tansy growls, spinning back, and flipping open the lid.

"For the first time, maybe ever, we are going to stand up for what's right!"

Pulling out a fatty beaded necklace with a large broach, Tansy says, "Is that what you tell yourself to feel better about the fact that WT's responsible for the murder of Francesca's family?" She layers my sweater with a few more necklaces and stuffs our fingers with a slew of diamond rings. *Oh*, how could I have failed to ask WT about Delilah? And Tim, her daddy?

"That's what I thought." Tansy adjusts her latest necklace with a trio of running horses mounted on the centerpiece.

"But Tansy, you murder people!"

"Oh, come, now! That body in the basement was already dead. I just stole him from the funeral home once upon a fortnight."

"But ..." I don't know whether or not I can believe her. I don't even know if I should ask how she was able to go to the funeral home in the first place.

"I may or may not have convinced you to go out ..." she says, expertly reading my mind. "Then, I up n' stole the memory."

When does it stop, the insanity? And when will we ever learn to work *together* and be on the same page?

"Trust goes both ways." Tansy eyes me while grabbing a tube of lipstick from the counter and applying it with the panache of a dancer on a Vegas stage.

She's just fastening a diamond and pearl comb in the side of our hair when her gaze hardens, and our upper lip curls. "Well, hello, there, sweet cheeks."

Never more alone, WT just stands there, arms held unusually close to his sides.

"As you can see," Tansy jeers, fastening her favorite hummingbird broach to the neck of my sweater, "I'm havin' a little heart-to-heart with G."

WT stuffs both hands in his pockets. "I can see that." He surveys my other half with a weightless gaze. But while I can hear the diplomacy in his voice, I know all Tansy can detect is the challenge to her authority. She's dubbed herself the queen of Hardin Mansion, replete with a dozen rose petal crowns to stake her claim.

"He isn't with them." I vainly try to calm her down while burning oil surges within our veins.

Hyperaware of each and every one of our movements, I watch, powerless, as Tansy treads up to our husband and sniffs his neck like he's a piece of meat. *"How* ... did you not die?"

He sets his jaw.

"I drugged you. Hung you. How are you ..." Suddenly wrapping our hand around his neck, she squeezes it with all her might. He grunts but doesn't lift a hand. Not even a spark of anger flares across his eyes.

"Knife," he eventually says through Tansy's grip before she releases his neck and traipses our hand along his chest in a tease.

"Ever the charmer," Tansy croons. *"Oh,* how the town's lamented the loss of their precious king."

Rubbing the back of his neck, WT takes a shaky step backward. His shoulder brushes against our dresser while Tansy skulks to the front of the fireplace.

"You know I don't care about that," he says. "We're here

to do what we should have done all along. Bury the Klan. Make sure they never again have a hold on Deep Creek."

Tansy makes a giant show of rolling our eyes. "We wouldn't *be* in this mess if you'd 'buried' them long before you met G."

Instantly, WT's shoulders sag as he hooks his thumbs through the belt loops of his jeans. "I would change a lot of what I've done if I could go back in time."

Suddenly jabbing him in the throat, Tansy shrieks, "And what about your precious Gemma? Are you *really* willin' to risk her possibly gainin' another alter? Another me?"

WT closes the distance between us. Takes up our hand as if swearing an oath for all to see. "We should all have a cause to believe in." His hand squeezes our fingers. "*Something* to fight."

Tansy drops his hand like there's a high likelihood that she'll contract leprosy. "The Klan isn't like an afternoon church luncheon, William. You cannot simply come an' go as you please."

I open my mouth to argue—make her see reason, some-how, some way—when Tansy grabs the granite wall between our consciousness, heaves it over, and flat-out buries me.

48

*S*heer will—unrelenting desire—is an extraordinary thing.

When Tansy put me away all those times, I went, bowed, almost willingly. But this time's different. I'm different. She may be covering me with the shame of how I never told on Edgar—how he murdered and destroyed that poor man's body—but I'm not him. I won't allow this granite to block the view any longer. Time to start seizing control and doing what's right.

Shifting the granite's weight, I try to heave it off, but it's heavier, slicker than I expected. I don't know how long I can hold on—stay cognizant of what's happening—though, for the first time in probably forever, I'm truly willing to fight.

With my palm pressing into the cool rock of the granite, I'm able to secretly tap into Tansy's side of our mind.

She's bending down. Shoving WT in the side of the knees with this mischievous look on her face. He staggers, but he still doesn't unleash his anger. Simply lifts his arm to cover his face.

Tansy lifts a vase. Chucks it at his head, and, almost like he's tempted to let her hit him, he ducks just in time.

She peels open his jacket. Snickers while slipping out an Apache gold pocketknife.

"Ain't this pretty?" Tansy tosses it in the air before flipping open the knife.

WT bites his upper lip, clearly doing everything in his power not to hurt me. Holding out his hands, he says, "All I need is for you to get in the car, Tansy."

Quick as a flash, she scrambles toward the settee. Hops on his back. Sinking her teeth into his ear, she whispers, "Well, aren't you a pair of fussy britches." Kicking him three times in the thigh, she then clambers off. "Catch me if you can!" She giggles before hightailing it to the hallway.

Grabbing pictures, lamps—anything she can get her hands on to prevent WT from coming within reach—she darts for the stairs before stumbling a little. But she rights herself. Oh, she needs to be careful if she doesn't want to trip and break our neck with this tomfoolery.

Luckily, WT's hot on our heels. Holds out his hands as if to catch her—if she would ever cooperate with such a thing.

"The difference between G n' me, William, is *I don't leave*." Tansy wrenches a sconce from the wall and hurls it straight at WT's face.

He ducks to miss the sconce. Ducks again to avoid a two-headed cat painting. "You can believe what you want. But you shouldn't try to stop Gemma from doing what she feels is right."

Hobble-hobble-flap.

Hobble-hobble, step-flap.

Looks like Tansy's impersonating a loon that's had too much to drink. Taking three more steps down the steps, she slurs, "What amazes me is you think you're capable of bein' redeemed! Actually, it's amazin' to me that you still wanna hold onto a sham of a marriage that never should have happened in the first place."

Swiping at a brass light dangling from a thick chain from the ceiling, Tansy adds, "Not like Gemma could be considered an ideal partner, considerin' the baggage I bring."

She fastens her hands on the rail; actually lifts up one leg. She's going to slide down, but she can barely *walk* down the steps, let alone balance this way.

WT seizes our arm. "You are going to kill her."

"That would be you, love. Not me."

Gently placing his hands on our hips, he lifts us from the rail while she kicks and screams. He bundles us up in his arms, and I wish Tansy could see how patient he's being. It would be much easier for him to march us straight to the door with us thrown over his shoulder. But he simply pins her gently yet firmly to the steps and leans forward with so much love in his eyes. "Tansy."

With the heel of our foot, she kicks him on the bottom half of his face.

Blood trickles from his chin, and he's going to have a fat lip. "Tansy, we both know that you keep Gemma locked up in here, because you are terrified of what's outside."

She tries kicking him again, but he pins her knee with his elbow, never once raising his voice. "You control her. Belittle her. You say you're protecting Gemma, but you stunt the amazing force for good she can be."

Fear, laser-sharp and focused, unexpectedly skitters down Tansy's spine. Suddenly, all she can see is WT, looming large above her, and *he's Edgar, who's going to whip us good if we don't clean out the stalls much faster. He has more chores for us to do if he ever again catches us reading those "useless" childhood stories.*

"Tansy." I try to console her. *"He isn't Edgar. You have nothing to fear from WT."*

Tansy gathers all the saliva in the recesses of our throat

and spits the biggest loogie of our life. "You never shoulda involved her in your filthy life!"

A mountain of regret shines in WT's eyes. He doesn't bother to wipe off the spit. Only when he lifts his elbow from pinning her, do I see that he's considering letting her do to him exactly what she's planning. "I have to repair what I've done. You're right."

Not about to look a gift horse in the mouth, Tansy head-butts him before opening the blade. "Now, *King*"—she licks our lips, deliriously greedy—"sit still while I cut out the both of your eyes!"

"*Tansy!*" I shout at her, but she's too busy giggling maniacally. True, I'd hoped she'd see reason, but now I can see that I *have* to intercede this time.

Putting his life in her hands, WT quietly releases her and scoots half a foot away. "I'll let you take both of them if it means you'll believe what I'm saying."

Now this is just crazy.

"*WT!*" I can't get my lips to work. "*TANSY!*"

I pound my hands into the granite, failing to get either of them to acknowledge me. Saliva builds up in the corners of our mouth; our entire body shakes.

Well, I can sit back and watch her turn Jeffrey Dahmer ... or I can *prove* that I'm ready to be in charge.

Using arm muscles I didn't even know I had, I grasp the granite wall and heave it to the side.

49

*G*ranite crumbles to a stormy, foamy sea.

The knife clatters to the ground, and I've barely registered that I've resumed control when WT clutches my arm.

"Gemma?" The duality of hope and fear war within his eyes. But there's no reason to fear—Tansy's already crawling back to her mental corner, head hung low, while she pulls the covers over her eyes. I don't know how long she'll be waving the white flag, but I suspect this is my moment. With or without her blessing, it's time to get out of this place.

Before we do anything else, though, I have to kiss the crease lines on WT's brow. "That's for not hurting her."

"I would never do that." He captures my hand like it's an elusive butterfly. Whiskers tickle my skin; he kisses my knuckles slowly.

"I know." I giggle for a moment—the emotion's so out of place—before drawing silent again. We have a mission—a *real* mission—and the first step to conquering it is tearing off these necklaces so I can concentrate.

Piling the rings, necklaces, then hummingbird broach on

top, I catch sight of WT smiling sadly. "You're certain you want to do this?"

"Never been more certain of anything in my life."

"But you do know she's just protecting you."

"I'm never going to grow or get any better unless I have the freedom to do as I please."

Ducking his head, WT extends a hand to me, smiling a little. "To not turning a blind eye."

I grasp his hand, lifting my chin. "To not turning a blind eye."

It only takes us about fifteen minutes to load up a pair of rifles and a dozen or so cans of gasoline. Matches, too—while keeping them a safe distance from the gas. I think about asking WT about the location of the property, but it's got to be within twenty or so minutes if it's in Wise County.

As WT peels out of the driveway, my eye catches on a familiar face. Cherry lipstick and no small amount of friendliness in her eyes—it's purple jogging suit lady. She still has her dogs, and their tails are wagging a million miles an hour—Jewel and Macy. What I would give to pet them again. Dig my fingers into their soft fur and pat their bellies.

She doesn't see us at first, but I wave at the dog owner as it occurs to me that I've adopted her *exact* same mindset—stop letting my fearful side from holding the reins. It's funny, it's like I didn't hear her before. But now it's the only thing I can hear, ricocheting through my mind.

Stop letting your fearful side from holding the reins.

We're still a package deal—there's no losing Tansy—but it's time to show her who's boss. I grip the front of my seat-belt. Come what may.

Goosebumps prickle from my arms as I settle back into my freezing seat. I knew I should have grabbed a coat before leaving the mansion. But I've just rubbed the backs of my arms when WT reaches in the back, pulls out a leather jacket, and spreads it over me.

Grateful, I pull the jacket close. "Thank you." I melt under the heavy feeling of the genuine leather and silk lining. "Will anybody know we're coming?" My fingers still feel like ice cubes, so I extend them and rub them in front of the barely blowing air vent.

WT spins a knob on the dash, sending the heater into overdrive. "There are cameras. Calhoun and Beauchamp like to keep an eye on the place. So, we'll have to disable them before—" His eyes dart to the rearview mirror where he instinctually scans all the supplies.

Honestly, I'm relieved he's prepared to go. We'll be working together. No matter what happens, I can say we're doing the right thing.

"How long has the land been in the family?" I'm not exactly sure I want to know the answer, but I listen while burrowing my arms into the sleeves' cool lining.

A sense of practiced calm exudes from WT's face. "Since about 1850." The side mirror gets another check from him, and I can't help finding comfort from how methodical he's being. "My third great grandfather bought it from the Governor. Pappi, my great-granddad dedicated it to the Klan after he and his friends strung up the Goatman in the '30s." His gaze hardens with disgust, and I can see that he has no love for this part of his family's history.

"You're standing up to them," I reassure him as I slip on the jacket the rest of the way. "Despite what happens, you— and I—are *finally* doing what's right."

WT presses his lips together, bowing his head in agreement. Still, it's become clear that he's not happy with how long it's taken him to take a stand on this, to fight. When we pass a billboard with a hen that says, "She's beauty and grace, she'll peck you in the face," my mind drifts to our own villains from the Klan.

"What are the chances that Calhoun and Beauchamp come before we finish burning down the place?" I steel my nerves against a shudder. "Will they just kill us the way they did with Francesca and Grammy?" Self-consciously, I make sure my hair's still tied back well enough with my hair tie. "Suppose we do get it done. Can't they just meet somewhere else in the county?"

WT's grip tightens as he cranks the steering wheel to a gravel road on the right. "Both Beauchamp and Calhoun are steeped in tradition. Neither likes deviating from the old ways. One big blow like destroying headquarters—while simultaneously teaming up with the feds—is not something either one will be expecting. Plus, they both keep going on and on about starting things up again with the children. Brainwashing them. The way Pa did to me."

My stomach plunges. "They're sick." An image of a dozen or so kids wearing white robes in front of a fire sparks in my mind.

Barreling down the road, WT drives us past a cluster of redbuds. Magenta blooms contrast sharply with our possible impending demise. Still, it's nice knowing we're doing what we can to fight evil—even if we are risking our lives.

I open my mouth to ask more about WT's involvement with Tim and Delilah when WT takes his foot off the accelerator and slowly turns to look me. His face muscles have relaxed and his pupils have dilated to twice their normal size. "Do you remember our first date?"

My heart reacts by pumping in overdrive. Nervous, I toy with the woven polyester of my seatbelt. "Pieces of it, but I don't think you understand the extent of what I've lost from my memories."

Sorrow crinkles WT's eyes. "I remember." His voice

comes out husky, though I remember more than I let on, since Tansy and I already talked about it.

Hula hoops hang and glide across an aerial, silk highway.

Trapeze artists catch and throw their friends, almost like none of them are real—just figments of our imagination. Dolls and toys. None of them human beings.

Cologne wafts heavily in the air while the vocals and trumpets take us to a land of enchantment and mystery.

"You gave me your jacket when Bass Hall was freezing," I admit quietly.

WT's shoulders soften slightly. His hands relax around the steering wheel as the truck slows. "You should have seen the look on your face. You"—his voice breaks off—"showed me the very definition of what happiness looks like."

A pair of longhorns graze near a trio of yuccas, and it occurs to me how innocent and naïve the cows look, without any attempt to know the difference between wrong or right.

"I should have been in the circus," WT says, only half amused, but full-on smiling. "Not that I care for an audience, but then I could have at least been honest about the times I had to lie."

"You're being honest about who you are now." Without thinking, I lean over and kiss him on the cheek.

I ... don't know what came over me. But my lips tingle like they're made of fairy dust, and my heart leaps as WT's gaze slowly drifts to mine. I'm "the bona fide imbecile" Tansy always talks about. Heat spasms and flushes up my cheeks. My head feels like I've just dived from the Empire State Building.

Suddenly nervous, I turn away, but before I know it, WT's cranking the steering wheel to the right.

At first, I think he's turning onto another dirt road, but he's pulling onto the shoulder.

His cell phone rattles from the console. Wheels kick up

dust, and we've disappeared into a fog of Indiangrass so tall, it shields us from prying eyes.

For what feels like eons, WT grips the wheel, refusing to say anything. Not that I blame him. My voice has gone by way of a Shelby Mustang.

I know what he wants to do—oh, I know what he wants to do—but I'm not there. Even if we are husband and wife.

Still, he reaches over, and I can feel myself melting into his embrace. He pulls me into his arms, and the fact that he doesn't ask for permission both terrifies me and is a relief. I want him to hold me. More than anything I've ever experienced. But how can that be right?

His hands are on my hips, clicking off my seatbelt, both luring and liberating me. I should pull back—it makes so much sense to pull back—but in this secret, hidden moment, he's too much of a temptation to fight.

Peeling out of the jacket, I nestle closer. He reaches for my sweater, and I giggle. Bat his hand away.

His eyes twinkle with amusement, but, instead, all he does is smile that boyish smile he only reserves for me. Digging his fingers into my scalp, he pulls me closer while a fireworks show rocks my every cell in my body.

I slip my hand around the crook of his neck. The other, I fasten around his shoulder, and, when he tugs me closer, we're so interconnected, it's like we're the same body.

I'm falling—to dripstones and cave pearls—and I wouldn't give up this moment for any amount of money.

Seconds stretch into minutes, and minutes could stretch into hours, but all too soon, we break apart, the both of us panting.

Seems as though my leg's gotten wrapped around the gear shift, and my sweater's twisted higher than I ever meant it to be. Straightening it—I note the fact that we've made the windows foggy.

WT's lips quirk into a smile, but, still, he doesn't say anything.

I thread my fingers behind his neck; nuzzle into the side of his face.

The timber of his voice is a poem in my ear when he whispers, so close, "I love you, Gemma Louise."

His skin is warm. Tanned, and my heart skips two happy beats. I love him. I know I love him—more than I can say.

Leaning back just enough so that I can look him in the eye, I rub my thumb along the side of his neck.

"You're *beautiful*," he says, his eyes lighting with blue-green intensity. "You grow more beautiful with each passing day."

Both of my hands, still fastened behind his neck, all but liquefy. I try scooting closer, when my pinky finger takes on a mind of its own and jabs him in the eye.

I gasp. "Sorry."

Laughing, WT uses his palm to rub his eye. "I've endured worse." As soon as he says it, though, he must assume I know he means Tansy, because he quickly takes my hands. "Not that I regret *anything*. Tansy's worth all the bumps and bruises."

While visions of Tansy hanging him from the roof hit me like a mace, I sag away from him. "How do you handle us?"

WT doesn't pressure me to come nearer. "She does keep things interesting." Tentatively, he trails a thumb down the side of my throat, never pushing too far, his touch continually feather-light.

"But we are more than you bargained for." My throat scratches as I try swallowing.

WT slips a comforting hand beneath my thigh. "What you have to know is, I'm not going anywhere. I may have made mistakes in the past, but we're *finally* doing what I born to do. Fixing the wrongs of my family."

"What if Tansy pops up again and makes things tricky?"

"Then we'll handle her." He grasps my hand again. "You're stronger than even both of us realize. Gemma, there may come a time when you doubt this, but I *need* you to know that I'm here for every facet of you—every side of Gemma Louise."

"How many sides are you expecting there to be?" I'm laughing.

Even harder, he clasps my hand. "Exactly the number you need."

I feel like he's telling me something with this, but he's probably just showing me his support, so I rise to the occasion and ask him about the one fear that's constantly plaguing both Tansy's and my mind. "What if I get too many?"

A river of empathy shines from the lines in WT's face. "Gemma, every one of us has hidden sides. You're just honest about who you are, and I love that about you."

All I can do is stare at my lap as more blood rushes to my cheeks.

WT lifts my chin. Pauses for me to look at him before saying, "I owe you all that I am. You gave me the courage to change."

A one-story house lurks like a phantom next to us on the gravel driveway. A broken cattle guard prevents us from pulling up farther, and thick brush obscures the entire place.

When WT grabs a rifle from the truck bed, he offers me a second.

"Just in case," he says. His hand lingers on my fingers, sending an electric shock through me, and I give him a small smile, almost wanting to smile wide. But this isn't the place or time.

While he gets to work unloading the truck, I drift closer and closer to the property. Knee-high buffalo grass and waist-high thistles dare me to believe this is a peaceful place, but a few paces off, the sight of a red rail fence juts through my ribs with a jackknife.

A hunter's stand hangs in one of the bur oak trees, which twists and conforms to an unseen presence, diseased. Much closer to where I stand is the remnants of an old bonfire with a few pieces of strip metal and ash—black and hunter green.

Behind the old fire, though, lies a strange three-by-six foot crate. Wooden bars. Human-sized.

Pushing back the nerves from dealing with Tansy again, I take the risk and turn to my other half. *"Last time I was here, what happened, Tansy?"*

She flops to the other side of her bed, covering her head with her arms to hide. *"Return home, G."*

But this is our time to actually stand up to the bad guys. *"I'm ready to know the truth. Ladybird ... you truly can tell me."*

When she rips off her blankets, I think she's about to get up, when she flips over and stares straight down into her mattress, insinuating she's not in the mood to listen to me.

But it doesn't take her long to roll back to her side. Flip her pillow. I know I've never tried working with her out in the open, but we *have* to do this to know how to move forward.

"Tansy, you know this is important to me."

In her room, a sparkle of light glints off a small pile of jade earrings. Amethysts. A heap of opals shine bright and metallic from another corner, as if whispering something.

Were they there before? I don't think so. Why would they appear now in her fantasy? What I do know is, it's clear that Tansy's not feeling well; she's not so much as wearing a pair of earrings. The only thing she's got on is a thin slip, making her look even more thin and vulnerable this night. I want to hold her. Hug her—not just because the weather's dipped back down to the thirties, but because we've gone through *so* much together. I don't know who I would be anymore without Tansy.

Wishing I knew how to get her attention, I tentatively straighten WT's coat. Zip it to my chin, biding my time.

After what feels like hours, Tansy throws out her arms and croons, *"Ladybird, ladybird, fly away home! Your house is on fire, your children shall burn!"*

Not exactly what I was hoping, but it's a start. "*I know this is difficult, Tansy, but, look, we're having a conversation right now, and we're not even inside!*"

Tansy plugs her ears, sticking out her tongue while WT clicks off a camera at the top corner of the house. I have to assume that he's the last thing Jesse and Calhoun saw ... or will see. *Please,* don't let them be watching the footage. We need time.

Grabbing the first of his jugs, WT douses the house and surrounding brush. He grabs another. Goes to work on a three-foot-high stump surrounded by a healthy batch of milkweed.

"*You don't care about the avalanche!*" Tansy's hair flies with static as she springs up from her bed, pouting.

At least she's engaging me in conversation, so I pause to lean the rifle against the fence, trying to think. "*Of course I care. But Tansy ... the Klan kills people. We have to expose this evil— for Francesca. And Grammy.*"

Once again, Tansy falls to her bed, thrashing her sheets. Kicking off her blanket, she induces another static whirlwind before sitting up and throwing her hands toward her canopy. "*You are goin' to regret this, G!*"

It's possible. I suppose I very much might regret poking the bear that is my subconscious mind. But Calhoun and Jesse could arrive at any second, and I can't risk *not* remembering.

While I was able to pry loose the other memories by visiting the places where they happened, I can *feel* this one, just itching to get out, to break free. But for whatever reason, I can't quite see it yet. And Tansy's holding onto it like her most treasured piece of jewelry.

No ... that's not what's going on. This is something else entirely. She's sitting on the center of her bed, holding fast to the final piece of truth ... not for herself ... but to protect me.

Shoulders sagging in defeat, she suddenly rolls off her bed, slip skewing to the side. *"You'll let me keep the house. Swear you won't go sellin' it out from under me."* But even as she says this, I'm not so sure that's what's been stopping her all this time.

She rips off the bedsheets.

The fleur-de-lis print glides through the air before kissing the ground and vanishing from sight.

Leaning down, she smacks her now-barren mattress. *"And you'll start bringin' home some old plasters n' gemstones for my art projects—whatsoever I like."*

Not exactly sure where I'll come up with said supplies, I nod, grateful that she's proving her ability to compromise.

Perching on the edge of her bed, she holds out our arms like she's about to summon the dead. *"Ladybird, ladybird, fly away home! Your house is on fire, your children shall burn!"* And face-dives into the mattress with more focus than I've seen her give anything.

Cotton meets teeth. I don't know how, but I feel like I'm right there with her as we get a nose-full of springs. It's possible that her only plan is for us both to asphyxiate to death when her nursery rhyme bleeds into something else— something with hoots and catcalls, and we spiral into the black forest of another time.

*L*ow, Gregorian-like chants slither across the grounds, twisting and feeding.

Mist. I'm surrounded by an ocean of mist. Brush so thick there's bound to be a copperhead or two in those weeds.

I seem to be currently on a gravel road, yes, but, no—a driveway. Just before a broken cattle guard are a row of vehicles.

WT's navy truck.

And Calhoun's fancy, white Mercedes.

A pair of four-wheelers with mud splattered on the tires front Jesse Beauchamp's police truck of black and white. What I don't get is why they're here, in the middle of nowhere, and out so late.

A burgundy truck with its front fender smashed in hunches on the edge of the road ahead of my Bimmer, which is safely tucked behind a pair of elm trees. About ten meters past the fence lies a bonfire that stretches its orange-hued fist to the smoky sky. No one tends the fire. I'm grateful for it. Don't need anyone knowing I've arrived.

Hoisting myself over the fence, I wade through the brush, my blouse catching on a honey locust's thorns. It doesn't take me long to tug myself free. My gaze lands on something wooden and unnatural ...

the most peculiar-looking tree—almost like a totem pole, with horizontal slats crossing the thick trunk and base.

While the bonfire crackles, I drift further and further into the property. A pack of dogs snarl from somewhere behind the house, and maybe that's why WT's come? To help the dogs? About five minutes ago, I followed him over, though I had to hang back half a mile or so for him not to spot me. Though I'm not in the habit of following my husband, he's been acting strange. More phone calls than usual. Fitful sleep. When he slipped out shortly after midnight, I knew I had to follow him, see if I could figure out what was happening.

But if this is an oil field he's been eyeing, he should be checking it out during the day.

When spurs jingle across the yard, I'm looking over to a lean man in a cowboy hat and Wranglers. Dwayne. He seems to be leading a muscular, darker-skinned man toward the totem pole tree ...

Pulling out a rope, Dwayne turns to the muscular man—like he means to tie him to the tree. But he can't really be doing that. The man obediently leans against the tree—until he swings a meaty fist at Dwayne.

I can help him—I'll help the man being tied!—when a longer-haired, drug-dealer-looking type—Olly—comes scrambling out of the bushes like a skunk on a chicken feast.

Olly catches the man by the neck with a long, hooked cane, and my heart's about to explode in my chest when his captive lets out a guttural scream.

Dwayne pulls out a whip, and he and Olly have never looked more demonic or sickly in the moonlight. This isn't real. None of this can be real. This is all a bad dream.

Their captive wails while a little girl screeches across the yard. "DADDY!"

But the little girl isn't near them—she's by me. And my heart jolts to my heart as I turn. She's in the crate, only a few paces away from me.

Lowering his whip, Dwayne scoops up a fistful of dirt and stuffs it between the man's teeth.

"Shut yer trap," he growls. "Don't wanna scare your little girl, right?"

His captive whimpers. Clearly tries to decide whether he should give up the fight, while the little girl wails again, "DADDY!"

I need my phone. I'll call the police.

But Jesse's here. Why is he here? Please tell me he's not involved in this some way.

Spinning, I head for the girl—thorns of the honey locust scrape my cheeks—while the little girl whimpers, so scared, from the crate just to my right.

I'm just lifting my hand to free her—somehow figure out how to unlock the crate—when a slobbery nose brushes along my hand and I'm reeling.

Long, droopy ears. Midnight fur marks off a seething face. Patches of skin hang from the poor bloodhound's side, and it's clear she's been abused; giant welts slice across her malnourished body.

Who *would do this?*

Where *is WT?*

When the bloodhound seizes my ankle, a shrill whistle rings through the trees. My breathing hitches as my ankle's freed. The bloodhound clambers back the way it came.

As the wind picks up, a new, unnatural caw cackles through the trees. I think it should be a Chupacabra for the unearthly noise it's making—but no. That's the sound of the devil at work as they hoot and caw, Olly and Dwayne.

"Gemma."

My heart lurches to my throat as I turn to place the hushed male's voice.

It's my husband, kneeling next to me in the scraggly weeds. He's wearing the antique leather Oxfords we bought last month. The same green blazer I saw him slip on this morning.

"*What are you doing here?*" His hands are on my shoulders as he gives me a gentle shake. His eyes have never been more wild or wide.

I think I'm finally going to get him to talk to me, when a dozen or so men come tearing out of the house, carrying white blankets, rifles, and long, rusted machetes.

But those don't look like blankets.

What am I seeing?

The group clears a path—through the brush, coming directly toward me. My heart hammers in my chest as my conscience twinges, warning me to hide.

"*Why are you here?*" I turn to my husband while another wail tears from the captive at the tree. "Are you turning them in? Working with Jesse?"

Three more men march much closer to us as machetes slice through the thistles' stems, purple heads beheading. At the front of the pack is Doctor Zebulun Calhoun. I think I may have had an appointment with him before ... it's hard to say.

With that blanket—or towel—slung casually over his shoulder, Calhoun looks about as troubled as if he were strolling on the beach.

Sticking his hands in his pockets, he says, "Well, boys, looks like our chosen leader forgot to mention he was bringing a dinner date."

On impulse, WT's fingers slacken around my waist. He shoulders himself between us. Seems to take great pains in mimicking Calhoun's casual speech. "Don't mind her, Zeb." My usually calm husband's shoulders are tensing. "Gemma, here, was just brushing up on some Hardin family history."

More wails break out from the captive. How can everyone just stand around when he's being tortured in plain sight? The girl's screams echo her father's, while a man with an enormous potbelly blocks my way.

Calhoun tilts his head. "You and I both know, William, it's against the bylaws to bring along your wife. Even if she is *Hardin royalty.*"

Easing me even further behind him, WT squares his shoulders.
"This is my land."

"Be that as it may"—*Calhoun reverently pulls his towel, which*
really a robe from off his shoulder like he's an ordained priest—*"Ms.*
Hardin looks ill-prepared to handle our little role play."

WT lunges at Calhoun, and I open my mouth to scream. Tansy
yanks me out of the memory.

Cotton from her mattress litters the floor in our head,
and several springs lay twisted and gnarled, never to be used
again.

"There," Tansy says breathing heavily. *"There is nothin' else*
you need to see."

But I have to go back. I have to go back!

The sight of Delilah's pink scrunchy flashes again in my
mind. I *have* to see if Tim and Delilah were set free.

Sensing Tansy's refusal to help me, I try to elbow my way
past her. I'll go to WT.

But Tansy groans. *"You n' I both know that there's no way*
Calhoun would have let Delilah and her daddy survive!"

All I know is, a mountain of phlegm fills my throat. I have
to know what happened, no matter if she's warning me.

Gas and other chemicals clog the air. A few paces off,
WT's got three separate fires going. Flames lick the newly
budded foliage, but if everything burns, I may never recover
my memory.

Sensing my panic, Tansy jabs a pointed fingernail in the
mattress. *"Can't see it, won't let you see it. Nope, nope, nopety!"*
Cotton spills around her like wasted ice on a snow cone
machine.

I try wrenching open her hand—maybe she's stuffed the
truth in that stuffing—when Tansy seizes one of the canopy
curtains, and tackles me with it, of all things.

I go down for maybe five seconds.

But she has to see she has to stop keeping things from me.

Knowing my best bet is with my husband, I tear off for WT. He's just past a mound of prickly pears, disassembling three large dog crates.

When I reach him, I seize his arm. "What happened?" I'm about to strangle his forearm. "Tell. Me."

The last thing I expect is to see tears shining in WT's eyes. He pauses like he's about to talk, when, all at once, he sets his jaw and marches directly toward the totem pole tree.

I scamper after him.

This is it.

I can feel it in my gut. He's going to tell me.

Stopping just short of the tree, WT lifts his boot just high enough to nudge Delilah's crate. "I wasn't sure how much Tansy would let you remember. You recall who was inside?"

I nod, the ever-widening pit in my stomach revolving.

"What about after that?"

All I can do is shake my head. I'd better not tell him where Tansy stopped the memory or he might assume I know more than I do.

Stooping for a red gas can, WT takes an eternity trudging even closer to the totem pole tree. Tilts the gas can downward, dumping the can's entire fuel at the tree's base.

Striking a match, WT flatly says, "I couldn't free them." I flinch as he lights up the entire edifice.

Flames lick wood; red-hot vultures, ravenous. Hungry.

"Nothing I said ..." WT stares at the dirt, eyes glazed over, unseeing. "Nothing I said made a difference. Calhoun's intoxication with power—his sick ideals ..." He hurls the gas at the fence. "I shot one of his men, then Tim—he started to get away, but the dogs—" He reaches up and wipes his nose with the back of his sleeve. "I tried getting them out, I swear to you, I did. Even tried drugging them before the others came. But Calhoun—" WT's voice breaks off. "He caught me."

Lifting a rock, WT hurls it at the back of the property,

reminding me of how he acted when we found Grammy. "Beauchamp trains the dogs to chase anyone"—he chokes back a sob—"who tries to escape."

I don't know if I can talk. "And Delilah?"

His face morphs into something unreadable. "With her, I was smarter. Told Calhoun he could have ten million. To set her free."

Despite the holes widening in my heart, I can feel the twinge of hope fighting to take hold of something. So ... she got away?

But from the way WT's standing, so stiff and holding his elbows so closely to his body, I can tell that there's something else he's not telling me.

Pacing to a dead, twisted tree, WT pounds his fist into the trunk. "I tried to make them stop, but they were obsessed with the old ways."

I'm still not sure what he means. Obsessed, how?

From the corner of my mind, Tansy casually places herself between her torn-apart mattress and me. She thinks she's being clever—coy—but she's not big enough to actually shield me from anything. Just to her left, lies a wooden box—a toy box—amidst the wreckage of the cotton and springs.

The box just sits there on the ground, right below where her mattress used to be, and it must house all the answers.

All the answers.

I dive for the truth while Tansy screeches—a bald eagle protecting her nest of eggs.

a painted ballerina adorns the top of the box, pink tutu stretching out like a tent, a full foot wide. While the pine prism boasts a ton of nicks and cracks, every fiber in my gut says I *have* to see inside.

Seizing me by the ankle, Tansy begs, *"Don't do it, G!"*

But it doesn't take me long to grip the smooth lid's edge. When I try to heave it open, though, it doesn't move or budge.

"You asked me to protect you!" Tansy pleads. *"You never wanted to see this. You* have *to believe me."*

Jiggling my foot, I try to shake her loose, when, like a demented Chihuahua, she cries out before sinking her teeth into my leg.

"TANSY!" With my other foot, I try to kick her off. Swiftly kick her three times. Guilt claws at me for doing it, but I *have* to keep going. Anything to see what's inside.

Tansy whimpers uncontrollably while I fiddle with the lock—a single, metallic padlock with a hint of rust on the side. I've just clicked it open when it disintegrates into dust.

I seize the lid. Flex my muscles to lift it high to find a little girl ... a little girl. And a squirrel and magpie.

Neither of the animals move—lifeless. Just like they were on the porch that day.

The little girl's hair's separated in twin, tight ponies, and my chest tightens as I track her sad, familiar eyes.

On her legs are the cutest pair of rainbow leggings. Pink and tan cowgirl boots wrap around her feet, and the baby unicorn on her shirt dashes under a rainbow, shaking its mane.

There's a blue and white handkerchief wrapped around the little girl's wrist, which sparks another memory. I know where I've seen that—tied by Grammy.

When the little girl stands, I find that my five-year-old self has a startling spray of freckles on her nose and under her eyes. A scab marks her left eyebrow—from slipping and falling after trying to catch a bunny.

"Close the lid," Tansy begs while the girl, just like the lock, dissipates.

"No!" I try grasping for her, but it's like hugging sand that's been blown out to the sea.

Tansy grabs the back of my sweater. Tries dragging me back. But I have to shake her off—haven't come this far to give up already.

Stepping inside the box, I force Young Gemma Louise to become me. It's a risk. I know it's a risk, but I have to do it while the wood's smooth and nicked. Not altogether sanitary.

I think maybe the girl will come out to greet me, when my spine suddenly contorts and pops, and I'm reminding myself of Smeagol in *Lord of the Rings*.

I know it's all in my head—it's all in my head!—but I can't help rolling with the motion. In my imagination, I shrink in size. It's now, but it's not. It's last year. Last year when I first arrived on Klan property.

My fingers shrivel; my tongue forgets all the fancy words I picked up while reading.

And the toy box vanishes. I'm on the ground *and the dirt and grass are very, very pokey.*

I don't know where they are, but I can sense them. The grownups ... they are watching.

I wipe the peanut butter from my hands. Gotta wipe it from my hands. Grownups don't like me being sticky. And oooh! A bonfire! A big, blowy, blowy bonfire with smoke and—and—maybe we'll be eating s'mores later once I find Grammy!

Tall man is standing way too close to me. He look like Edgar 'cept he's got no scratchy hair on the bottom of his face. He puffy-puffs on a cigar. The smoke has me coughing.

"Mizz Hardin," Tall Man say. The fatty cigar sticks like a popsicle between his teeth.

I don't know a Mizz Hardin, but he's a lookin' at me, so I swishy-swash across the grass. Can't give him lip, or Edgar—he will smack Grammy. He do it yesterday. He say, "If ya tell yer meemaw what happened, I will KILL her, do ya HEAR ME?" He say that. He say that right after he bend my wrist back and we bury chopped man's body.

Now Tall Man nods at a big, BIG muscly man who's tied to a broked telephone pole tree. Tied man looks like he need a hug, cuz his lip is soooo puffy.

"Hang him," Tall Man say. He sound like Edgar, but I will certainly do no such thing. Tied man needs to be taken to a hospital. Needs shurgery.

Tall Man hands me a rope. It's heavier than a veloshiraptor. A tank! And he's a lookin' at me. So I take it. I take it. It's awfully scratchy but I have to do it, I have to do it or Edgar, he will smack Grammy.

Tall Man give my head a patty-pat, which makes me feel silly. "You'll be a good girl, won't you, Gemma Louise?" He nods at tied

*man, and ohhhh, he wants me to put the rope on tied man's neck, but I
don't wanna do it. I don't wanna hurt nobody.*

*"You must do this if you are to save the child's life," Tall Man say.
He nods at a pretty, sad girl I don't wanna see cry. Her hands have so
much dirt and her face is sooo splotchy.*

*But Tall Man, he won't let us go till I loop tied man's head with—
with jewelry.*

After I put it on, I'll take it off.

Take it off ...

Raising the choker, I close my eyes.

Gotta save the little girl.

Gotta save Grammy.

WT yanks my arm so hard, every single person in my
vision spills to the wind, becoming fairy dust the trees. What
exactly is WT trying to do? Force me to *forget* what I did?
Forget how I reverted to my five-year-old self, Young Gemma
Louise?

"Gemma." WT's voice has never sounded so terrified.

But my arms have become limp as WT shakes me. He
takes me by the shoulders to try to see into my eyes, but I
shake him off. Bite my lip, because blood's the only thing I
should be tasting.

I'm a *killer*.

There's blood on my hands. I took a life.

Without really thinking about it, my body shifts taller. I
stand broader as I come to terms with what I did that day.

"Gemma," WT pleads. He reaches for my hand. "Please
talk to me."

All I can do is take a step back as he attempts to cup
either side of my cheeks.

I don't know how to respond. Don't know how to say it.
How to say it? My mouth—the muscles have stopped
working.

I swallow back the bile. "You—*knew* ..." I lean over to dry heave. "You knew I hung Ti—" I take a breath. "Delilah's daddy."

WT takes a shaky step forward as I slug him with a fist. "All along, you *knew* it was me." I bite my lip, wanting nothing more than to bleed.

I lifted the rope.

Killed a man who *didn't deserve* to die. He was a good man who was raising a little girl all alone. Francesca was going to find them, and they were going to be reunited as a family.

I'm the killer.

All along. To think I thought it was Tansy.

Tansy's teetering on the edge of her bed, wringing her hands, clearly at a loss as to what to say.

While WT foolishly tries to pull me closer, I snarl, "I DIDN'T ASK YOU TO LIE!"

He flinches while Tansy shrinks back.

"*Both* of you!" I stammer. "All this time ..."

I don't care if they feel bad. They should feel great pain. They *knew*. And they kept the truth of what happened and locked it away from me.

Knocking her back into the bedpost, Tansy says, *"I did it for you! What you just remembered could prove your destruction, G."*

But all I can do is pound and pound away at what I've just seen. The criminal act. So much hate. The *disgusting* truth that I acted on the Klan's orders.

And the avalanche already came.

Digging into his jeans pocket, WT pulls out a photograph of a little girl with a bright pink scrunchy. Delilah looks just like her mommy. Same front gap in her teeth.

Pointing repeatedly at the photograph, WT says, "You *saved* her." He crinkles the photograph, knuckles turning white. "They weren't going to let her go, but *you* agreed to—" he lowers the picture, obviously not wanting to say what I did to Tim. "Because of you, she survived!"

All I can do is stare at my hands. At the filth. My crime. They tingle from the touch—they know all too well that I lifted a rope to take a decent person's life.

WT's hair sticks out in every direction while he shakes the photograph in front of my face. "She lives in Houston with her aunt, see?"

But my fingernails ... they still remember the scratchy fibers of the rope. My palms itch from the coarse strings. Eyes won't forget, won't stop burning.

I saw Calhoun and believed it to be Edgar, and they both forced me do unspeakable, heinous things.

My breath ... I'm not breathing. I grapple with WT's coat. Rip it off. Tear at my sweater. Can't. Breathe.

"Gemma"—WT digs his hands into his hair—"you *have* to see that Calhoun didn't give you a choice. You were *coerced*!" Hesitantly, he holds out his hand. He wants to touch me, but I'm not worthy of being touched.

"He enjoys messing with your head." WT's eyes shift back and forth as he searches my face, trying to explain things to me.

But I'm tired of excuses.

I took a life.

Lifting a fist toward the sky, he shouts, "He's a *psychopath*, babe!"

But he doesn't truly understand what I did. I committed the worst of the worst, an unpardonable hate crime. I deserve to be locked up. Abandoned forever.

Erased.

Beneath my skin, I can still feel her—Young Gemma Louise. She wants to regain consciousness and part of me wants to let her. Why not let her? I've already done the unthinkable anyway.

"*G ...*" In the secrecy of our room, Tansy holds out her

hands for me. *"I'm sorry I lied. But I did it to protect you. I'm your bodyguard, my sweet."*

But now I know the answer. A few paces off, there's a lone jug of gasoline. And like a magnet, it pulls me. I stride over, and, really, it's light as a watering can—all innocent-like, sitting amongst the primrose and milkweed.

I lift the can. Mind goes blissfully blank.

The red handle gives me the water of a shower as bitter liquid washes down my teeth.

I'm just reaching out my hand—gotta connect with the still-burning hanging tree—when WT wails, "NO, GEMMA! STOP, PLEASE!"

I turn to smile and say I love you. Time to say goodbye.

BOOM!

A gunshot tears across the property, and before I know it, I'm scanning the yard, searching for where the bullet lodged in one of the nearby trees.

I slap my chest. My damp chest.

Seems whoever made the shot didn't hit me.

And I didn't touch the fire. That's a relief. But the boom ... why the boom?

WT groans as he stumbles into Delilah's crate.

53

I rush to my husband, my hand connecting with something wet on his chest. Blood. No ... it has to be Tansy's red paint, while smoke and ash barely conceal three stalactite figures lurking in the driveway.

WT grabs my arm, but he's still on the ground, suddenly oh so weak. "Put her back." His gorgeous eyes are so blood-shot this has to be a bad dream.

Who does he want me to put back?

Her. Young Gemma Louise.

When WT starts to say something else, he chokes on his own blood, and no. No—this isn't happening.

"You're *strong*." More blood gurgles in his mouth. "Gemma, you *know* you have to fight."

But all I can see is the fiery inferno of Satan's flames. The adversary telling me to give up and die. He says that *I'm no good, no good* ... and I'm dangling in his clutches. I really was ready to die.

Sweat pours down sweet husband's face. So many foul chemicals worm their way across the grounds, pillaging the twisted, diseased trees.

But I can't let him go. Won't let him go. "Let's get you to the truck." I pull on his arm, but it's like tugging on another stalactite. "You'll be fine!"

Tears smear the corners of WT's eyes. He shoots me another adoring look, sending me to *the clock on the mantel. It doesn't tick, so he plucks it up while introducing me, for the very first time, to his library.*

I'm amazed by how many books there are. Running my fingers over the leather spines, I pretend not to be aware that he's looking at me.

The wind rustles the curtains while he sneaks up behind me. Wraps me in his arms. "This is my safe haven," he says. "You are welcome here anytime you like."

Coughing, WT sprays his shirt with another dose of Tansy's red paint.

"In my pocket," he says, but I can't look away from his gaze for even a moment. I need to freeze time.

When WT's gaze trails to where my hand's resting uselessly on his thigh, I know this is important. So I reach for the narrow pocket in his jeans.

Digging into the fabric, I suck in a breath as my fingers connect with something small, round, with a princess-cut diamond on top—my wedding ring.

WT's breaths come in shorts spurts. He shudders, heaving himself up. "I was going to give it back when you were ready."

Tears won't stop flooding my eyes.

WT takes my hand, and I know this is it. This is really it. "Tell them it's *your* turn to keep them safe."

His head lolls back, and NO. He's not allowed to die.

"Oooh, that's it!" Tansy cheerily claps her hands while WT lies, lifeless, against the crate. *"I was goin' to say it, but it really is time for you to be the queen of the clan! Er, 'clan,'"* Tansy sputters, truly embarrassed. *"Always to be spelled with a 'c.'"*

But I can't think—do—anything.

I've lost him. I've really lost him when I was just beginning to see who he was to me.

We talked about children.

He never really cared if our first was a girl or a boy.

And now he's gone—never again to go to Palo Duro, or eat breakfast in the garden with me.

I wrap my arms around my husband's chest while the fire around us grows, sadistic and hungry. If we don't get up soon, Tansy and I will be burned alive.

Shooting me a sorrowful look, Tansy eventually says, *"Ready to bury her, my sweet?"*

I would give anything not to deal with our other alter right now—Young Gemma Louise. But there's still at least three guys out there who want us dead. And I'm in the mood to see somebody pay.

54

*P*roblem is, Young Gemma Louise doesn't want to go away.

Lights flicker—actual lightbulbs burst—from every single corner of Tansy's and my mind.

The toy box appears—flickers in the back left corner.

The right.

It's going in and out of focus and I'm worried if we don't strap her down now, she's going to reemerge even stronger next time.

The child mutters something from her back corner while another gunshot booms across the yard.

"What is she saying?" I steel my nerve while I ask Tansy.

"She's searching for chopped man's body ..." Tansy eyes a pile of bracelets peeking out from under her canopied bed. *"It's why she comes out. Remember the time you got lost in Boyd?"*

"Before all of this?"

Tansy nods.

"Yeah, Calhoun said he helped me ..."

"Stuck his fat nose in where it didn't belong, he did. The goon poked and prodded like we were a science experiment! Gemma, he

was truly fascinated by Young Gemma Louise. That was the first time she took over—since Tim's hanging." Glancing back at the glowing embers of the hanging tree's fire, she adds, *"The second time, of course, was with the squirrel n' magpie. Fact is, Calhoun and the others are waitin' for us, and we still have to tuck ol' Young Gemma Louise away!"*

"Do you know where the Klan buries their bodies?"

Tansy shakes her head, hair staticky. *"I imagine those threads will unravel the minute the police start pullin' the string."*

"Okay"—I try to find my gumption, but it isn't exactly easy. All I have left is a giant hole in my chest ever since WT …

But, any second, Calhoun or the others will shoot me. I know I have to put Young Gemma Louise back, but I don't see how I can tackle not being shot while wrangling yet another alter in my mind. Not wanting to admit I can't do it alone, yet also seeing there's a reason why I created my other half, I turn to Tansy.

"I need you to put her away."

We veer around a burning stump, a piece of scrap metal that's seen much better days.

"I know she wants answers, but we don't have them yet. Maybe you can tell her that we'll know the location of chopped man and the others once they're uncovered by the FBI."

Tansy wrings her hands. *"You don't happen to know how to lock her up? She's a tad bit squirrely."*

I survey the gigantic pile of necklaces that seem to be growing on Tansy's side of our mind.

"Bury her."

Tansy's eyes widen before she sets the pile of jewelry in her sights. *"Oooh! I did that sorta thing to you all the time."*

"We'll talk about that later, but, for now, you are my ladybird—built to sound the alarm when the bad guys are coming."

Tansy stares at me, stunned. *"At long last, you finally remember the nursery rhyme!"*

"Took me a while. I forgot it was from one of the tours we gave in D.C."

I smile, until it sinks in that Tansy's more interested in thinking about nursery rhymes than losing WT. But maybe that's good thing; she can rationally perform her newfound mission. And I can focus on not being shot while holding onto WT's last gift—my wedding ring.

Smoke flares over the grass; I guess it's been a while now that I've been coughing. And now the Klan's patch of land has become nothing but a scratched-out, yellow Crayola painting. Too many overgrown candles threaten to swallow me whole. Ash mingles with singed bark. The entire land smells of campfire, and I won't feel the need to go camping for a very long time.

Wildfire tugs beads of sweat from every inch of my body. When I duck beneath a tree branch, it crashes to the ground. Fumes wash across everything.

Shuddery breaths ripple from my chest, when, all at once, the smoke clears, and *right there* are Calhoun, Dwayne, and Jesse.

They're still standing in the driveway. I'll reach them in about twenty feet.

While Calhoun raises his rifle to shoot me, I have to wonder if he felt any remorse about shooting WT. Or has his conscience been squashed altogether? Actually enjoys forcing innocents to get their hands dirty.

As my chest expands, Tansy peeks out from a curtain she's pinned up between her and my side of our mind. Her hair's a little singed and a fair amount of soot blackens her eyes, but her smile's ginormous.

"I did it!" she says. *"It may have taken a Titanic-amount of broaches n' rings, but I put her back. I knew I could do it, G!"*

My smile is genuine. *"Way to go, Tansy."*

But right when I expect her to barrage me with the play-by-play, she lifts her arm and points at a spot through the smoke. *"Look, look, lookety!"*

Black clothes, black helmets, big guns ...

I think I might be imaging things, but SWAT team officers are stationed behind one of the few unburned oak trees. One's training a submachine gun on Calhoun—while Calhoun's stationed himself between Dwayne and Jesse.

From their smug expressions, though, it looks like none of them have any idea their fates are about to change.

Suddenly stiff, I climb over the fence. Briefly wish I could turn the rifle on Calhoun for all he's done to me.

But I can't think about my own vendetta.

This isn't about a vendetta.

I have to play this right.

Tansy and I step over a hollowed-out log; we spot yet another dark-clothed officer—hiding behind one of the bur oaks at the corner of the property.

Three more officers are stationed on the other side of WT's truck.

Another's hunkered low behind Calhoun's Mercedes.

I'm just trying not to smile while Calhoun cocks his rifle, testing me. "Still want to run off with her when she helped her scum husband burn Klan property, Dwayne?"

Dwayne's fat bottom lip puckers. Reaching over, he yanks the rifle straight out of Calhoun's hands. "Don't you *dare* shoot my future wife!"

Tansy bristles, and I have to call out my other half. *"How come you never strung Dwayne up like you did to WT?"*

She crosses her arms from her bed, full-on pouting. *"'Cause of my ridiculous feelin's. I was gonna give him what he had comin', but I never found the right method, right time ..."*

"So you're over him?"

"Oh, you have no idea."

Calhoun and Dwayne grapple over the gun—Calhoun's just getting it back—when the SWAT team officer from behind the bur oak yells, "Weapons on the ground, hands in the air!"

All three men go still, eyes stretched unusually wide.

Calhoun's shoulders stiffen, and it's clear he's still planning on using the gun on somebody, so the officer yells again.

"Gun. Down. NOW!"

Arms impossibly stiff, Calhoun raises his gun—like he's going to use it on me—when the officer behind WT's truck picks him off like we're playing airsoft. But every single one of those guns is as real as Jim Bowie's hunting knife.

Calhoun hits the ground, eyes blank. Dwayne and Jesse pause for maybe two seconds, when Dwayne scrambles for the gun and flies backward the minute a string of gunshots hit him in the chest—right where his heart is supposed to be.

Tansy gives the motherlode of all gasps but quickly recovers herself. *"Couldn't imagine a more rightful ending."*

Now there's only one Klan leader left. Jesse. Question is, how's he going to react to being surrounded today?

Putting his hands in the air, he looks at me, eyes as cool as ice.

Two police officers are already putting him in handcuffs and dragging him away.

When an officer with a crewcut and a face like a squirrel tentatively stalks toward me, the world suddenly goes still. It's Agent Spence. And he wants to talk to me.

"Ma'am?" he calls out to me. While I'm finally out of the fire's clutches, I'm half-tempted to turn around and join WT.

"Ma'am," he repeats. "Ms. Hardin. Are you all right?" Thin arms, thin hair. Agent Spence is certainly on the gangly side.

I'm tempted—*oh*, I'm tempted to tell him that yes, everything is just fine. Tansy and I could return home. Squabble over what to wear while she chooses the subject for her next macabre painting.

But that wouldn't be fair.

Not to everyone else.

Taking a deep breath, I stick my hands in the air.

"I need to turn myself in," I say.

EPILOGUE

There's something oddly invigorating about running with Tansy. She knows who I am. Knows the decisions we've had to make. She's even contented herself with wearing a small pair of hoop earrings while we endure our time in Millwood—the mental health facility the judge chose for Tansy and me.

We took a plea deal. I get to stay here in exchange for everything I know about the Klan in Wise County. My lawyer says I may even be able to get out soon. If I keep up with my good behavior. We'll see.

Sure, settling in at Millwood has been a little bit tricky, but now that I have my daily runs, it's getting easier to manage my frustrations. I get thirty minutes on this squeaky treadmill every morning.

Tansy's been a trooper, though she misses the mansion and Jerusha and Hawkins. Luckily, Natalie's volunteered to take care of the cats. She takes care of our yard, too, though Tansy insists that the less work, Natalie does, the better—in the name of keeping the tourists away.

Inside this weight room, the fogged-up window has a

great view of a huge rose bush outside. Sometimes I like to pretend WT's standing out there—pruning the roses to keep an eye on me. Honestly, I dream about him all the time. We're usually in Palo Duro or dancing outside on the Fourth of July. I've even started reading some of his favorite books —*1984* and *Band of Brothers*. *Dracula*, too, though Tansy claims Mina's a sissy.

Oh, that's why the treadmill squeaks—the belt's on crooked—not to mention the bashed-in electronic display. At least Big Henry, the orderly posted outside the door, never gives me any trouble. As long as I keep Tansy's and my conversations inside our mind.

In Group, I've learned that I still carry around a lot of guilt for the people who've died. My therapist likes to remind me that I was coerced—Calhoun made me take Tim's life. But sometimes I'd give anything to know that I'd fought back. Stopped myself from becoming Young Gemma Louise in some way.

Of course, I never would have needed to form any alters if Edgar hadn't exposed me to "chopped man" in the first place. And I never would have split from Tansy even further if Calhoun wasn't consumed with "resurrecting the old ways."

But it did happen. And I've come to terms with the fact that even though things aren't exactly ideal right now, God's justice is *always* just—even if it means I have to wait to see some of that justice in the next life.

Thankfully, WT set up his will to not only take care of me but Delilah, who's also undergoing intense therapy. He also willed a huge portion of his fortune to helping orphaned kids. Another chunk to the NAACP.

When my treadmill's timer goes off, I know my run's complete. Feeling a smidge of regret, I slow my speed.

Big Henry, in his gray scrubs and pockmarked face, isn't much of a talker, but he also never freaks out when I pull my hair into a pony. Technically, hair ties aren't allowed here—but he's also seen the hair fiascos I end up with after tossing and turning all night with Tansy.

Holding out his hand, Big Henry doesn't say a word when I hand over my hair tie before we're spotted by the other orderlies.

Our rubber-soled, Velcro shoes scuffle along the tile almost peacefully. And the plain, cream walls are a minimalist's interior design dream. I used to get breakfast in bed—until I started exercising.

The halogen lights do tend to flicker, but that just adds to the ambiance of the place.

After we pass the file room, and three more doors, Big Henry stations himself outside my room with this faux tough look on his face.

Inside my room, the utilitarian bed is firm as ever with its unforgiving, plywood frame. More cream walls form the backdrop, and, really, I don't mind it. Though the lack of color around here makes Tansy go absolutely batty.

"They don't even have pastels," she whines. *"Hurry on up and take your meds. I'm soooo ready to hibernate."*

Dutifully, I stride over to the desk where my breakfast awaits. The ham here may have absolutely no flavor, and the eggs may taste a bit plasticky, but I'm just tickled to eat anything besides split pea soup or lemon chamomile tea.

It's the red and blue envelope at the back of the breakfast tray, though, that gives me pause. Ooh, what's this? A letter from Natalie.

Snatching up the note, I rip the thin paper open. Natalie and I have been corresponding for ages—from the moment I got put away. Turns out WT was right—she just needed to figure out how to stand up to the Klan and Jesse.

"Signed, sealed, and delivered," Natalie's jaunty handwriting says.

Looks like she finally did it—found her grit and divorced Jesse.

Not only has Natalie been excited about shedding the Beauchamp name, but she's also been working tirelessly with the FBI. After digging through Jesse's old papers, she was able to ascertain the locations of both tied man and chopped man's bodies. Francesca's, too. I don't even know how to feel about it—all of them, including a few others, dating back to before the '90s—were all at Edgar's place.

It makes me feel ill, thinking about Grammy.

I believe Natalie when she says she didn't know the Klan was killing people. She says that was also the same case with Grammy—though Grammy had her suspicions. But neither one of them ever found any proof, so they didn't go to the police.

Jesse supposedly confessed to killing both Francesca and Grammy. What I can't figure out is if he actually did it, or if he *wanted* to appear guilty as a way to put himself at the top of the Klan hierarchy. I'm guessing he had help, namely from Dwayne. Or, who knows, maybe Olly. All I know is, Jesse's been put away for life.

Olly ran for Mexico the moment he heard about the feds taking Jesse into custody. Word is, he was sipping on a margarita when the feds pulled up, oblivious to the fact that he hadn't actually cross the border. Trial date pending.

As for the other Klan members—the ones with the four-wheelers and Potbelly—a few ran to Arkansas. One got pulled over for a DUI.

When all's said and done, I do have to be grateful that I never willingly embraced the Klan's ways. If they were inducting children, Edgar could have easily inducted me. I suppose he did, off the books, by forcing me to help him bury "chopped man's" body. But I'm trying to make amends in that area, too. I've learned Edgar's victim's name's actually Omer, and I'm slowly putting the pieces together to get in touch with his family.

Settling my gaze on the paper cup with my small red pill inside, I linger a bit longer—not exactly ready for Tansy to go away for the day.

"Are you sure you don't want to recite any new nursery rhymes?"

Tansy pats her latest rendition of a mattress—a waterbed with satin lavender sheets. It's not a bed I would have ever picked out, but she insists that Young Gemma Louise is much less likely to break through if there's a hint of water blocking the way.

Not sure what that's about, but I'm glad Tansy takes her status as "ladybird" seriously.

Stretching her arms out with a yawn, Tansy says, *"I gotta say, I'm really broken up about missin' Bingo night ..."*

"Hey, I never play Bingo."

"Next, you're goin' to claim you never ended up chattin' with Agnes over a game of Gin Rummy."

Agnes may be old enough to have ridden on the Titanic, but she's practically a prodigy with all the tricks she can do with her dentures. Not to mention all her adventures in Tahiti.

"Oh, before I forget," I tell Tansy. *"I wanted to tell you that the autopsy came back. John Doe really was already dead. They've finally confirmed that we didn't murder that bog body."*

"Told you!"

"I suppose he really was a grifter from Abilene."

"And now that fact's gonna help us get released!"

"Maybe ..." I pluck up the paper cup with my meds. *"But not if you go and do that again."*

"Wha—? Why? I will never risk doin' anything that prevents us from goin' back to the estate."

I know that's true. And it feels good, knowing that Tansy and I have a place to go when we're all healed up and ready.

Which brings me to our final goal—our loftiest and most pinnacle dream. It's a plan I've been telling our doctor Tansy and I have been concocting for ages. We're going to do it once we're released.

The breeze ruffles our hair as we hunker low on WT's motorcycle while we fly down Highway 199. Our mission is to expose the truth about the Klan—small town after small town, large city after large city.

We distribute flyers. Staple them to telephone poles, power poles— just about any available surface we can find. On the papers, we've included a bulleted list of Klan telltale signs. Also about thirty different phone numbers for state, local, and federal police.

We work on speeches. Deliver said speeches. Maybe even write a book about how to break from the status quo and stand up against racial injustice and hate.

I'm just reveling in the dreamy sound of the engine, when Tansy leans back on her pillow with a sigh. *"It's a good dream."*

"It's more than a dream." I raise the cup while she tucks her blanket under her chin.

"You know I'll go with you, my love"—she closes her eyes, preparing to drift off to sleep—*"just as soon as we're released."*

"We are *going to do it,"* I vow. *"You, me—"*

WT grabs his helmet for his motorcycle. "And me."

AUTHOR'S NOTE

A year or so ago, I saw an old, derelict house that was once owned by the local KKK. I didn't want to see it, but my friend insisted a couple of us take a look, and, maybe, she insisted, this was my next story.

The house itself looked to be built sometime in the '30s. A few paces off from it were these strange, oversized wooden dog kennels, and several twisted, diseased trees. Near the house, was an odd totem pole tree. While I don't know what it was for, if you've read this book, then you know what my instincts whispered to me.

What cannot be denied is the undeniably dark feeling of the place. While my friends and I didn't climb the red-rail fence, we did spend a bit of time in the grass, pondering the horrors that might have happened on the property

A few miles south of the house, a pair of oak trees currently stand with metal rods and brackets, about fifteen feet high. The trees are in front of an old church that has been converted into a funeral home. It was as if even the trees were ashamed of their past—growing over the rods, hiding what no one wants to believe happened in that county.

Several miles northeast of the town, my friends and I visited a local attraction, Goatman's Bridge. Years ago, in the '30s, the Klan's said to have taken a young Goatman's life for being too successful in his business dealings.

Days later, a few of us visited an old cemetery down the road from the Klan house. Surprisingly, the cemetery had a very different feeling. The birds were out, and throughout the grounds stood these majestic cedar trees. All the while, I couldn't help wondering, "How come the cemetery feels peaceful when the Klan house is so near, under a mile away?"

Before any of these visits, a group of us visited an old, boarded-up Victorian mansion with a high cupola that sat on the dead end of a once-thriving Main Street. All of us yearned to see inside. We dug up old phone numbers, trying to contact the owner. We even joked about breaking in. This interaction became one of the many seeds for the book: "Who lives inside? With the sordid history of the county's past, might the residents have been party, somehow, to the Klan's crimes?"

As a person who's visited often with two people who've had to dissociate from trauma, I'm here to witness that our minds and bodies are jigsaw puzzles none of us fully understand. Though we *have* come a long way. The book, *Life Reinvented: A Guide to Healing from Sexual Trauma for Survivors and Loved Ones* by Erin Carpenter is an invaluable resource. If you have endured trauma of *any* kind, I would suggest that you give it a look. If you've had to dissociate from the horrors of your past, I want to tell you, you are *not* alone. You can survive. Despite all that's happened, never underestimate the force for good you can be.

Which brings me to my final comment. Because of the theme of dealing with racial injustice as a white woman, this book truly terrified me. Shouldn't we leave this topic for those who can speak in their #ownvoices? But, as I thought and wrote and researched, and then after seeing the heinous crime that happened to George Floyd, I knew that the manuscript I'd written was something I wanted to edit and share with others who might be on the fence about how to act or what to say. Racial inequality is an issue for which *everyone* should strive to get a stronger knowledge base. Discrimination is real. It happens all around us, as evidenced from my little field trip to former Klan property.

Christian religious leader, Russell M. Nelson says, "We are brothers and sisters, each of us the child of a loving Father in Heaven. His Son, the Lord Jesus Christ, invites all to come unto Him—'black and white, bond and free, male and female.' It behooves each of us to do whatever we can in our spheres of influence to preserve the dignity and respect every son and daughter of God deserves."

My sphere of influence, however small, is the writing community. And I live in a state where these types of crimes continue to happen. Just like Gemma, I'm not willing to turn a blind eye. Plus, I've always tended to tackle the hard topics when I write.

Our duty is to stand against evil, *no matter* its shape. I'll tell you what I told my husband when he asked me if I really wanted to tackle this story. "Ignoring the Klan gives them power." What's funny is, a few days later, I was listening to a podcast with Tim Ballard, founder of Operation Underground Railroad, where he said the exact same thing. He said human trafficking continues to be as widespread as it is *because* people aren't willing to talk about it. It's time to open up the dialogue and look for opportunities to provide healthy change.

If you would be open to learning more about the injustices that are happening in our country and see what you can do to stand up for racial equality, I would highly suggest that you read *Just Mercy* by Bryan Stevenson. This book truly changed me. I had no idea that so many tragedies have happened in our justice system. We can continue to fight to make it more just and merciful for *everybody*. Apart from that, starting right now, we can listen to other peoples' points of view. Love and serve different races. Take action at local levels and vote. Call out racial slurs of *any* kind.

Racial equality will only become a reality when *we* do our part. Let's use our voice.

ACKNOWLEDGMENTS

Toni, THANK YOU for giving me the pieces. I needed a story, and you jumped on it like you do everything—with love and loyalty. Karin, you keep reading my books! I love your reader brain. Thanks for supporting me with your kind words, reviews, and time. Penny, you told me you didn't like creepy books, then you fearlessly read everything I've ever written. Thank you. You show me what support looks like. Barbara, thank you for telling me *Our Sweet Guillotine* was mesmerizing! I reminded myself of that every time I needed to encourage myself to keep writing. Debra, thanks for your example and perspective on boosting black voices. I read your posts and was touched. You're a class act, every day.

Vanessa, I asked you what I should write next, and you said to go older. I did. Thanks for challenging me! Katie, thanks for being so complimentary of my last release—*The Ripper of Monkshood Manor.* Boy, did your enthusiasm help me keep my head up and keep striving, and thank you, thank you for wanting to read an early copy of this story! Jerusha! Thanks for your unending support of all things Monster Ivy (and for lending me Tansy's kitties' names). Cammie,

THANK YOU for helping me figure out how to write that twist the story needed so desperately. And for rockin' the cover! I adore your creative mind. Lydia, thank you, thank you for helping me see how to go the distance with Gemma's transformative ending. I didn't know how to do it without you, so your help was a godsend on this one. Siyhani, thanks for your fresh, brave perspective. Travis, thank you for being the spreadsheet ninja we need you to be! And Mom, thanks for showing me who you are. You're honest, selfless, and kind.

Monster Ivy authors, you are my peeps. You inspire me to be a better author, editor, marketer, publisher. You make me want to spend time with you guys. I wish we could all rub shoulders more often and live in the same state.

Monster Ivy reviewers, thank you for taking a risk on our books. Thanks for your support as we try to grow this often tricksy "Edgy, Clean" niche.

Dear reader, thank you for reading. I sincerely hope you were able to feel the love and hope amidst all of Gemma's pain. Many of us endure hard things in life. Uncomfortable things. Thanks for sticking with me.

Lastly (and firstly), Heavenly Father, *thank you* for helping me along, showing me I'm loved, and for blessing me with THE blessings you know I need. If my kids and husband happen to read this, you all make me the world's happiest mom and wife. I love your laughs, your experiments, and each of your interests. You make my world full, rich, textured, and complete.

ABOUT THE AUTHOR

Mary Gray balances dark and twisty plots with faith-based messages. Some of her best ideas come when she's lurking in the woods, experimenting with frightening foods, or pushing her kids on the tire swing. She is the co-owner of Monster Ivy Publishing and has written several fiction and nonfiction works.

ALSO BY MARY GRAY

HUSH, NOW FORGET (SISTERS OF BLOODCREEK #1) - two sisters team up with a pair of hottie hunters to unveil the truth about the Blurred Ones and what they really are.

SLEEP, DON'T FRET (SISTERS OF BLOODCREEK #2) - the Abram sisters head out to New Orleans to contend with some witch doctors and Raylan's ruthless sister.

RISE, TAKE FLIGHT (SISTERS OF BLOODCREEK #3) - Unwilling to stand around and wait while Eva's been taken over by one of the Despairity, Frost works tirelessly with Beau and Leo to figure out how to free her sister.

THE RIPPER OF MONKSHOOD MANOR - never go into Monkshood, unless your goal is to meet your Maker...

OUR SWEET GUILLOTINE - a young executioner falls for the daughter of a woman he had to kill...

HER DARK FANTASY: A PREQUEL TO OUR SWEET GUILLOTINE - Young Tempeste witnesses an executioner break apart her mother's feet in an attempt to extract a confession.

THE DOLLHOUSE ASYLUM - a group of teenagers are granted asylum from the apocalypse, only to be forced to reenact some of the most famous, tragic literary couples... or die.

THE DEVILS YOU MEET ON CHRISTMAS DAY - a short story anthology about the outliers, the murderers, the misunderstood, and the forgotten.

HOW TO WRITE FAITH-BASED MESSAGES FOR A SECULAR MARKET - for secular writers who hope to incorporate messages of hope and faith.

HOW TO WRITE CLEAN YET SCINTILLATING ROMANCE - bodice rippers are some of the most lucrative books in the industry. So what if you write books that aren't as steamy?

HOW TO WRITE DARK AND TWISTY BOOKS TO SHOWCASE THE LIGHT - in this brief nonfiction booklet, Mary discusses a psychological and scriptural basis for tackling darker books, some of her favorite techniques for mastering the craft, and how to show the strength of God's light.

CPSIA information can be obtained
at www.ICGtesting.com
Printed in the USA
LVHW040841290920
667266LV00013B/676